Praise for the works of Lo

### *Astrid Inside/Out*

From page one, I felt at home in this story. McBain does a nice job creating its world and populating it with relatable characters. Astrid couldn't feel more familiar, and the confusion she experiences over the sudden change in her appearance is the perfect jumping off point to address personal insecurities and society's obsession with outward appearances. Astrid and Simone fit so well together. Their romance develops in an easy fashion. It's joyful and relatively angst free. Everything about this romance fits and highlighting caring for the environment is a bonus.

-*The Lesbian Review*

### *Claiming Camille*

The characters are amazing, the dialogue is perfect, the romance is off the charts, and I laughed multiple times throughout the story. At several points while reading this lovely story I realized my face was hurting from smiling for so long. Not to say that there isn't plenty of drama and intrigue because there is, but overall the story gave off a fun and sexy vibe that was perfect and entertaining. A supremely great read.

-Kris W., *NetGalley*

### *Maybe Charlotte*

Like *Claiming Camille* before, *Maybe Charlotte*—which can be read as a standalone despite being set in the same universe—is a light and sweet read. Both Charlotte and Lily are good people who only want the best for everyone. They have their flaws too, but they act like adults and communicate instead of making assumptions, and that's really refreshing.

There's also a great ensemble of secondary characters, especially around Charlotte. A lovely romance with very lovable characters, both main and secondary. I'm looking forward to more by this author.

-*Les Rêveur*

With each book McBain's growth as an author and storyteller is unmistakable, and *Maybe Charlotte* is the best proof of it. It is a full-blooded romance with very charming and likable protagonists who have great chemistry together. There are also numerous perfectly done secondary characters who give the story depth and interest. The writing is very good with an interesting plot, nice dialogue and pacing.

Overall, this is a lovely book very well worth reading. I recommend it, and am looking forward to the next romance by this author.

-Pin's Reviews, *goodreads*

*Maybe Charlotte* by Louise McBain is wonderful! ...one of the most enjoyable reads I've had in awhile.

Charlotte and Lily are both looking for love, but it starts off a little chaotic. The story really explores Charlotte's family and her ex girlfriend Madison, and it turns into this delightful, funny, witty and charming story!

I don't want to give too much away, but the family of Charlotte's twin brother, their great aunt (and her two male friends), just bring so much heart and love to the story.

I highly recommend this book!

-Emma A., *NetGalley*

This is the first time for me reading a Louise McBain book, and I wasn't disappointed. *Maybe Charlotte* is a good read, a romance with some funny moments thrown in. Great story with an added bonus of fantastic secondary characters.

-Cathy W., *NetGalley*

What sets Louise McBain apart for me is that her books are so funny, but it's not artificially hilarious sitcom dialogue funny. She sneaks in random observations that maybe some readers don't notice, but I found myself chuckling several times. Some terms that have completely new meaning now are Madness, Charlie Pie, The Geoffrey Problem, and Laurel Jaguar.

I loved the entire cast of characters—not only the MCs Charlotte and Lily, but Charlotte's twin brother Daniel is really a MC too. Maddie, the obsessed ex, and Wellesley and her two house mates all added interest and depth. This book is set in the same universe as *Claiming Camille*, and although it can totally be read as a standalone I would highly recommend reading Camille first—I loved it so much.

-Karen C., *NetGalley*

This is a lovely romance about two women who have been very unlucky in their past relationships.... *Maybe Charlotte* is listed as a sequel to *Claiming Camille* in the blurb, and this book does take place in the same "world" as the former with some of the same characters, but honestly, you could read this book as a standalone if you haven't read the first one yet. However, both are excellent romance novels, and I recommend you read both in order. I certainly enjoyed them both.

-Betty H., *NetGalley*

On a
wing
and a chair

# On a wing and a chair

## louise mcbain

BELLA
BOOKS
2022

Bella Books, Inc.
P.O. Box 10543
Tallahassee, FL 32302

Printed in the United States of America on acid-free paper.

First Edition - 2022

Editor: Cath Walker
Cover Designer: Sheri Halal

ISBN: 978-1-64247-386-5

*PUBLISHER'S NOTE*

# Acknowledgments

*On a Wing and a Chair* was inspired by personal experience. When I was an active member of Alpha Delta Pi sorority at the University of Georgia, our chapter discovered that the twelve founding members of our sorority had each been given their own commemorative chair. The UGA chapter owned two of the ornate, heavily carved monstrosities, which had been shoved in the mailroom until a sister from a neighboring chapter told us of their significance.

I don't know if ADPi ever tried to find the rest of the founders' chairs. In fact, I don't even know if this story is absolutely true. But I'm thankful to the woman from the Brenau chapter for putting this idea in my head.

Writing *On a Wing and a Chair* was a fun trip to the south without the bother of gnats or humidity. It was my first time writing dual points of view which was more difficult than I anticipated. I am beholden to my stalwart beta readers for their invaluable feedback. I gave them limited turnaround time and they came through quickly with helpful focused notes. Many thanks to Linda ReVeal, Maggie Menditto, Dr. Eliza McGraw, T. Elizabeth Bell and Cade Haddock Strong. Your big brains made this book so much better. My thanks also to John Menditto, Mary Stapp, Stacy Lynn Miller, Florence Williams, Michele Woodward, Yong Lee, Eleanor Palm, Kat Menditto, Cal Menditto, Meg Dawson, Doug Dupin, Lauren ReVeal, Fran Calhoun, Toba Greenbaum, Sophie ReVeal and Anne Beyersdorfer. Your love and support keep me afloat.

Finally, a big thank you to my fabulous editor, Cath Walker. Your attention to detail is unparalleled. You continue to improve my craft.

Louise McBain
July 2022

# PROLOGUE

*Two years ago*

*East Village, New York*

Katie spooned coffee beans into the grinder and snapped the lid into place. She hated to wake the sexy, older woman asleep in her bedroom but there was no way around it. Katie had to be at work and needed caffeine to get out the door. The coffee grinder echoed loudly in her tiny East Village kitchen and she closed her eyes. Last night's gallery opening had gone much later than she'd anticipated. But what right-minded individual anticipated staying out until two thirty in the morning on a Thursday and bringing home a complete stranger for a marathon session of recreational sex? A year out of graduate school, Katie was still getting a handle on the rhythms of the adult world. Fortunately, there was coffee.

"Good morning."

Katie opened her eyes to see the woman—Lauren? Lorraine?—was no longer in bed but standing in the living room with a sheet draped seductively around her gorgeous body.

"Good morning," Katie said, and went to kiss her cheek. There was little chance she'd see the woman again but she wouldn't be rude. The night had been fun and Katie hoped Lorraine/Lauren had enjoyed herself too.

"Are you rising and grinding without me?" Lorraine/Lauren said, and pulled Katie against her chest. "I hoped we might do that another way."

"Unfortunately, I don't have time," Katie said, and let herself be held for a moment before gently letting go. "I have a meeting in forty-five minutes."

"Tell me about your job?" the woman asked, and propped her elbows on the counter that separated the kitchen from the rest of Katie's apartment. Katie didn't know what Lorraine/Lauren did for a living but her interest in the art world seemed authentic. She'd purchased two paintings at last night's opening and seemed to be on a first-name basis with everyone at the gallery.

"I think I told you, I'm finishing the first year of my fellowship at the Whitney Museum," Katie replied. As always, she loved the way the words sounded coming out of her mouth.

"Yes, but what do you do every day?" Lorraine/Lauren asked, looking genuinely interested.

"Right now, I'm learning the financial side of curating an exhibit," Katie replied, happy to talk about the job she loved. "I'm checking receipts, tracking copyrights, that sort of thing. I've also taken over social media and that's fun. Our curator is Bruno Laredo. He's very talented."

Lorraine/Lauren blinked happily. "Dear, odd, little Bruno," she sniffed, looking nostalgic. "I bet it's wonderful working with him."

"You know Bruno?" Katie asked, wondering why she hadn't mentioned this the night before. If Lorraine/Lauren knew Bruno socially, Katie might be put in a compromising position of having her boss know her private life. Mixing work and pleasure was unavoidable in the art world, but there were boundaries that shouldn't be crossed.

"We were in the same class at Brown," Lorraine/Lauren replied and accepted a cup of coffee. "Now he works for my husband," she said, and stirred in a splash of creamer.

"Husband?" Katie said, though she wasn't truly surprised. Part of her had wondered if the socialite might be married.

Lorraine/Lauren flashed a giant diamond solitaire. "I thought it was obvious." She shrugged. "I wasn't trying to hide anything."

"Yeah, okay," Katie said, and moved onto her primary concern. "If Bruno works for your husband, does that mean your husband works at the Whitney, also?"

"Heavens no," Lorraine/Lauren laughed, as if the idea were preposterous. "Thomas doesn't work at the Whitney. He just gives the museum money, so they give him input."

"Your husband is on the board of trustees?" Katie asked, and calmly set down the coffee cup so she didn't throw it across the room. "I wish you'd told me that last night."

Lorraine/Lauren wrinkled her nose. "If you'd known Thomas was a trustee you might not have invited me home with you."

"I definitely wouldn't have," Katie replied. She moved out of the kitchen to look for the woman's shoes. The quicker she was in them, the quicker she'd be gone.

Lorraine/Lauren grabbed at Katie's arm as she walked by. "Don't worry about Thomas, he's skiing with friends upstate and won't be back until Sunday. We could have the long weekend together. Want to come to my place tonight?"

Katie shook her head. "Last night was great, but I can't risk my job."

Lorraine/Lauren dropped her hand. "Bruno is lucky to have found such a dedicated assistant."

"Please don't talk to him about me," Katie said, and Lorraine/Lauren locked her mouth shut with an invisible key.

"A quick shower and I'll be out of your hair," she said, but then lingered in the doorway longer than necessary. "Unless you'd like to join me?"

"No, thank you," Katie said, but watched reluctantly as she disappeared into the bathroom. Yes, Lorraine/Lauren was a bit of a liar, but she also had a Pilates body and a straight woman's pent-up fantasies.

Katie sponged off as best she could in the kitchen sink and then went into the bedroom to dress. Taking off the T-shirt and boxers, she stuffed them in a drawer and pulled a short, black dress from the closet. When the doorbell rang, she was standing in front of the hall mirror applying makeup to the faint circles under her eyes.

"Rachel?" she called, as her grad-school friend was the only person who ever visited this early. When no one answered Katie called again. "Hello?"

A low, masculine voice came back. "It's not Rachel."

"Just a minute," Katie said, and walked toward the door. If it wasn't Rachel it had to be the maintenance guy, Carter, who probably needed to do some sort of system test. Katie loved living in a building that had an onsite supervisor but was still getting used to his unscheduled pop-ins. She unbolted the lock but peeked through the hole before slipping off the chain. It wasn't Carter, but a tall, thin man balanced on crutches. "Who are you?" she asked, worried she already knew the answer.

"It's Thomas Carlisle," the man said, confirming her fears. "I've come to collect my wife. I understand Laurent left the gallery with you last night."

*Shit.* Katie looked down and saw the man's leg was wrapped in a plastic boot and knew the trustee must have suffered a skiing accident. *Double shit.* Even if he and Laurent had some sort of understanding that allowed for private recreation, he wasn't likely to be in a good mood. Katie had no idea how he'd gotten her name and address but knew the chances he'd come inside to share a companionable cup of coffee while his wife finished her shower were slim. Katie wanted to climb out the window but she couldn't leave an injured man standing in the hallway.

Taking a deep breath, she took the chain off the door.

# CHAPTER ONE

## *The Jump-Start*

"I'll have a Bloody Mary, please," Katie Simmons told a bored-looking waiter in the dining room of the Metropolitan Club. Katie had no idea why her grandmother had summoned her to the elegantly laid table in midtown Manhattan, but had decided to make the best of it. "With a twist of lime please."

"Very good, miss," the waiter said and turned to Flora. "Anything for you, ma'am?"

"I'll have the same," Flora told him. "And my name is Mrs. Simmons. I'll be staying in the Kennedy suite tonight."

"Welcome to the Metropolitan Club, Mrs. Simmons." The waiter nodded politely. "My name is Chad. I'll be back shortly with your drinks."

"Thank you, Chad," Flora said, and sipped from her water goblet. A man with a silver chafing dish approached and Flora allowed him to place a popover on each of their plates and then told him not to come back. She shook her head. "They want to fill us up on bread so we'll go light on the buffet."

"Good luck with that," Katie replied, eyeing the bountiful table in the back of the room. "I can't wait to introduce myself to the fried oysters."

"I saw those, too," Flora said, eyes sparkling. "And the lobster tails."

Katie smiled. Her love of rich food could be traced directly back to her years under Flora's care after her mother had died. "Thanks for inviting me to lunch." She raised her glass. "This is a real treat."

"It's my pleasure," Flora said, and knocked her goblet against Katie's.

Katie couldn't remember the last time she'd been to a restaurant that served both food and wine. Her mouth watered at the smell of the prime rib she spied at the end of the buffet table. She was truly looking forward to the meal, although she wondered at Flora's motives for inviting her. What was her grandmother doing in New York and how was it that Flora was staying at the Metropolitan Club?

"How did you get a room here?" Katie asked, tearing into the popover. "And why are you in the city? Is there a new Broadway show I haven't heard about?" This was entirely possible. Since losing her fellowship at the Whitney, Katie had stopped paying attention to things she couldn't afford. If there was a hot new show on Broadway, she'd be the last person to know.

"Is this how you greet your sweet, little, old grandmother? With the third degree?" Flora waved a hand dramatically and Katie caught the familiar scents of talcum powder and Dior perfume.

"Flora, it's so good to see you," Katie corrected herself. Of the three descriptors seventy-five-year-old Flora had used, old was the only one that was applicable. There was nothing little about her or, heaven forbid, sweet, unless you counted her addiction to key lime pie and tiramisu.

"It's wonderful to be here, dear," Flora replied, still avoiding Katie's question. "I've missed your face."

"You saw my face at Christmas," Katie reminded her grandmother. She'd driven her beloved Mini Cooper up to her dad's house in Syracuse where Flora had joined them for the holiday. Katie remembered it particularly well as it had been the last road trip before she'd sold the car to a woman, who'd said she was buying it for her cleaning lady.

"Christmas was two months ago," Flora said. "I want you to come to Beaumont to visit me. You haven't been back to Georgia since graduating high school. I'm starting to take it personally."

"You know it isn't you," Katie replied. Her late mother often said that a little bit of Georgia went a long way. Katie was inclined to agree. The four years she'd spent at Beaumont Central High School had filled Katie up to the top of her curly red head. Maybe if she and Beth were still in touch she'd feel differently. When Katie conjured the South, all she remembered was diving insects and feeling out of place.

"How do you like living in Brooklyn?" Flora asked, changing tack.

"It's okay," Katie hedged, thinking of the couch she was currently renting at her friend Rachel's. It was fortunate Flora had wanted to meet Katie at the Metropolitan Club. She couldn't imagine what her proper, southern grandmother might make of the four-story walk-up Katie had been calling home since giving up the lease on the East Village apartment she'd optimistically taken after finishing grad school. "Rachel is really nice."

"Is Rachel your girlfriend?" Flora asked. She'd never had any trouble with Katie's sexuality but often bemoaned Katie's lack of relationships. Married to Katie's late grandfather for fifty years, Flora's only child was Katie's dad, leaving Katie the only hope of great-grandchildren. Many of Flora's friends in Beaumont already had this honor, as Katie had heard more than once at Christmas.

"No," Katie responded firmly. She and Rachel had hooked up a couple of times, but it had just been sex. She certainly wasn't Katie's girlfriend and no one Katie wanted to introduce to Flora.

"What did you do with your furniture when you moved out of the Village?" Flora asked, now looking a little concerned.

"I got rid of most of it," Katie said, leaving out the fact that she'd also sold the Mini Cooper. "Rachel already had everything. It was easier to just move in."

"I hope you kept your mother's lamp," Flora said and Katie imagined she heard a touch of judgment.

"I didn't get rid of everything," she said, now feeling defensive. The last two years had been humbling enough without her grandmother taking a swing.

"Of course, you haven't," Flora said, and patted her arm.

Katie sighed. It wasn't Flora's fault she'd been fired from her fellowship at the Whitney Museum. Friends from grad school, who hadn't derailed their careers by fucking inappropriate women, were doing exciting things. Katie went to their openings, shook their hands and enjoyed their wine.

"Living with Rachel makes better financial sense. I mean, until I find a better job," she admitted.

"And how is that going? Any new leads?" Flora cut right to the chase.

"Not since I saw you at Christmas," Katie replied, and forced a smile. "I'm still working at the preschool. Still picking glitter-glue out of my hair every night."

"I'm sure the children love you," Flora said tactfully, but did not pretend to be impressed.

"The kids are great, but as you know, it's not my dream job," Katie said, and hung her head. "Honestly, I'm starting to worry a museum career is never going to happen."

Flora looked thoughtful. "From what you've told me, it's a very competitive field."

"That's true," Katie said, and tried to keep the waver out of her voice. She didn't want Flora to know her true desperation. But it was becoming more difficult to keep a brave face. Everyone in her grad-school program who hadn't bailed on New York was now working at a major museum. Katie wasn't sure how much longer she'd be able to endure the proximity to her dream jobs without finding one herself. Cheerleading her friends' successes simply wasn't enough. "There are a limited number of positions and more applicants every year."

"You must keep trying," Flora said. "You can't score a touchdown if you don't call a play."

"It's not that easy," Katie said. "And you still haven't told me what you're doing here."

"It's very simple. The Metropolitan Club has reciprocity with my club back in Beaumont," Flora said and paused when the waiter returned with their drinks.

"Okay, but that still doesn't explain what you're doing in New York," Katie said when the waiter was gone.

"Isn't it enough that I wanted to see you?" Flora asked, sipping her cocktail.

"Yes, but why in February?" Katie asked. "You only come to New York in the summer. This is making me nervous. Is something wrong with Dad?"

Flora sighed. "If you must know, yes. He's worried about your financial difficulties. We both are."

"What did he say?" Katie asked, feeling her whole body deflate. Her father had promised not to mention the sale of the car. "I can't believe he called you."

"Believe it," Flora said, and put down her spoon. "My son is incapable of keeping a secret. The sooner you learn that the better."

"He didn't need to call you," Katie said, and crossed her arms tightly over her chest. "I've solved the problem on my own. It's all worked out."

"You had to sell your furniture," Flora countered.

"I still have Mom's lamp," Katie said as if this made a difference. "And I won't be at Rachel's forever. I've got some ideas," she lied.

"I'd like to help," Flora said and took something from her purse.

"I told you, I'm doing fine," Katie said, wondering how much money Flora would try to give her. Katie was too destitute to say no but knew it would only be a Band-Aid on the real problem. Until she got a job working in her chosen field of study, Katie wouldn't be truly happy.

Flora placed a set of keys on the table. "I bought your car back," she said, and slid the keys across the table.

Katie recognized the Colgate College fob and went very still. "You did?" she asked incredulously. Gingerly she picked up the familiar-looking key chain. Turning the key in her hand Katie marveled at Flora's generosity. Buying back the Mini Cooper would not solve Katie's problems but it would go a long way to lift her spirits. Perhaps Katie would drive to Beaumont after all. "Thank you so much. I don't know what to say."

Flora looked confused. "The car is not a gift," she said, surprising Katie. It wasn't like her grandmother to be stingy or cruel. Why buy back the car if only to tease her?

"Then why did you buy it?" Katie asked.

"I thought the car would make an attractive signing bonus," Flora replied and took another object from her purse.

"A signing bonus?" Katie asked, staring at the pen in Flora's hand. "What is it that I'm signing?"

"An employment contract, hopefully," Flora replied. "I've come here to offer you a job."

# CHAPTER TWO

## *The Air is Full of Wishes*

"Come in for a second, and listen to something I'm working on?" Syd called to her friend from the stoop of her recently purchased Grant Park bungalow. "I've got cold beer."

Joe paused in front of Syd's walkway and squinted up at her through the glare of the unseasonably warm Atlanta afternoon. "When did you get back to Atlanta? How's your grandmother?"

"Come in and I'll tell you everything," Syd replied, touched at his concern. Though she'd known Joe a long time, their relationship had always revolved more around music than personal matters.

"What kind of beer do you have?" He asked, starting up the steps. "I can't have anything too bitter. Your songs are bitter enough already. Last time you played me something new I had to go home and eat a cookie."

"The beer is an IPA," Syd replied, slightly stung. "Where are you going, anyway? It's hotter than Jessica Rabbit out here."

"I was going to the movies to get out of the heat," Joe said and paused to allow Syd to enter the house first.

Though he dressed like an aging hipster and smelled of Aqua Velva, Joe had the manners of a southern gentleman. He always wanted to get the door and the check. Syd knew this should rankle her feminist sensibilities but could never bring herself to care. How did paying for drinks and insisting on driving diminish her power? It felt like free booze and chauffeur service to her.

"God, your air conditioner feels good. Lori refuses to turn ours on out of principle because it's February." He sat down on the couch and crossed his legs. "I'll listen to one hundred revenge songs for this air-conditioning."

"I don't write revenge songs," Syd protested, but knew Joe wasn't far off the mark. Her last album had coincided with her divorce and some of the bile had spilled over into the lyrics. It was undeniable.

"Your lyrics have been savage," Joe confirmed, and wiped his forehead. "Maybe moving back to Georgia will mellow you out." He looked past Syd into the kitchen toward the refrigerator. "This climate will certainly slow you down after ten years in LA."

"I don't mind the heat so much," Syd said and rose to fetch the drinks. "It's weird that it's so hot here in February. What movie were you going to see?"

"I forget," Joe said, and flicked a hand in the air. "Someone said free beer and everything just flew out of my head."

"Who said it was free?" Syd laughed. "You have to listen to my song." She opened the fridge.

Joe's ear for music had not happened by accident. A drive-time DJ at Atlanta's alternative rock station for twenty-five years, he now co-owned a small performance venue in midtown Atlanta with his wife, Lori. Syd had known the couple since her early days as a young musician and had not purchased a house in their neighborhood by coincidence. For all its many charms, Atlanta's traffic was almost as bad as LA. Syd had been thrilled to find a recently remodeled 1930s bungalow with a pool but would have settled for something less worthy if it meant being in Grant Park. Her manager, Colette, also lived in the neighborhood and it was easy access to Interstate Twenty, the highway Syd took to get to her hometown of Beaumont.

Handing off Joe's beer, Syd perched on the edge of a chair and picked up her custom-made Rockbridge guitar. She could always count on Joe to tell her if she'd inadvertently borrowed a guitar riff or poached a lyric. It was an easy mistake for a solo artist. When Syd was fronting Ache and Bake, she'd had Paul or Carrie to tell her if she'd stolen something. Then Carrie had left her for Paul. Now Syd had Joe.

"Here's to your grandmother getting out of the hospital," Joe said, and leaned forward to knock his beer against Syd's.

"Thanks." Syd smiled thinking of Honey propped up among the goose-down pillows they'd brought from her cabin on the lake. "She's now at the rehab facility where my sister works."

"Sounds like a tough lady."

"She is," Syd agreed. Honey's small stroke had given them all a big scare. Syd had decamped to Beaumont until the doctors had cleared Honey to go to Green Acres where Debra was an administrator.

"That's good luck," Joe said.

"That's good insurance." Syd smiled, and strummed the guitar. "And I'm certainly happy about it. But I've also just been happier in general. It started before Honey recovered from the stroke."

Joe looked confused. "It's the move back to Georgia, genius. It's got to be nice not having to worry about running into your ex-wife and ex-drummer at the grocery store."

"Thank you, Dr. Phil," Syd said. "But I haven't seen those guys in months. I hope I've been over Carrie for a while."

Joe made a snorting noise. "There's no timeline where love is concerned," he said, and set his empty bottle on the table next to the couch. "We all move at our own pace. Like I drink more quickly than you."

Laughing, Syd gestured to the fridge. "Help yourself."

"Thanks." Joe rose to his feet. "Now, tell me about this new song."

"Okay," Syd said and plucked the first chord on her Rockbridge. Choosing not to use a guitar pick had required hours of practice, and given her crescent moon-shaped calluses on the tips of her fingers. It was the price she'd paid to be closer to the music. On good days, she could feel it flowing through her body like a current. "I'm still just messing around with lyrics. It's called 'The Air is Full of Wishes.'"

"That doesn't sound bitter." Joe's voice echoed inside the fridge.

"Well, it's for Emma's birthday, so I hope not."

"Emma, your niece?"

"Who else?"

When Joe looked up, there was a devilish smirk etched into his lined face. "I was hoping you'd finally hooked up with one of your groupies, turned her into a gropey." He laughed at his own joke.

"What? No." Syd shook her head.

"Stop pretending you don't notice all the starry-eyed, young women hanging around your shows. Last time you played the Third Pig, Lori caught a naked woman in a trench coat trying to pick the lock on the dressing room."

"No way." Syd laughed, surprised she hadn't heard the story before. Both Joe and Lori loved to spin a yarn.

Joe walked back into the living room and sat down. "It's true. Lori had to drag her out by her ponytail."

"You're making that up," Syd said.

He didn't deny the embellishment. "How long has it been since you've let someone keep you company?"

"Too long," Syd admitted. "I think I've forgotten how to talk to women. I wouldn't know what to say."

Joe gave Syd's shoulder a fatherly pat. "Say as little as possible. Let your music speak for you and it'll happen. Especially if you've stopped writing revenge songs."

"I don't write revenge songs."

"Whatever you say." He swigged the fresh beer.

"Will you please just listen to the song?"

"Let her rip."

"It's called 'The Air is Full of Wishes.'"

"So, you said. Play me the song."

Syd closed her eyes and played the song she'd written on her hike the day before. It was a complete departure from the material Syd was known for, but it made her happy, so she'd decided not to question it.

*When a ladybug lands on your finger*
*It's just a wish that's stopped to linger*
*Shooting stars streaking through the night*
*Are brand new wishes burning bright*
*Isn't it delicious?*
*The air is full wishes*
*Like a school of flying fishes*
*or a penguin blowing kisses,*
*there's no need to wash the dishes*
*When the air is full of wishes*

Finishing the first verse, Syd looked up to see that Joe had an odd look on his face. "What?"

He shook his shaggy head. "That's fucking sweet."

"You say that like it's a bad thing." Syd put her guitar down and tried not to feel defensive. Joe was here to give her feedback on the song. She'd hijacked him off the street and bribed him with beer expressly for this purpose. It wasn't fair to argue with his opinion.

"I don't think it's a bad thing at all," Joe said, evenly. "It's just cotton-candy sweet and completely different from everything you're known for."

"What exactly am I known for?" Syd asked. She had some idea of what he might say but still wanted to hear the words, if only to remind herself.

He scoffed. "For being a fucking badass. You're a southern-fried, extra crispy, angsty, lesbian rock goddess."

"Angsty lesbian rock goddess?" Syd laughed as Joe continued to spin, now using his professional DJ voice.

"Yes, some people call you Syd Clitious, but that's an insult. You're a total original. You wrote 'Woman at War' and 'Deja Boo' and won three Grammys by age twenty-one."

"I did." Syd smiled thinking of Ache and Bake's breakthrough album.

"You wrote 'The Sky is High' and then performed it topless at the Fox Theater on Halloween with Mick Jagger," Joe went on.

"I was wearing duct tape on my nipples." Syd wagged a finger at him, though she continued to laugh. Her early days had been wild. With Carrie by her side dreaming up endless ways to push boundaries, they'd gained a huge following across the southern US before moving to Los Angeles and gaining a national following.

"You were flaming hot," Joe said, dramatically, and swigged his beer. "I love that photo of you dancing with Mick. Y'all look like twins."

"Um, thanks, I guess," Syd said, and picked up the guitar. "For the record, the new song is supposed to be sweet. I write something for my nieces every year on their birthdays."

"Then you hit the mark. That song gave me a toothache." He rubbed his jaw and Syd glared at him.

"I wasn't planning to open my next set with it."

"When is your next gig?" Joe was quick to ask.

"The one Colette set up with y'all in late April," Syd replied, referring to the one solo show her manager had talked her into performing later in the spring.

"Not until April?" Joe asked, clearly disappointed. "Is this because Colette's on maternity leave? I'm happy to give you another night at the Pig. You can have as many as you like."

"Thanks, buddy," Syd said. "Lori said the same thing. I'll let you know when I'm ready."

"Don't wait too long, or the public will forget you," Joe cautioned and took a sip of his beer.

"I'll keep that in mind," Syd said, slightly annoyed, though she knew Joe was just looking out for her. Her last album, a solo release called *Florida Man*, had sold extremely well, though she'd done little touring to support it. Her stated rationale was her grandmother's illness, but it wasn't the only reason Syd was dragging her heels. At thirty-three she'd been fronting a trio for more than a decade and found it odd to suddenly be onstage alone. Other musicians had reached out, but Syd wasn't ready to collaborate. If it wasn't for Colette relentlessly pressuring her to perform, Syd might be happy to hide out in her new house indefinitely.

"I'm serious, Syd." Joe looked worried. "The public has a ravenous appetite. Feed them consistently or they'll find somewhere else to eat."

"I'm playing a private house concert in Beaumont the weekend before Memorial Day," Syd replied, happy to have another gig to report. "Does that count?"

"It won't hurt," Joe said. "Who's hosting the party? Must be a good friend if they talked you into performing below the gnat line in May."

Syd shuddered, thinking of the incessant little black bugs. "The show's inside," she told Joe. "And, you're right. Jennifer is my childhood friend. The show benefits the local humane society."

"Good vibes." Joe nodded. "If you've got to give something back, you may as well give it to dogs."

"Or cats," Syd said, thinking of Annapurna, the cat she'd left behind in Los Angeles. "I worked at the Beaumont Humane Society in high school. They still have the same director. I'm looking forward to seeing her, too."

"Her?" Joe asked, his voice hopeful.

Syd almost choked on her beer. "Dude, get your mind out of the gutter." She shook her head. "Jane is my grandmother's age."

"Grannies can be hot," Joe told her. "Don't forget Lori's son has two boys."

"Lori is smoking," Syd agreed. "I've just never thought of Jane that way, or heaven forbid, my own grandmother."

"Be glad your grandfather did," Joe cracked.

"I'll drink to that." Syd raised her beer once more. Maybe when Honey was safely out of rehab, Syd would feel like touring again. She went to sleep, dreaming of Honey's garden and woke up to a ringing phone.

It was Deb, calling from the rehab center. Honey had suffered another, more severe, stroke. This one had been fatal.

# CHAPTER THREE

## *Zapped*

"Of course. I'd love to see the Eagle Chair," Katie said, and strove to keep her foot from tapping against the polished wood of the chapter room floor. Seated before the twelve-member, national Board of Directors for Zeta Alpha Pi sorority, or ZAP, she had to remind herself that the meeting wasn't an interview, but a formality. The contract had been signed yesterday. Katie already had the job. Still, she was nervous.

The women at the table, though ranging wildly in age, were all possessed of the same inscrutable poise that Katie found intimidating. She tended to clam up in the company of perceived sophisticates like this or, worse yet, make horribly inappropriate comments. Rachel liked to say that Katie was an equal opportunity fuck-up. Perhaps this was the real reason why, until Flora had swooped in last week with a job offer, Katie had been unsuccessful in securing a position which reflected her education and experience. Now that she'd been given another chance to prove herself, she'd need to put her best foot forward and stop bouncing it under the table. "Is the Eagle Chair here, or do we need to go next door to see it?" she asked.

"Arthur just picked it up," Flora informed her. "The ZAP chapter, from Georgia Southern college, had been using it during their member meetings." she shuddered, as if this were a horror not to be borne. "We located two more chairs in Atlanta and another at our own Nancy Littlejohn's house." She gestured to a tiny woman seated to Katie's left.

"It has cardinals on it," Nancy volunteered, brightly. "We had no idea the chair was so important until the ZAP founders' portrait was discovered last year." She pointed to a medium-sized painting of eight women seated in giant throne-like chairs hanging in a place of honor over the fireplace. "Imagine my surprise? I used to hang the dry cleaning on it," Nancy confessed, drawing titters from other members of the board.

"Nancy is a direct descendant of Tamara Fenwick Tilden," Flora explained, and Katie recognized the name from her own pledge year at Colgate. "Her family has the distinction of having the only unbroken legacy line in ZAP history."

"Congratulations," Katie said, as this seemed the expected answer.

"My granddaughter pledged ZAP at Georgia Tech last year," Nancy informed Katie, proudly.

"Wasn't Tamara Fenwick Tilden from Monroe?" Katie asked, and was rewarded with a huge smile. It was ironic. Never would Katie have imagined the arcane knowledge she'd learned as a first-year sorority member or pledge might someday benefit her career. A key activity of hell week, or *swell week* as they'd called it, because the event had been held at someone's parents' swanky, New York mountain house, had been to memorize the names and hometowns of the eight original founders.

*Hailey Cooper Lawrence, Fontaine Maguire Ferguson, Alethea Albright Buchannan, Mildred Samuels Bonewright, Tamara Fenwick Tilden, Hortense Duquesne Baker, Bernice Wolfe Calhoun, Martha Westminster Carroll.*

"She was!" Nancy took a photo from her purse and passed it down the table to Katie. "The Cardinal Chair came from

Tamara's estate. Until the portrait was discovered, we'd no idea that the other ZAP founders had special bird chairs too."

Katie studied the photograph. Tall and boxy looking, the chair indeed looked like a throne. The cardinal carvings only made the appearance a tad more delicate. "Where is the chair, now?" Katie asked.

"It's already in the exhibit room, at Maguire House." Flora nodded toward the house next door. "We also have the Hawk and Owl chairs. A ZAP alumni found the Hawk Chair at an estate sale in Augusta and the Owl Chair turned up at an antique store in LaGrange," she reported, with a gleam in her eye. "There are four more chairs out there. Katie's first job as our Museum Director will be to find them."

Katie looked at the portrait of the founders over the fireplace. If it truly was the original, her first job as Director of the new Zeta Alpha Pi Sorority Museum would to be to remove it from the damaging sunlight. She managed to keep this to herself and just smiled instead.

"How exciting," said a woman in a powder-pink suit. The other women made noises of agreement. Katie marveled at their collective deportment. They were all so tidy and perfect looking. Dressed in various shades of pastel they sat up straight, like pins in a packet. Next to them in her short black skirt and matching jacket, Katie felt like she was going to a funeral. What had seemed chic in the mirror looked dire juxtaposed to their tasteful colors. She took a deep breath, reminding herself again that she already had the job.

"I'm pleased to report that Katie has agreed to the terms of our contract," Flora said, as if reading her mind. "Does anyone have a question?"

"I do." A woman at the far end of the table raised her hand.

Katie held her breath. If asked for facts about antique bird chairs, she'd have to wing it. Her museum science was curating. The little research Katie had done on the ZAP founders' chairs suggested they were part of a royal revival design craze that occurred in the United States in the third quarter of the nineteenth century. That was all she had. If the board member wanted more information than that, she'd have to wait for the opening or Google it herself.

"Did y'all have fall or spring rush where you went to school?" the woman asked and Katie flashed to the swirl of parties that resulted in her joining Zeta Alpha Pi.

"Oh, it was in the spring at Colgate," Katie answered. That ZAP was also her grandmother's sorority was only a happy coincidence. Collegiate sororities were a bit like restaurant franchises. Though separate chapters were governed by the same parent body—using the same Greek letters, bylaws and secret handshake—they varied drastically in size and popularity. Some schools had new member, or pledge, drives at the beginning of fall semester and some waited until spring.

"Rush should be held in the spring. That way girls can truly get to know each other." The lady gave a delicate sniff leading Katie to suspect someone close to her had been disappointed with the outcome of their sorority rush experience. It happened more frequently than not. Dashed expectations could be devastating. Who knew this better than Katie?

"The ZAP Board of Directors has no say when different chapters open their membership windows, Betty Anne. You know this," Flora said. "There are many things about new member recruitment we'd change if we could. It's just not within our power."

"It's still wrong."

"I don't disagree."

Betty Anne seemed satisfied by Flora's answer and another hand went up. Flora nodded at a woman midway down the table.

"Can our new Museum Director drive a pickup truck?" she drawled in a thick southern accent. The question drew appreciative murmuring from the rest of the group. The speaker, a woman in late middle age, didn't wait for Katie to respond. "I live in Atlanta, but we've got an old Ford on the farm we're not using. It'll be great for hauling chairs."

"Sure, I can drive a pickup," Katie replied, automatically. She'd driven a truck exactly one time in her life, when she and Beth had chauffeured the hayride their junior year of high school.

"Wonderful." The woman looked pleased, and Katie congratulated herself on giving the correct answer. Furniture moving was not an aspect of the job she'd considered until now, but she dismissed it as a minor logistic. How difficult could it be? They'd already located four of the eight chairs, one of which was coming through the door right now on a dolly. The woman smiled. "You can pick it up any time you like."

"I'll let you know," Katie replied, wondering where this farm was and how she was supposed to get there. She was hoping to see Beth this weekend. It had been almost eight years since they'd spent any real time together. This seemed impossible to Katie, but there it was. The thought was interrupted by the young man pushing the chair through the doorway.

"Where should I put it?" he asked Flora.

"Just over there, Arthur," Flora said, and pointed to a spot in the middle of the room.

"Yes, ma'am," he said, and did as she'd asked.

Katie wondered at his presence in the chapter room. Men hadn't been allowed inside the ZAP suite at Colgate. It had been one of her favorite things about being a sorority member. She looked around the lavish front parlor of the mansion that housed the Beaumont chapter of Zeta Alpha Pi. Though it was the same sorority as the one she'd belonged to in New York, it seemed like a completely different place.

"That's perfect. Just leave it right there," Flora directed him.

"Yes, ma'am," Arthur answered, his southern accent deep and deferential. Katie gauged his age to be late teens or early twenties. He was likely a student at the college but what was he doing inside the sorority house? "Do you need anything else?"

"Close the door on the way out," Flora started to dismiss him and then, once again as if she were reading Katie's mind, called him back. "Wait a moment."

"Yes, ma'am?" Arthur repeated, sounding like a windup doll.

"I'd like you to meet my granddaughter, Katie. She'll be working next door, in Maguire House. She may need your assistance from time to time."

"Yes, ma'am," Arthur said, a fourth time. Walking over, he gallantly offered Katie his hand. "I'm Arthur Mobley." He smiled with the confidence of someone who knew he was attractive. "ZAP houseboy, at your service."

Katie struggled to hide her surprise. Houseboy? Was that really a thing? Once again, she was reminded that the ZAP experience at Beaumont was far removed from her own in New York. "Nice to meet you, Arthur." She took his hand.

"The painters finished yesterday." He jerked his head toward the two-story dwelling. "Smells a lot better. Are more girls going to live there?" He looked excited. "Are you the new house mother?"

"No, I'm not," Katie said and looked to Flora for help.

"The property next door will serve as the Zeta Alpha Pi Founders' Museum and National Headquarters. Katie is our new Museum Director," Flora replied.

"I heard they were going to make it a Crispy Fried Chicken Shack," Arthur said.

The woman on Katie's right brightened. "I love Crispy Fried's coleslaw. My husband says it's better than mine."

"That can't be true." A woman across the table shook her head. "I don't believe it."

The first woman smiled. "You're sweet, but there's a special ingredient I can't put my finger on. The Crispy Fried people are super secretive about it. My niece and her husband own a franchise in Raleigh. I can't even get her to tell me, and she's my goddaughter."

"I love their fried pickles," the woman on the other side of Katie offered and half the table moaned with pleasure.

Flora waved a hand. "We were never going to let a Crispy Fried Chicken Shack move in next door to ZAP House, no matter how delicious their fried pickles are. We've been on the lookout for a new national headquarters and Maguire House is perfect." She turned to Katie. "The current headquarters is in Atlanta."

"*That* was pure politics," Nancy Littlejohn said mysteriously.

"It never made any sense," Flora agreed. "Zeta Alpha Pi was founded in Beaumont. The headquarters should be here, too. Buying the property next door was an easy choice. We couldn't have a fast-food restaurant adjacent to the ZAP House. Think of the rats."

"I'd rather not," Katie said. As far as she could tell, the absence of rats in her daily life was one of the only positive things about leaving New York. She still couldn't believe she was here. When she'd left for college eight years ago, she promised herself to never again live in Georgia. Katie hoped the thrill of landing her dream job, together with rent-free accommodation at Flora's, would be enough to counter the humidity and the conservative thinking.

"We make our pledges shoot the rats over at my fraternity house," Arthur offered and the smirk on his handsome face made it clear he was hoping to shock them.

"I bet," Katie replied. She'd no doubt he was telling the truth. Many of her classmates at Beaumont Central High School had hunted as a hobby, shooting whatever happened to be in season. It was not a reach to imagine them popping alley rats.

Flora gave Arthur the reaction he was looking for. "That sounds horrible," she said. "You'd better give Katie your number in case she has any problems at Maguire House."

"I swear I'm telling y'all the truth," Arthur said. Beaming with masculine mischief, he swaggered toward Katie and held out his phone. The women at the table tittered with approval and Katie felt like she was back in high school where being tall, male and Caucasian counted as spendable currency. "I thought more girls were moving in next door because the upstairs still looks like bedrooms."

Katie shook her head. It was a reasonable assumption. The renovated apartment had been offered to her as part of her employment package, but she'd turned it down. Why would she stay in the thumping heart of campus, next door to a popular sorority house, when a suite at Flora's was also an option? Three buffer blocks away from the university, the location was perfect.

"Cool," Arthur answered. He tapped the screen of his cell phone. "I just airdropped you my contact information. Text me if you need anything else." He gestured to the shrouded object on the wheeled platform. "I'll come back later for the throne."

"Thank you, Arthur," Flora said, and Katie could tell by the tone in her voice she approved of him. She wondered if it was because his clothing met her expectations of how a young man should dress. The basic uniform required no thought, only compliance. With his blue buttoned-down oxford shirt, khakis, loafers and a belt, Arthur checked all the boxes of southern-boy bingo.

"Yes, ma'am," he said one last time. Ducking out of the room, he closed the door behind him.

Flora rose from the table. "I apologize for being so dramatic." She approached the shrouded object. "It's mostly for my own benefit. I haven't seen the Eagle Chair and I'm very excited."

Katie looked up to find the Eagle Chair in the portrait. Hailey Cooper Lawrence was easy to spot as her chair was taller than the rest and positioned at the head of the table. Katie wondered if the eagle carvings were personal to Hailey and if she had been the one who'd had the chairs commissioned. Perhaps there was a connection to a local furniture maker? If accounting ledgers existed from the period, a record for the sale might exist. It was exciting to think about and why Katie loved museum studies. Every uncovered fact opened a trail to another.

A hand went up and Flora nodded at a woman sitting midway down the table.

"Have you decided on a conservator yet?" the woman asked and Flora stood up a little taller, giving Katie the impression she was steeling herself for a fight.

"As I told you in my email, yesterday," she said, sounding leagues less enthusiastic than moments before, "choosing a conservator will be Katie's job and she won't make her decision until after all eight chairs have been located. We can't possibly know the restoration needs of the collection until we have all the pieces."

"But my…" the woman tried.

Flora cut her off. "Katie has the number of your nephew's conservation shop in Savannah," she said and Katie nodded as if this were true. "Fortunately, the three chairs at Maguire House are all in fairly good condition. As you'll see in a moment, the carvings are intricate but the oak makes them sturdy. If there are no more questions, I'd like to see the Eagle Chair, now."

"Yes, let's see it."

"Don't keep us in suspense."

"Pull the drape, Flora."

The women began to banter and someone laughed.

"Okay, then." Flora jerked off the piece of fabric and the group grew silent. Only Katie said a word. Two words, actually.

"Holy shit."

# CHAPTER FOUR

*Roma, if you want to*

"Please tell me that's not more fried chicken," Deb said, and leaned over the kitchen counter to peer at the aluminum foil-covered platter that Syd had found on the other end of the doorbell. "Every time a person dies in Beaumont, the whole town dusts off their cast-iron skillets. You'd think it was law." She poked a manicured finger into the foil. "If I eat another drumstick, I'm going to sprout feathers, I swear."

"Let's see," Syd replied. She wasn't going to make any promises about what was under the foil. There *had* been an impressive amount of fried chicken delivered to Deb's two-story colonial during the past two weeks. Personally, Syd thought the traditional southern fare was the perfect comfort food. Agreeably versatile, it could be eaten hot or cold, put in sandwiches or salads, and tasted equally delicious whether store-bought or homemade. Syd had nothing against fried chicken. Still, there had been a lot of it. Pulling back the wrapper, she found thick slices of perfectly ripe tomatoes layered with fresh mozzarella cheese and basil leaves. She whistled with appreciation. "I don't know the proper name for this, but it's not fried chicken."

Deb looked suspiciously at the platter. Picking up a tomato slice, she ate it whole. "It's a caprese salad," she muttered, "and Margaret Mullins is responsible. I just know it."

"Who?"

"Margaret Mullins." Deb made a face. "She went to Italy last spring and won't let anyone forget it."

"Well, her salad looks delicious," Syd said, and opened a drawer to get forks.

"It's a ca-pre-se," Deb said in the worst approximation of an Italian accent Syd had ever heard. She plunged a fork into a chunk of cheese, expertly spearing a basil leaf as well. Disdain would not stop Syd's dauntless older sister from enjoying the meal. Smacking her lips, she picked up a tomato. "Every time I see Margaret, she kisses my face, twice and says *ciao bella!* Owen hasn't kissed me in five years."

"That's not true," Syd called her out on the lie. Deb and Owen were Syd's model of a successful partnership. What she'd thought she'd had with Carrie, and one day hoped to have with someone else, existed in her sister's marriage to her high school sweetheart. "I saw y'all making out like teenagers last night in the gazebo."

Deb didn't deny the accusation but barreled on with her rant. She pointed her fork at Syd. "You're not supposed to say Roma if you're not in Italy. There is literally an idiom about this specific thing. Margaret's all 'Roma' this, 'Roma' that."

"Roma, if you want to," Syd laughed, happy to egg Deb on. In no way did she believe her sister cared about Margaret Mullins's trip to Italy or the fried chickens flocking on their doorstep. The steam she was blowing off was coming from somewhere else.

"It is not okay! The woman is working my last nerve," Deb seethed, and a piece of tomato slid off her fork and landed on her crisp white blouse. "Shit."

"Don't you mean *merda?*" Syd asked, careful to play out the second syllable. "And you brought that on yourself." She loaded her fork again. "What do you expect to happen when you bad-mouth this gorgeous salad?"

Deb wiped at the tomato flesh on her shirt with a damp dish towel, making the stain even worse. "It's not a-karma it's a-fiasco," she said, using the ridiculous Italian accent again. Shrugging out of the shirt, she bumped Syd away from the sink and, standing in her bra and slacks, plunged the stain beneath the running water.

"Not sure that's going to make it better," Syd laughed, and was surprised when Deb turned back with tears running down her face. "Oh, sweetie, what's wrong?" she asked, but she knew. Syd had arrived in Beaumont two weeks ago, and Deb had broken down at least once a day since.

"Honey died." Deb gulped, and visored a hand over her eyes. "And you're leaving me here with the vulture."

"I'm sorry," Syd said and also began to cry. She moved forward to wrap her big sister in a hug. A head shorter than Syd's lanky five-ten, Deb nestled comfortably against her shoulder. They held each other for several moments and Syd wondered if dealing with the enormity of Honey's loss would ever get any easier. She was thankful for the time they'd had together but always thought they'd have much more. Being closer to Honey had been one of the primary reasons Syd had moved back to Georgia. "I'll be back next weekend. I promise."

Deb held her more tightly. "I don't want to meet with the lawyers, today. It's too soon. Why can't Great Aunt Arlene relax? No one wants Honey's crazy old stuff, anyway. Mom just rolled over and let Arlene set up the meeting."

"I know," Syd agreed. Patting her sister's back, she inhaled the familiar scent of her perfume. She didn't know the name, just that it was French, and that Honey had given it to Deb on her sixteenth birthday. Syd wouldn't bring that up now. "I think Aunt Arlene is grieving in her own way."

"You're too nice," Deb said, sounding disgusted.

Syd pushed forward. "And it does make a little bit of sense to meet while Mom and Dad are still here. Maybe give Great Aunt Arlene a break?"

"Genius idea. Which arm?" Deb joked.

Syd sighed. "When Carrie left, I needed to get rid of everything that reminded me of her. It was out of sight, out of mind. I think that's why it was so easy to give up the house and move back here."

"Carrie is a bitch from hell," Deb repeated the phrase that had become her go-to since the online gossip magazine *Spill* had posted a photo of Syd's ex-wife kissing her ex-drummer outside an Austin nightclub. "You're so much better off without her."

"I know," Syd agreed, though at one time, she'd hoped they'd grow old together. "I'm just saying, this might be what's going on with Great Aunt Arlene."

"What's going on with Great Aunt Arlene"—Deb pulled back from the hug and looked Syd dead in the eye—"is that she's judgmental and vindictive. She never could stand Honey's taste in furniture and wants us to donate everything to her church."

Syd held her gaze. "I'm confused. Didn't you just say you didn't want any of this stuff?" She tried to picture Honey's ornately carved pieces of Bavarian, pre-war furniture in Deb's house and failed. "Where on earth would you put the squirrel-and-acorn dining room set?"

"That's not the point." Deb ran a hand through her shoulder-length, black hair. "I don't want the acorn table. What I want is for Great Aunt Arlene to give me a minute to catch my breath."

"I get that," Syd said, quickly. Deb had been closer to Honey's death than anyone else in the family. As an executive working at the rehab facility, Deb had been called to the bedside the moment Honey had suffered the second fatal stroke. She'd held her hand as she passed. Last week, she'd delivered the eulogy and then hosted the reception. It was all too much. Syd felt guilty about going back to Atlanta and leaving Deb to deal, but she'd allowed Colette to schedule a small gig. It had been four months since Syd's last performance, and she was ready to get back on stage. Maybe it was Honey's death, but Syd felt restless in a way she couldn't articulate. She tried a different tack. "Did you tell Great Aunt Arlene how you feel?"

"I did," Deb said. "But you know how self-righteous she is. She insisted we meet today to review the will. Next, we have to go through Honey's furniture and make picks like it's the NFL draft. I hate her."

"No, you don't."

"Yes, I do. She's been nasty to us since we were children."

"You're almost forty," Syd pointed out and Deb started to cry again.

Syd pulled her back into the hug. It had been two long weeks of intense grieving. Just because Honey's death wasn't entirely unexpected, didn't change the degree of loss. As Deb had observed at the funeral in front of a packed congregation at the First Methodist Church of Beaumont, the girls had hit the grannie jackpot. A warm and gracious woman, Honey, or Virginia Clairmont as the rest of the world had known her, had always been present in their lives. Every holiday, every birthday, every graduation, Honey had been there to celebrate their milestones and then take them to lunch afterward. It was hard to imagine her not being around to hand out the stockings Christmas morning or the bon mots at cocktail hour.

"I'm just so sad," Deb hiccupped.

"Me too. It's okay," Syd said, and squeezed her tighter. "We'll get through the lawyer meeting together. I'll come back soon and we'll go through her stuff. It might be fun, who knows?"

"I know."

"You do not."

Honey had served as their daycare provider until they'd been old enough for preschool. Not because their parents, both math professors at Beaumont University, couldn't afford daycare, but because Honey had insisted on doing it. As a child, Syd had thought her the most beautiful woman on earth. As an adult she'd revered her wisdom, coming to her for guidance before, during and after her marriage to Carrie. After a long fruitful life, Honey's death wouldn't be considered tragic, but she would be sorely missed.

Someone coughed, alerting Syd that she and Deb were not alone. Syd turned to see her ten-year-old niece Emma standing in the doorway with Ray, the family dog.

"Um, y'all look weird," Emma said, as Ray wandered into the kitchen.

"Um…you're weird," Syd replied. Releasing Deb, she picked up the damp dish towel, lying next to the sink, and hurled it across the room. A shortstop on every softball team she'd ever played on, Syd's aim was predicatively accurate.

The towel hit Emma square in the head and caused her to shriek with delight. She fired it back at Syd but was wide of the mark. Bouncing off the refrigerator, the towel hit the floor where it was immediately snatched up by Ray who ran out the doggie door like he'd just scored the Hope Diamond. There was a brief moment of silence and then Deb began to laugh. Deep and throaty, it was one of Syd's favorite sounds on earth because it meant everything was going to be okay. Maybe, it was only going to be okay for a moment, but sometimes a moment was all you needed.

"Here's how it's done," Deb said. Balling up her shirt, which was now a sodden mess, she threw it at Emma but landed it on top of the light fixture instead.

"Nice, Mom!" Emma cracked up.

She was still at an age where she was not yet embarrassed by her mother though Syd was on the lookout for any sign of change. Emma's older sister, Grace, had gone through a prickly phase from fourteen to sixteen, and was still known to roll her eyes from time to time. A sophomore at Beaumont University, Grace was a near physical duplicate of her mother so also bore a striking resemblance to Syd.

"What's going on in here?" Syd's brother-in-law walked into the kitchen adjusting the collar of his Beaumont University golf shirt. Tall and broad-shouldered, Owen looked like the retired college football player he was.

"Mom's going crazy," Emma said, and ducked under his arm.

"Is that right?" Owen asked, ruffling her hair.

Though injuries had squashed his dream of going pro, being the player who caught the winning pass in a national championship game had been enough name recognition to launch a successful Toyota dealership. Intelligent and kind-hearted, Owen was a loving husband to Deb and a wonderful father to Emma and Grace.

"Is the lawyer meeting still happening?" he asked, eying his wife's shirtless state. "Grace said she'd take Emma to her Girl Scout meeting, but she's not excited about it."

"No one is excited about today, besides Great Aunt Arlene," Deb said, and squared her shoulders. "It's going to be all hands on deck when we go through Honey's things. We can't let Arlene take everything. She and Honey barely spoke."

"Why don't we take all the furniture to Syd's new house?" he asked, looking around their own tastefully decorated kitchen. "Honey's cuckoo clock collection is not exactly our style."

Syd shook her head. "I don't want Honey's cuckoo clocks, and Deb doesn't either," she explained. "We just don't want Great Aunt Arlene to have them."

Owen tilted his head. "So, this is a clock-block?"

"Exactly," Deb said. "That's exactly what we're doing. *Thank you*. We can't let Arlene take our legacy."

"Fine by me," Owen said, as if it now made perfect sense. He was no fool. Syd knew he was happy to scapegoat Great Aunt Arlene and her furniture lottery if it meant deflecting Deb's frustration away from himself. His strategy was impressive to watch. Choosing his battles, he asserted opinions only when absolutely necessary. "You wearing that?" he asked her now, nodding at her off-white, lace-front bra.

"Maybe," Deb replied, eliciting a horrified squeal from Emma.

Her long blond ponytail bounced in protest. "No! Mom! Put on another shirt. Please?"

"Your wife had a small accident," Syd offered. She fixed her gaze on the light fixture. "There was some fallout."

"Do I want to know?" Owen asked her. Craning his neck, he tried to get a better look at what was hanging on the light.

"I don't think you get a choice," Syd said, smiling.

She'd known Owen since she was a starry-eyed preteen, staying up late to wait for Deb to come home from her date with the quarterback. Owen had always treated Syd like a little sister, calling her Kid or Squid, or any other variation of her name that came to his mind. He smiled gently at his wife. "What happened to your shirt, baby?"

Deb adjusted a bra strap. "It's all Margaret Mullins's fault."

"I heard she went to Italy," he said, and she stuck out her tongue.

"Margaret had the audacity to bring us food," Syd reported and Owen's eyebrows shot up. Scanning the room, he honed in on the now covered caprese salad.

"Is that fried chicken?" He asked, hopefully, and stepped up to the platter.

"Mope," Syd said, using the family shorthand for a regretful no.

"Y'all cannot possibly want more fried chicken," Deb said, and tried to snatch her blouse off the light fixture.

"Nice try, Mom," Emma said. She climbed on a barstool but couldn't reach the shirt until Owen lifted her beneath the arms. Freeing the sodden blouse, she flung it directly into Syd's face. The shirt landed with an audible smack and stayed there, covering Syd's head like a hood. She knew how comical she must look and played the moment for all it was worth. Making no effort to remove the shirt, she spoke calmly through the shroud.

"Good one, Emma," she said, and gave her niece two thumbs-up. "Your training is coming along well. First rate."

"That was awesome," Syd heard Owen say. She shook off the shirt just in time to see him give his daughter a high five.

Emma looked thrilled and Syd marveled at the amount of space this child took up in her heart. She ran a hand through her closely cropped short dark hair. Being hit with a wet shirt wouldn't affect her appearance. She didn't wear makeup and her hair was so short it looked about the same wet as it did dry. Deb was a different proposition. Though she'd only been wearing the simple, white blouse with her fitted black slacks, Syd knew that both time and thought had gone into her appearance. Choosing a replacement outfit could take a while. Syd was itching to get through the lawyer's meeting so she could begin the two-hour drive back to Atlanta, if only to recharge so she could return and be of more help to her sister. After they divvied up the furniture, they'd need to clear out Honey's house and get it ready for sale. None of it would be easy.

"We really should get going," Syd teased Deb. "You don't want Aunt Arlene to be mad at you."

"Let her wait," Deb said, moving at a languid pace. "We'll get there when we get there."

"She's going to figure out how to take all the cuckoo clocks," Syd called out after her.

Deb shouted something back, that sounded like *pucker*, but was probably something different.

# CHAPTER FIVE

## *Discovery*

"Will you be home for dinner tonight?"

Katie looked up from her laptop to see Flora standing in the foyer holding her car keys. Dressed in a pair of dark slacks and a lavender silk blouse, her most casual outfit aside from nightgowns and tennis togs, Flora was going out to run errands.

"Yes, I think so," Katie said, wishing she had another plan. During the two months she'd been in Beaumont, Katie had eaten dinner with her grandmother almost every night. The only exceptions had been when Flora wasn't available. Unlike her pathetic granddaughter, she had a life outside the house.

"Wonderful, I'll pick up crab cakes from the club after my bridge game. How does that sound?" Flora asked, and flashed Katie a sympathetic smile.

"It sounds yummy," Katie replied, feeling like a charity case. Two months ago in New York, she'd gone to parties and art openings most weekends, and had the occasional date. Sure, her career had been parked at the kids' table, but her life had been exciting and the people she talked to almost never mentioned arthritis or critiqued obituaries.

"Have you heard from Beth?" Flora asked.

Katie winced. "I did, actually," she said, and looked back at her computer screen.

"Oh?" Flora brightened. "Did you all make plans? I'd love to have Beth over one evening."

"Nothing firm yet," Katie said, and wished she had a different answer. "I know Beth is busy with the twins."

"I'm sure that's true," Flora agreed, and looked politely into the hall mirror, pretending to fix her lipstick. The pity she felt for Katie was palpable but her code of conduct did not allow her to weigh in unless expressly asked. Even then she might be stingy with advice. Katie's father operated under the same laissez-faire approach. Katie mostly appreciated the freedom, but right now her inner child wanted bold comfort. Beth's resistance to reconnect hurt deeply. Since arriving in Beaumont, Katie had texted her former best friend once a week, suggesting they meet for a drink. So far, Beth had been completely unreceptive. The first two times she hadn't even offered Katie an excuse. Once she responded *no*, and once *I don't think so*. Lately, she'd been issuing more polite rebuffs, which Katie took as a good sign.

Flora seemed to think the way to reunite the old friends was through music. "I hope you'll reach out to Beth again. I saw that singer you two liked was playing a benefit for the local humane society next month. I hate to think of you here, all alone, when I'm visiting your father. So, I bought two tickets."

"What benefit? What singer?" Katie asked, and felt a small thrill start in her chest. There was only one singer whom she and Beth had obsessed over in high school. It could only be one person.

"Syd Collins," Flora said, and did a little shimmy. "She's playing a solo show at someone's private home on the lake."

"You're kidding," Katie said, though this was exactly whom she'd suspected. She wondered if this would be enough to tempt Beth and then sighed because the rift was all her fault. Why should Beth respond to her now when Katie had stopped responding eight years ago?

"I understand Syd's recently divorced and has moved back to Atlanta," Flora continued, as if someone like Syd Collins would look sideways at Katie.

"I heard that, too," Katie said, her mind racing at the prospect of seeing her favorite singer in a private venue. The last time Katie had seen Syd Collins perform live, the alt-rocker was still fronting Ache and Bake. Katie had never seen Syd perform solo. She wondered if Beth had been more fortunate. Flora wasn't overstating when she'd said Katie and Beth had been obsessed with the singer in high school. Senior year, they'd followed the band up the east coast, like migrant farm workers. "Are you sure you won't be back to go with me?" she asked.

Flora waved her off. "I won't be back until the tenth," she said. "Invite Beth and do it soon. Give that young mother time to find a babysitter."

"I just may do that," Katie hedged. "Thanks for buying the tickets. I'm really looking forward to it. And don't worry about me being alone when you're visiting Dad. I've got plenty to do here." Katie nodded at her laptop where she was updating the social media campaign she'd launched to find the chairs. So far there'd been no traction, but with thousands of ZAP alumni nationwide and only four lost chairs, Katie was hoping to turn up some viable leads.

"Anything to report?" Flora asked.

"Not really," Katie said and felt a stab of shame. Flora was too polite to complain but Katie sensed her grandmother was getting impatient with her progress and anxious to report some good news to the board. "I already told you there was nothing at the ZAP headquarters in Atlanta," she said. Katie had driven the Mini Cooper up a few weeks ago to review the scant archive and found she already knew every detail in the file.

"Why didn't you get the truck when you were up there?" Flora asked. "Ginny emailed me the other day wanting to know when you might come by the farm."

"You mentioned that," Katie said. Trying not to let her frustration show, she made a joke instead. "It doesn't make sense for me to pick up the pickup, until I have something to pick up."

"And won't that be exciting," Flora said, betraying the smallest amount of emotion. "Don't you have any leads at all?"

Katie searched for something to share with her grandmother. "I've an appointment later today at the Beaumont University Library with a special collections librarian. I've found an archived collection of nineteenth-century business ledgers from Gerald County. They have accounting books from two different furniture makers. If the ZAP chairs were made locally, there'll be a record of it."

"Really? How exciting," Flora exclaimed, and Katie felt guilty. Finding a sales record of the chairs was far more possibility than probability.

"Well, I've got my fingers crossed," she said, and watched Flora's smile falter. As much as she wanted to please her grandmother, Katie would not be untruthful. "I'll let you know if I find anything."

"Please do," Flora said, and opened the front door. "We're all very invested in your progress."

"I'm checking under every stone," Katie called, "and thanks again for the tickets," she said, but Flora had already gone. "Shit," Katie swore under her breath. Who knew it would be so difficult to find four giant bird-themed chairs? Two months into the search and Katie hadn't found a thing. Flora's constant questions only exacerbated the self-doubt. Katie was looking forward to her grandmother's vacation to New York almost as much as if she were going herself.

She looked back at the screen where she'd posted renderings of each ZAP chair as if they were listed on a wanted poster from the American old west. The four chairs in their possession were x'ed through as if they'd already been apprehended and the four others had a reward listed beneath them. Twenty-five hundred dollars per chair. This was the complete allotment for the acquisition, but cash was the most likely thing to flush the woodwork out of the woodwork. Katie was hoping her post would go viral. So far, she had sixteen likes and a comment asking if this was *for realia Sheila.*

Katie slid the laptop into her messenger bag. The Beaumont University Library archive wasn't likely to yield big results.

Even if, by some miracle, a sales record was listed, it would be a far cry from finding an actual chair. Still, the ledgers were a solid lead and Katie needed some progress. This was probably why Flora was so eager for her to collect the old Ford from Atlanta. An empty truck was better than nothing.

An image of the high school hayride popped into Katie's head, and she impulsively pulled out her phone. So far, she'd only invited Beth out to lunch or to meet for a drink. What would Beth say if Katie invited her to see Syd Fucking Collins?

*Any interest in an extra ticket to see Syd Collins perform at humane society benefit concert next month?*

Three dots appeared immediately, indicating Beth had read the message and was forming a reply. Katie stared at the dots, willing them to turn into a sign that moving back to Georgia hadn't been the most ridiculous thing she'd ever done. The dots hovered for several seconds and then disappeared completely. Katie was surprised to feel tears prick the back of her eyes. It wasn't like her to get emotional. Her father liked to say she'd cried all her tears the year her mother died. The dots appeared again, and Katie held her breath.

*Thank you. I already have tickets.*

Katie deflated. If Beth wasn't responsive to a Syd Collins's show, then Katie didn't have a shot at reconnecting. At least now she knew for certain. The phone beeped in her hand.

*How about dinner next Tuesday? Simpsons 6pm*

Katie texted back before the invitation could disappear.

*Looking forward to it.*

Pocketing the phone, she wondered at the choice of venue. Simpsons was the type of restaurant where a family might eat after Sunday morning church. They had an early-bird special, paper placemats and a buffet. Katie wondered if Beth was sending her a message. There were so many old haunts they might revisit, places that held meaningful memories. Katie had no recollection of ever going to Simpsons with Beth, but it was better than no plan at all. She celebrated by Googling Syd Collins.

Images flooded the screen, showing Syd from almost every angle. Katie selected a recent candid of Syd's face and zoomed in. Still as striking as she'd been eight years ago, there was now a haunted look in her eyes that inspired protective feelings in Katie, and probably ever other queer woman on the east coast. Syd's divorce to bass player Carrie Outlaw had been reported in all the tabloids. Was that the connection Katie was feeling? Of course, losing her mother wasn't the same as Syd divorcing her wife, though the cancer had been a cruel and quick shock.

Syd's new album, *Florida Man*, was a scathing indictment of love. The title track was a hilarious takedown of the man who'd taken Syd's wife. Katie liked to sing it really loudly in the shower. She was touched that Flora had thought to get tickets for the benefit. If she and Beth were friends by then, maybe they could go together.

Katie's day got better when she arrived at Beaumont University Library, and met Ernest, the aptly named librarian. Not only had he pulled Gerald County's mid-nineteenth-century business ledgers for Katie, he'd laid them out arranged by date in a climate-controlled room. Standing discreetly inside the door, he handed Katie a pair of white dust gloves.

"Good luck with your research, young lady," he said, but made no move to leave.

"Thank you, Ernest," Katie said, and slipped on the gloves. "I'll let you know if I find anything interesting."

"Please do," Ernest replied, still hovering.

Katie was not bothered by his presence. Curiosity was an excellent trait in a librarian and she never discouraged it. When she'd called to reserve the archive, she'd made sure to tell Ernest all about the search for the ZAP founders' chairs. If something escaped her attention, there was a chance he would think of it.

"Hope you find a record of the sale," he said and gave a little bow. "Come find me if you need anything."

"I will," Katie said. She ran her finger down the spines of the ledgers, which were conveniently marked by date. ZAP had been founded in 1868. Katie would start with the ledger marked 1870 and go from there. Laying it carefully on the cloth, she positioned it under the light. Flipping the pages, she saw two columns written in faded pencil. They were only legible if magnified so Katie placed a clear plastic sheet over the first page. In the left-hand column, names were written. On the right side, was the item purchased and the price. Katie ran her finger down the column of names, looking for one of the eight ZAP founders and didn't find a match. The next page was more of the same, and the one after that. Katie spent three hours looking through the ledgers. Ernest checked in on her several times providing moral support and fresh gloves. It wasn't until Katie was paging through the last book that she finally found an entry that sparked her interest.

*Ida Bonewright x eight*

She held her gloved finger down on the entry. Mildred Samuels Bonewright was one of the three ZAP founders, originally from Beaumont. Could Ida be a nickname for Mildred? Could the women be relatives? Surely the "x eight" referred to eight items? Katie looked back at the ledger. The total cost of the items purchased was three hundred and twenty dollars. Divided by eight, made forty dollars per item. But for what? It was then that Katie realized, that unlike the other books she'd scrutinized, this ledger didn't list the actual item purchased. Closing the book, she read the name on the spine. Why hadn't Graham and Sons recorded what furniture had been commissioned? There were unusual letter pairings attached to each entry but no mention of what had actually been made.

Katie went to find Ernest. The librarian might have an opinion about the letters next to ledger entries. Katie would also request a copy of the page mentioning Ida Bonewright. The files she'd copied at ZAP headquarters in Atlanta may have mentioned Ida among Mildred Bonewright's family. If the information wasn't there, Katie could check the US census or newspaper archives. If Ida Bonewright was related to Mildred Samuels Bonewright, Katie was confident she could verify it. It wouldn't be conclusive proof that Graham and Sons had made the ZAP chairs, but it would be more information than Katie had when she'd started.

The special notations by each entry had to be references to what piece of furniture was being made. What was the point of keeping a record if you couldn't discern what you were recording? Perhaps pages were missing from the book or maybe Katie had missed something.

Ernest wasn't in his office so Katie returned to the room where she'd left the ledgers and found him standing over an open book. "There you are," he said, and Katie wondered what was going on. He was wearing a pair of dust gloves and had a hand on the ledger.

"I was just looking for you," she said, forcing herself to stay calm. What was he doing with the ledger?

"You found me," Ernest said and splayed his gloved fingers in a wave. He took a step back and Katie saw the ledger wasn't on the page she'd left it.

*What the fuck was going on?* Katie struggled not to let the thought escape her lips. It wouldn't do to alienate the person in charge of the one potential lead she'd discovered regarding the ZAP chairs, no matter how small or unsubstantiated it was. She worked to mask her frustration. "I was hoping to get a copy of a page in the Graham ledger." She pointed to the book opened on the table in front of him.

"A page?" Ernest said and looked surprised.

"I assume that's allowed," Katie said. "I found what I think might be a relevant entry."

Ernest nodded as if this made perfect sense. "I put your ledger over there," he said, and indicated the stack of books to his right. "Don't worry, I marked your spot."

"Thank you," Katie said. Confused, she studied the ledger open on the table. Looking closer, she saw the pages weren't filled with names and numbers but, what appeared to be drawings and diagrams. "What are you looking at?"

"It's a companion ledger to Graham and Sons, a type of index," Ernest explained, and beckoned Katie forward. "I'm embarrassed to say the book was left on my cart. There's no excuse except that I was so excited to get you started, I overlooked it."

"That's okay," Katie said, straining to see the pages better. "Does it have a record of the ZAP chairs? I found a three-hundred-and-twenty-dollar commission, from Ida Bonewright, in August of 1871. That's the entry I want copied."

Ernest stepped aside. "It won't be a problem," he assured Katie. "And, I'm fairly certain it won't be the only copy you'll need tonight." He gave her a little wink.

"What do you mean? Did you find something else?" Katie asked, and Ernest nodded.

She looked down and felt the world shift on its axis. On the page in front of her, drawn in a fine hand, were detailed diagrams for the eight Bird Chairs of Zeta Alpha Pi.

# CHAPTER SIX

## *Careful*

"What the hell are you doing here?" Syd asked, looking at her ex-wife in disbelief. Framed in the doorway to Honey's cottage, Carrie hovered like a bad smell.

"I've come to pay my respects," Carrie said, and made a move to come inside.

Syd blocked her passage. "I don't think so."

Carrie looked bemused. "Let me in, Syd," she said, as if they were five years old playing queen of the castle. "It's hot out here."

"Then get back in your car," Syd suggested, and took a step forward just as Carrie did the same.

Suddenly, they were inches apart. So close, Syd could smell the nervous cigarette Carrie had smoked on her way over and the orange mints she'd eaten to cover it up.

"I'm here for Honey," Carrie whined.

"Her funeral was two months ago," Syd said, holding her ground.

Carrie took a reflexive step back. "Well, no one called me," she muttered, looking angry.

Syd didn't know how she was supposed to respond, which was often the case when dealing with Carrie. Her modus operandi was to do shocking things and then dare you to pretend it wasn't normal. There was only one possible reason for her to show up at Honey's cottage today. Syd wondered if Carrie would be bold enough to admit it. "Why are you here?" she said, and Carrie shifted her eyes toward the ground. It was as much as an admission.

"We sold the LA house. Paul and I are staying in Beaumont with Mama until we decide what to do," Carrie replied, as if she and Syd were old acquaintances, and not high school sweethearts who'd once declared to love each other until the end of time.

Syd took a deep breath. There was no point letting Carrie rile her up. Her ex-wife thrived on drama, and would push the scene as far as Syd allowed it to go. Syd couldn't imagine anything tackier than to have a family member see them catfighting on the front lawn. She steadied her voice. "Okay, but why are you here?"

"Me and Mama saw your Aunt Arlene at the TJ Maxx." Carrie smoothed a hand over her pin-straight, red hair. "She mentioned y'all were going through Honey's stuff, today. I thought I'd come by."

Though Syd had suspected the furniture lottery might be the reason for Carrie's appearance, the idea that Great Aunt Arlene had been the person who'd invited her was laughable. "You took that as an invitation to participate?" Syd asked and wondered how she'd ever loved someone so selfish.

Carrie shrugged her narrow shoulders. "There's a mirror I've always loved, I thought…"

Syd cut her off. "You've got to be kidding," she said, tamping down the rage. All morning she'd been trying to come to terms with the dismantling of her grandmother's estate. Carrie Outlaw had not been part of any solution she'd imagined.

"Well, I loved Honey, too," Carrie said, and made a pouty face. "You weren't the only person in her life, you know."

"Yes, but Honey was *my* grandmother," Syd said. "When you divorced me, you lost all rights to my family *and* their furniture."

"I only want one mirror," Carrie persisted. "We both know that house is full of crap. No one will miss that mirror."

Syd held her ground. "No."

"Honey wrote to me after the divorce. Did you know that?" Carrie said, and Syd squeezed her hands into fists. It wasn't a stretch to believe Honey might have corresponded with Carrie following the breakup. A prolific letter writer, Syd's grandmother had not been afraid to pick up a pen. She had an entire armoire stuffed with a lifetime's worth of her correspondence. Honey had written to anyone who inspired her, and often received letters in return. Still, Syd hadn't known she'd written to Carrie, and the knowledge stung.

"Show me a letter that tells you to come and take a mirror," Syd said, working hard to not lose her cool. "Otherwise, I need you to leave."

"Don't be so stingy," Carrie said, as if Syd were denying her a stick of gum. "No one's going to miss that tiger mirror. You know, I've always loved it."

"You love any mirror," Syd said, quietly. Tired of arguing, she moved to close the door. "I gave you everything you were going to get in the divorce. You took the house, the car, the cat." She gave Carrie a sad smile. "It's all done. Now, go away."

"Well, you got all the music," Carrie sneered, and it took all of Syd's willpower not to slam the door in her face.

"I took what belonged to me," she said, calmly. "Now, please, leave. You don't want to be here when Deb arrives, I promise you that."

Carrie glanced nervously over her shoulder. The long gravel driveway leading to the road was clear of vehicles. The only other car in the small parking lot besides Syd's Prius was the vintage Mercedes Syd recognized as belonging to Carrie's mother.

"Don't you dare threaten me," Carrie spat. "After your last album, I should be the one calling the police. Paul was really injured by the title song. The other tracks were just spiteful."

"I've no idea what you're talking about," Syd said, now on full alert. For all she knew, Carrie was recording their encounter and planning to sell it to the tabloids. There was already too much speculation regarding the inspiration for "Florida Man" to add more fuel to the fire.

"You wrote those songs about me," Carrie snarled. "Just like you wrote all the Ache and Bake songs about me. I'm your muse. I've always been your muse. You've said it a million times. It was in the *Rolling Stone* interview. You tattooed my name on your arm, for fuck's sake. There's no getting rid of me."

"You're wrong," Syd said, and tugged at the shoulder of Honey's lumpy old cardigan she'd been wearing around the cottage all morning.

When Deb had first suggested Syd remove the Carrie tattoo, she'd been torn. Syd's sleeve was not a slapdash collage. It represented her journey, of which Carrie had been a significant part. But last week—Syd still wasn't sure why—she'd had a change of heart. Even Deb didn't know she'd done it yet. Syd supposed it was poetic justice that Carrie should be the first to see. Pulling off the cardigan, Syd showed Carrie the artful edit.

The tattoo had been changed from *Carrie* to *Careful*.

For a long, satisfying moment Carrie's face froze into a mask of horror, but she recovered quickly. "Look how clever you are," she said, feigning indifference but Syd could tell by the jut of her jaw that she'd struck a blow.

"Please, just go," Syd told her, and yanked Honey's sweater back on.

"Not until you admit you wrote "Florida Man" about Paul," Carrie snarled, and gave Syd a little shove.

Syd knew from past encounters that when Carrie got violent it was time to bail. There was no chance of Syd admitting who had inspired the songs on *Florida Man*, but maybe there was another way.

"Fine, take the mirror."

"Really? I can have it?" Carrie brightened instantly. The change was so swift, Syd took a step back.

"If you'll leave, then yes," she said, thinking it couldn't be soon enough.

"Thank you," Carrie said. Lunging forward, she tried to hug her.

Syd fended off the advance by shutting the door in her face. "Don't touch me," she said, and twisted the lock.

Carrie didn't deserve so much as a taxidermied squirrel from Honey's house, but if a mirror got her off the front porch, Syd was resigned to give it to her. It hadn't been an overstatement to say that the cottage was full of furniture. Syd wasn't sure a day would be enough to sort through the items in the living room alone. Moving too quickly down a cluttered hallway, she banged her shin on a huge, wooden chair and had to limp down the back hallway.

The tiger mirror was hanging just inside the door leading out to the deck. Syd went to lift it from the wall and paused when she caught her own angry reflection in the glass. How dare Carrie show up demanding a keepsake from this house? What was the matter with her? Syd let go of the mirror and took a moment to think. There was no way Arlene intended for Carrie to join in the lottery. Just yesterday Deb had had to argue to let Grace and Emma participate. What had Great Aunt Arlene hoped to accomplish by telling Carrie about the family gathering? Was she just being spiteful? Did she hope Carrie would show up and cause a scene? What made people so hateful?

Syd pushed open the back door and stepped onto the deck. Why couldn't everyone understand that Honey's legacy was more than just a pile of stuff? She felt tears prick the back of her eyes and cursed Carrie for making this already difficult day even harder to bear. Honey was gone. Every time Syd thought about it, she felt a shot of pain deep in her chest. None of the things in the house, even if added all together, would be worth a single afternoon in Honey's company. Carrie didn't get this and she never would.

Swiping at her eyes, Syd wondered how she was going to make it through the afternoon. Maybe she could steal off to the little island where she and her friend Jennifer had played as kids. Owen had pulled a canoe from the shed the day before and there were paddles under the cottage. Facing water snakes was preferable to interacting with her ex-wife and great aunt. Syd let out a guilty giggle, wondering if Carrie was still standing on the front porch. How long would she wait until she realized Syd wasn't coming back?

The sound of gravel crunching on the driveway told Syd that Carrie might not be her problem for much longer. Someone was coming down the single-lane drive toward the cottage. If Carrie was still on the premises, and Syd was almost certain that she was, she'd be forced to confront whichever family member had showed up early for the lottery. Syd's money was on Arlene who had an unusual fixation on Honey's possessions. It was probably the reason she'd blabbed the date to Carrie and her mother at the TJ Maxx.

Stepping off the deck, Syd crept around the azalea bushes hedging the east side of the cottage. There was little chance she wouldn't have to involve herself in whatever drama was about to go down. It didn't matter that it was Great Aunt Arlene's fault that Carrie knew about today's gathering. She was still Syd's mess to clean up.

The incoming car wasn't yet visible when Syd reached the side of the house, so she waited in the shrubbery. Part of her wanted to remain anonymous to see how the family member would greet Carrie without Syd present. Apparently, Great Aunt Arlene had no problem chatting up Carrie in shopping malls, and Honey had been a pen pal. Who else was still friendly with Syd's ex? Deb talked a good game, but she and Carrie had once been friends. Maybe they met secretly once a month to drink margaritas and paint each other's toenails. What did Syd really know about anything?

The car came into view and Syd saw it was her parents' old sedan. Shit. What were they doing in Beaumont so early? When Syd had spoken with her mother the day before, Barbara had said they weren't leaving their retirement community in Florida until ten thirty. Her father had been very clear about wanting to play nine holes before their drive. Syd wondered what had changed.

The car came to a stop and Syd took a reluctant step forward. It wasn't fair to ask her quiet, introverted parents to deal with Carrie. They'd never articulated their feelings, but Syd knew they were mortified by her ex-wife's exhibitionism. Syd's own wild side, tamer by degrees, had been problematic enough for the academic couple. If Honey hadn't been around running interference and offering guidance, Syd might not have survived adolescence. Syd touched the side of the house, wishing her grandmother were here now.

Syd's mom got out of the car and stared at the house. Syd could tell from her mother's body language that Carrie was still on the front porch and said a silent prayer that she'd get in the Mercedes and leave. The driveway was now clear, leaving an easy exit. But Carrie remained obnoxiously on-brand. Appalled, Syd watched as her ex-wife walked boldly forward to greet her parents.

"Hey, Barbara. Hey, James. How are y'all doing?"

"That can't be Carrie," Syd's mother said, and visored a hand across her forehead.

Syd looked back over her shoulder, wishing she'd gone with her first impulse and escaped in the canoe. Where did Carrie find the entitlement to treat the world with such impunity? How dare she put Syd's mild-mannered parents in the awkward position of having to greet her? Did she expect Barbara to invite her in for sweet tea?

"It's been a while since I've seen y'all," Carrie said, and stopped a few feet away. Syd tried to move but found her feet glued to the flower bed.

"We certainly didn't expect to see you here today," Barbara replied, and Syd's father squared his shoulders in solidarity. Walking around the car, he came to stand behind his wife.

"Arlene told me the family was getting together today," Carrie continued, her voice now a tad uncertain. "I'm in Beaumont, staying with Mama, so I thought I might help out."

"How very kind of you," Syd's mother replied. She turned to James, "Did you hear that? Carrie wants to help."

"We don't need Carrie's help," James said, and gave his head a little shake. Syd had never seen her father be anything but scrupulously polite and wondered what he would do next.

"But I'm here," Carrie said, and held out her hands as if the family were cleaning oil off of penguins and couldn't afford to turn away volunteers.

James made a twirling motion with his finger. "And now, you can go."

"Don't be like that," Carrie said, and looked to Barbara for assistance. "Syd doesn't care that I'm here. She's inside the cottage, right now, getting a mirror Honey wanted me to have."

"I don't believe you," James said, simply, while Barbara leapt forward and pointed a finger in Carrie's face.

"You stay away from our daughter," she said, her voice shaking with anger. "How dare you intrude here today? Haven't you caused enough pain? What's the matter with you?"

Carrie looked as if she'd been struck. "I just want one mirror," she said, and turned toward the cottage as if she expected Syd to appear any moment. "Syd said she'd be right back."

"It doesn't look like she's coming to me," James said. He made the twirling motion with his finger again. "Now get on."

Syd watched in fascination as Carrie did as bid and retreated to her car. Never, in a million years, would Syd have believed her docile parents capable of knocking steam-engine Carrie off the tracks. Yet somehow the Mercedes was disappearing down the driveway without the mirror or Syd's dignity in the back seat.

Syd saw her parents embrace and stepped back into the bushes to allow them a moment of privacy. She knew, firsthand, how unsettling it could be when Carrie forced you out of your comfort zone. Just because you were up to the task of defending yourself didn't mean the confrontation didn't take a toll. Syd dropped down to her knees. It was possible her parents might want to reframe what had happened in the driveway. Maybe they'd prefer it if Syd knew nothing of the encounter at all. What Syd did know was that her parents had earned the right to make the decision for themselves.

Quietly she stole around to the back of the house and slipped inside the cottage. Walking down the hallway, she was careful not to bang her leg on the giant chair again. She'd known before coming today that she'd likely leave here with treasures. She hadn't imagined the gift she'd just received in the driveway. Opening the back door, Syd followed her mother's voice through the house until she found her arms.

# CHAPTER SEVEN

## *Maguire House*

"Are you sure it's okay for us to be here?" Beth asked, quiet as a guilty conscience in Katie's ear. Walking up the newly refurbished stone path to Maguire House, the two old friends paused to discuss trespassing.

"This is my legitimate office," Katie said, not bothering to keep her voice down. "Why would coming here be a problem? Explain that to me," she asked, marveling at how normal it felt to talk to Beth after eight years' estrangement. Watching the honest, blue eyes process the question, it was as if Katie had seen Beth yesterday.

"I don't know," Beth admitted, and then glanced nervously over her shoulder at the ZAP House looming to their right. Built before the Civil War by a wealthy planter as a gift for his new bride, the mansion looked like a fancy wedding cake. Next door, Maguire House, though of the same period, was infinitely more modest. "When I was in ZAP, they threatened to put us on membership probation if we got caught over here."

"Well, there's a new sheriff in town," Katie said, and jangled her keys for emphasis. "I told you at dinner. I'm their new Museum Director. They pay me to be here."

"But at night?" Beth said, still sounding doubtful. Katie knew not to take it personally. Beth's reticence to come inside Maguire House had nothing to do with her belief in Katie's ability to do her job. Beth, as always, was worried about breaking the rules. Katie took care to put her mind at ease. If she were truly going to make amends with her old friend, she could start by alleviating her anxiety about spending a night in jail.

She turned the key in the lock. "Trust me. I'm allowed to be in here, any time I want. They even offered me the upstairs apartment."

"Really?" Beth said, and tilted her head toward the house next door. "When I lived at ZAP House, the other sisters used to sneak up there to have sex and smoke pot." She stepped hesitantly over the threshold into the tiled entrance as if the house mother was going to pop out at any moment and bust them for rules' violations. "I heard there was even a mattress."

"But you never used it yourself?" Katie teased and was rewarded with a snort.

"Lord, no! I never would have come in here." Katie flipped on the light, illuminating the grand foyer, and Beth whistled with appreciation. "It really is pretty, isn't it?" she said and craned her long neck to peer up at the original tin-tiled ceilings. "Our old house mother used to say it was haunted."

"Really?"

"She told anyone who'd listen," Beth replied. "It was probably just a ploy to scare us away."

"Maybe," Katie agreed. She paused to allow Beth to take in the details of the room.

In addition to the refurbished ceiling, the foyer boasted the original wainscoting, painted bright white, and black-and-white checkerboard flooring from the 1930s. Katie knew from the board meeting that ZAP had paid a hefty sum to restore the exterior of the property in accordance with the exacting standards demanded by the Beaumont Historical Society. The result was understated and elegant. Despite the small issue of breaking her private vow never to move back to Georgia, Katie loved working in the gracious old home. The recent renovations had included the installation of a central air-conditioning system that she kept on blast, justifying the cost as a preservation expense. Everyone knew antiques fared better in lower temperatures and humidity. So did Katie's hair. Right now, she had the unruly mop of red curls corralled into a bun that Rachel called her librarian hair.

"I don't think it's haunted," Katie assured Beth, and then, as if on cue, heard a small thud overhead.

"Then what was that?" Beth crossed the short distance between them and stood next to Katie.

"Raccoons?" Katie guessed, looking up at the ceiling. "Or maybe just the house settling?"

"That's probably it," Beth agreed, but grabbed onto Katie's arm.

The weight of her hand felt wonderfully familiar, and Katie reached up to squeeze Beth's fingers. Spending time with her tonight had been like a homecoming. When dinner had ended, Katie had offered to show Beth the renovations made to Maguire House and been delighted when she'd accepted. It had been too long since Katie had smiled into Beth's big blue eyes.

Something creaked again, and Beth gave her a worried look. "I never would have come here in college."

"Of course not," Katie agreed, carefully, as she had little idea what Beth had done in college. Leaving Beaumont after high school, Katie had never looked back. Losing contact with Beth was her only regret. For years Katie had justified their estrangement as a mutual drifting. They'd never had a fight, never even argued. But after months of getting the cold shoulder, Katie had been forced to admit that the blame was on her. She'd been the one who'd left, after all.

They walked through a door to the left and Katie turned on the light in the exhibition room.

Beth stopped short. "Wow, are these the chairs you were talking about?" She gasped. "They're so big. I had no idea."

"That's why some people called them throne chairs," Katie said, smiling. She was much happier to discuss the exhibit in progress than the guilt she felt for abandoning her best friend.

She flipped on the lights installed beneath the chair's pedestals.

"The carvings are wild," Beth observed and leaned down to examine the figures on the Eagle Chair. "They look like something out of *Hansel and Gretel*. And they're so big," she exclaimed. "I thought nineteenth-century people were supposed to be smaller in stature."

"Yes, I was surprised by the size, too," Katie admitted, remembering her embarrassing reaction to the unveiling of the Eagle Chair. Fortunately, none of the board members had taken issue with Katie's colorful language when she first saw how enormous the chairs were. Some of the women had even laughed.

Beth scrutinized the birds on the back of another chair. "Are these hawks?" she asked, and Katie nodded.

"All the chairs have bird themes."

"That's so interesting," Beth enthused. "Do you know which chair belonged to which ZAP founder?"

"I do." Katie smiled. "The Hawk Chair belonged to Hortense Duquesne Baker."

"Hortense Duquesne Baker, from Augusta, Georgia?" Beth responded, and Katie laughed out loud.

"The very one."

"I still have all the ZAP founders committed to memory," Beth said, and blinked her big blue eyes. "I was so scared that I was going to fail my pledge test, I studied those eight names incessantly. My schoolwork may have suffered."

"Why am I not surprised?" Katie smiled, remembering Beth's attention to detail. "I still can't believe we pledged the same sorority."

"It always made sense to me," Beth said, softly. She shrugged, and her long blond hair caught the light. "We were already best friends. Sisters was the obvious next step. At least that's what I thought at the time."

"Yeah, I want to talk to you about that. I'm really sorry about how…" Katie started but paused when they heard another noise upstairs. "Did you hear that?"

"I told you the place was haunted," Beth said, matter-of-fact. "Maybe Hortense wants her chair back."

"Shh," Katie quieted her. They paused to listen but heard nothing.

Beth changed the subject. "Have you personally found any of the chairs?"

"Not yet," Katie admitted, vowing to revisit the subject of their estrangement. "But it's only a matter of time. These women are motivated. I've also got a social media campaign going through ZAP National."

Beth nodded. "Great idea. The more people involved in the search, the quicker you'll find the chairs."

"Absolutely," Katie agreed. It felt good to discuss her job with someone other than Flora, who was also technically her boss. "The problem is the search started a year ago, without me."

Beth frowned. "It sounds like a head start to me."

"Yes, but no one kept records," Katie vented. "So, I'm doing a lot of backtracking. It seems like every place I call has already been contacted."

Beth nodded. "How do you know this chair belonged to Hortense Duquesne Baker? No offense, but there must be other chairs in this style."

"That's a good question," Katie said, and walked over to the original portrait of the founders she'd taken from the wall in the Zeta Pi chapter room. "This was our first piece of evidence," she said, and pointed to the second woman from the left in the portrait.

"Is that Hortense Duquesne Baker?" Beth asked and moved closer for a better look.

"Yes, photos from her estate confirm it. Now look at this," she said, and pointed to Hortense's chair. A portion of the hawk was clearly visible.

Beth looked from the portrait and back to the chair. "Okay, I can see it."

"That's not all," Katie said. "I traced the genealogy of the owner of the estate where our board member found the chair and found a direct connection to Hortense."

Beth looked impressed. "That was smart."

Katie smiled. "Thank you. It's important because the second source authenticates the artifact."

"That's so interesting."

"It's the professional standard," Katie explained, warming to her topic. "But I really got lucky last week, when I found a third source."

"You found another source?"

"Do you really want to hear about this?" Katie asked, suddenly worried the evening had revolved too much around her. They'd spent most of dinner discussing Katie's life in New York and now her job was taking center stage. She'd hate Beth to think she was the same selfish person who'd left town eight years ago. "We haven't talked about your kids yet, or your job. I want to know about what's going on with you."

"My kids are sweet as pie, and my job is boring as hell," Beth put her off. "Your sleuthing is so much more interesting. It's like Nancy Drew and the search for the gargantuan chairs. Tell me what else you found."

Katie laughed. "Okay, Sensei," she replied, using Beth's old nickname from their one semester of karate. Beth let it pass without comment or her usual response. Katie had a momentary twinge but pressed ahead, sharing her big discovery of the Graham and Sons ledger from the Beaumont University Library.

"Flora must have been over the moon," Beth mused.

"She was thrilled," Katie agreed. "The renderings are meticulous. Every detail is listed, down to the cost of wood and genus and species of the bird."

"Did the library give you the ledger?" Beth asked and looked around as if the book might be somewhere in the room.

Katie shook her head. "I'll get the book on loan when the exhibit opens," she explained, and picked up a folder. Opening the file, she spread the contents out for Beth to see. "The librarian let me make copies, so I don't have to keep running back there."

Beth bent over the table. "These are incredible," she said, and picked up a page to examine more closely.

"Right?" Katie agreed and peered over her shoulder at the specifications for the Snowy Egret Chair. One of the four chairs remaining to be found, it had belonged to founder Bernice Wolfe Calhoun and was Katie's favorite.

"I love that all the chairs have bird themes," Beth announced, looking enchanted. "This is such an interesting project."

"I think so too," Katie said, nodding. The floor creaked overhead, but this time she ignored it and pointed to a notation on one of the copied pages instead. "I discovered in the ledger that they were known as the bird chairs of Zeta Alpha Pi and commissioned by a woman named Ida Bonewright."

"Was she related to Mildred Samuels Bonewright, by any chance?" Beth winked and Katie cackled.

"Your pledge trainer would be so proud."

"Thank you."

"Ida Bonewright was Mildred's mother and a Graham by birth. Thomas Graham was her brother," Katie continued. The information had not been in the files she'd collected from ZAP headquarters in Atlanta but easily found in the town archives.

"This really is like Nancy Drew," Beth said, incredulous. "Your job is so cool. Nothing interesting ever happens at the copy store."

"You're a very talented graphic artist," Katie said, not willing to let Beth put herself down. The copy store she was referencing was actually a full-service print shop owned by Beth's parents. Beth had been working there since high school and now oversaw design. "You must get some interesting projects," she said, trying again to draw her out. Beth kept her at arm's length.

"Not really," she said and then startled at the sound of another, much louder, noise upstairs. Katie followed her gaze to the ceiling.

"Those are some big raccoons," she said, and then grew quiet as the noise turned to footsteps, followed by a giggle. A toilet flushed.

"At least they're house-trained," Beth whispered, her eyes now huge.

"Fucking college kids," Katie muttered and then smiled at the unintended pun. "Literally, fucking college kids."

"Are you going to bust them?" Beth asked. "I'm not suggesting we call the police or anything, but it might be funny to…"

"Scare the shit out of them?" Katie asked.

Beth nodded. "It would only be fair. They had me terrified to step foot on this property."

"You're still scared to step foot on the property," Katie reminded her, and agreed to the plan. If Beth wanted to bust the fucking college students, then a-bustin' they would go.

"Let's do it."

Footfalls on the stairs suggested they would be too late for an ambush. Beth shot Katie a nervous look. Any moment, whoever had been using the bedroom would see lights on downstairs and know they weren't alone in the building.

"What should we do?"

"Introduce ourselves," Katie said, and strode purposefully into the foyer.

"Are you sure that's wise?" Beth asked, close at her heels.

In the end, introductions weren't necessary. One of the flushed young faces they met in the foyer belonged to someone Katie knew, and the other was known to Beth.

"Arthur?"

"Grace?"

"What are you doing here?" Katie asked Arthur.

"Checking on some stuff," Arthur said, his face red.

The ZAP houseboy had helped Katie several times during the past two months and, despite his alpha-male entitlement, she'd grown quite fond of him. He had a unique way of making her feel included in whatever mischief he was manufacturing. Right now, he was holding hands with a slim young woman who was wearing a midriff-baring top and looking at Beth nervously.

"Hi, Mrs. Kennedy," the girl said, her cheeks a bright pink. "How are Justin and Davy?"

"Fine, Grace," Beth said and smiled, as if she'd run into her at the drugstore and not on a walk of shame. "They got haircuts last week."

"I bet they look so cute."

"They really do," Beth replied. "Are you still enjoying college?"

"Yes, ma'am," Grace responded, and Katie had to stop herself from laughing. Everyone was acting as if it were completely normal for Grace and Arthur to be skulking around Maguire House on a Tuesday night when it was clear they were using the empty room upstairs. The situation was incredibly absurd and incredibly southern.

Beth turned to Katie. "This is Grace Parker. Grace goes to our church and babysits the boys sometimes. Grace, this is Katie, we were friends in high school."

*Were friends?* Ouch. Katie absorbed the blow and greeted the girl. "Nice to meet you, Grace. Are you a Zeta Pi here?"

"No, ma'am. My great-grandmother was in ZAP, but I didn't rush."

"Call me Katie, please," she told the girl, firmly. She'd never liked formal prefixes and wouldn't attach one to herself.

There was an awkward silence, and Beth cleared her throat. "I don't think you know Grace's mom, Katie, but you definitely know her aunt."

Katie wondered at the edge in her voice. "Was your aunt a Zeta Pi here, too?"

"Um…no," Grace said. "Aunt Syd went to college here, but she didn't pledge a sorority. She was in a band?"

"What band?" Katie said, wondering at the almost comical look on Beth's face.

"They were called Ache and Bake?" Grace replied, her voice rising in question, as if Katie might not know who she was referencing.

Katie shot Beth a look as an image of a woman strutting across the stage with a guitar strapped against her long lean body flashed in her mind. "Your aunt is Syd Collins?"

"Yeah, she's a solo artist now. Syd just moved back to Georgia from LA," Grace informed them as if Katie hadn't scoured the Internet for any piece of news regarding the scandal that had rocked the lesbian music world last year. "Ache and Bake broke up."

"I think I read about that," Katie demurred, and Beth laughed.

"I bet you did," she said, grinning. "When we were in high school, Katie was a total fangirl. She even dressed as Syd for Halloween one year. Dyed her hair black with shoe polish and ruined her grandmother's pillowcase. I tried to get her to go as Carrie because they both have red hair but she wouldn't hear of it."

"I would never dress as Carrie Outlaw," Katie said, horrified at the suggestion. But she was happy to have stumbled onto a conversation that made Beth smile. She should have thought of it sooner. Ache and Bake represented nothing but positive memories of their friendship. *Deja Boo* had been the soundtrack to their last year in high school. "You were just as into the band as I was," she pointed out.

Beth laughed again. "I was into the music. You were in love with the lead singer."

"I really was," Katie admitted.

Grace smiled, "You know she's playing a show in Beaumont next month?"

"My grandmother actually bought me tickets," Katie confessed.

Grace laughed. "You guys are hilarious. I can't wait to tell Aunt Syd about this."

"Tell her that Katie had a poster of her hanging over her bed."

"I did."

"Syd's really pretty," Arthur chimed in, and Katie knew he was hoping to avoid the trespassing conversation.

"Was it the one of her with the guitar over her head?" Grace wanted to know. "I have that one in my dorm."

"It was the one with the dog collar," Beth and Katie said in unison, prompting a "jinx" from Arthur.

Beth kept talking.

"One time, we camped out on the sidewalk for tickets."

"You never told me that." Grace gave Beth a surprised look.

"It's true, we were a little fanatic."

"Aunt Syd is the best," Grace smiled. "I think Katie probably needs to meet her."

"Me?" Katie asked, her mouth going dry at the thought. She glanced cautiously at Beth. Her former best friend certainly knew Katie was gay though they'd never discussed it. It was a big part of why their estrangement felt so strange. What if Beth was put off by Katie's sexuality?

"Is Syd single?" Beth asked. Katie felt a quick jolt of happiness that was immediately diffused by Grace's look of confusion.

"I wasn't suggesting a date," she backpedaled. "I want you meet Aunt Syd because…"

"Oh, I never thought…" Katie scrambled to save the situation but forgot all about her pride when she heard the next words out of Grace's mouth.

"You have to meet Aunt Syd because she just inherited two hideous chairs that look exactly like the ones in the other room."

# CHAPTER EIGHT

## *The Third Pig*

"You've got something in your teeth, honey," Lori told the young woman chattering away in Syd's ear. It was an hour before her set and Syd had slipped in the back door of the Third Pig to watch Profane Jane, a new thrash band with a reputation for sick beats and outrageous lyrics. Syd had been curious about the trio from lower Alabama for a long time. Now that she was back in the South, she hoped to check out the local talent that had developed since she moved to Los Angeles. The steady stream of conversation coming from the star-struck young woman next to her made it difficult to focus on the music.

"In my teeth? Where?" The girl's hand flew to her face.

Syd gave her a sympathetic smile. She'd no idea how the young woman had managed to slip past Joe, who was standing on the other side of the partition that cut off the last two stools from the rest of the bar. With Colette on maternity leave, both he and Lori were being overly protective tonight. The bar was packed with fans who'd come from all over to see Syd perform. Colette had forwarded Syd an email from a group in Ireland who'd booked tickets six months ago.

Lori waved a vague finger in the girl's face. "It's on the left side. No. No. That's not it." She shook her head.

The girl dug at her teeth with a fingernail, and then looked hopefully back at Lori. "Did I get it?"

"Sorry," Lori said.

Syd couldn't see anything in the girl's teeth but waved goodbye when she pushed off the bar stool on a stated mission to figure it out.

"Works every time," Lori said, smugly, when the girl was out of earshot.

"You made that up?" Syd laughed, incredulous and more than a little impressed. "You really had me going. I was ready to get her a toothpick."

"That puppy was not for you," Lori said and shrugged her broad shoulders as if lying to strangers about dental hygiene was a legitimate means to an end. "We needed her gone. I don't know how she got by Joe in the first place." She craned her head around the partition to look for her husband.

Syd took a sip of her warm tea. Shot through with a splash of high-test bourbon, it was her ritual, preshow drink. "Maybe he did it on purpose," she offered. "I mean that girl was cute."

Lori shook her head. "Joe knows better," she said, and her large, gray eyes filled with concern. "I know you've had it rough, but I hate to see you sniffing around someone like that."

Syd blinked at her. "When exactly did I become a dog?"

"We're all dogs when it comes to sex." Lori blinked back. "How long has it been since you got laid?"

"Carrie," Syd admitted, and winced at the look of pity on her friend's face. It was almost as bad as the memory of the weepy, breakup sex she'd had with her ex-wife.

"That's just sad," Lori said, and excused herself to greet a familiar-looking blonde who'd just taken a seat a few stools down on the other side of the partition. Enrico and Eduardo were working the bar tonight, but Lori and Joe were working the room.

Syd peeked around the beam, but couldn't place the blond woman, who was now talking intently to someone next to her.

Syd wondered if she knew the woman and took another sip of her tea.

"The blonde says your niece Grace is her babysitter." Lori was suddenly back on the other side of the partition.

"Really?" Syd glanced over her shoulder. "She must be from Beaumont. I thought she looked familiar." Syd started to wave but Lori grabbed her hand.

"I told her it wasn't you."

"What? Why?"

"You're on in thirty minutes." Lori checked her watch. "You can flirt with your fans after the show."

Syd looked around the partition again. "You said she was Grace's boss. Why can't I say hello? It's not like I'm going to try to fuck her."

Lori pursed her lips. "Colette told me to watch out for you tonight. Talk to the blonde after the set."

"Okay fine," Syd said. "Send her back to my dressing room with a double bourbon," she teased, but she was only half joking. Syd had never taken advantage of her star status to score women. Maybe it was time.

"I will," Lori promised. "Her friend said she needed to talk to you anyway."

"She did? What friend?" Syd looked around the partition again. "I thought you told them I was someone else?"

"Don't quote me. You need to focus. You can score women after the show." Lori threw up her hands and stepped away to talk to Eduardo. When Syd had arrived an hour earlier the Third Pig had only been at half capacity but was quickly filling up. It was Syd's favorite kind of crowd. Everyone was hip, young and urban. Best of all, the women outnumbered the men three to one. Syd checked her phone and saw a text from Colette. Her long-time booking agent was three weeks into maternity leave and still monitoring Syd as if she were backstage.

*Play the songs from Florida Man*

Syd replied *maybe* and flipped her phone over on the bar.

She knew it was a better marketing decision to play the tracks from her latest release, but she just didn't feel like it. Not that she wasn't proud of the music. Syd didn't need the cover of Atlanta magazine or glowing reviews, both of which she'd had, to know the music held up well to her earlier work fronting Ache and Bake. The songs that Joe called bitter were well-crafted and well-received. Every time Syd performed them, the audience shouted the lyrics back at her, as if Carrie's betrayal had hurt them as much as it had hurt her. Syd loved these songs. She just didn't want to play them tonight.

Lori sidled back to Syd with unexpected information. "The friend wants to talk to you about chairs."

"Oh, right, the chairs," Syd said and looked over her shoulder to where the other woman was only partly visible. "I'm supposed to meet someone named Katie tomorrow about Honey's stuff. I didn't know she was coming to the show."

"You're selling your grandmother's furniture?" Lori looked aghast.

Syd thought of the giant chairs taking up all the room in her garage. Just yesterday she'd banged her shin on the one with pheasants carved on it and now had a nasty bruise. "I won't miss these chairs, believe me."

"What's the matter with them?" Lori wanted to know.

"They look like big, wooden thrones with birds carved into them," Syd explained. "Colette called them renaissance-festival chairs last week."

"I thought Colette was on maternity leave," Lori replied.

"Colette needed leave from her maternity leave," Syd explained, and Lori nodded.

"I get that," she said, and then her eyes widened a fraction. "Don't turn around."

"What?" Syd asked, and then realized Lori was tracking an approaching fan. She started to swivel her stool when Lori grabbed her arm.

"Syd, stay," she commanded.

"Again, with the dog references?" Syd asked but did as she was told. She'd been performing long enough to know that listening to the bar owner was usually the smart thing to do. Syd's first set began in a little more than a half an hour and would last ninety, high-octane minutes. It took a lot of energy to command a stage, especially by yourself. Talking to fans, though important, and sometimes really fun, could be exhausting. Without Colette, Syd was lucky to have Lori running interference.

"When did you become such a good liar?" Syd asked, when Lori returned to her side. "I heard you tell those people I was on a tour bus. When did I get a tour bus?"

Lori cracked a smile. "It's the job. Tell me more about these chairs and this woman coming to your new house tomorrow."

"Grace set it up," Syd said, and told Lori what she knew of the chairs' significance to Zeta Pi sorority.

"Did she mention a price?"

"Five thousand for the pair."

"Not bad for a day's work." Lori clinked her iced tea against Syd's spiked one. "Congratulations."

"I'm giving half the money to Deb and I'm happy to be rid of them." Syd smiled. She'd gotten Honey's spittoon and a few other pieces that worked nicely in her house. There was neither the room nor the sentimental attachment necessary to foster two refrigerator-sized chairs. Deb had been tickled when Syd had told her about the Zeta Pi connection. She'd seemed to relish the thought of Great Aunt Arlene, who'd been a ZAP during her own time at Beaumont, hearing about the acquisition through the grapevine.

Syd looked at the women seated down the bar. "Is the woman closest to us wearing an original, *Deja Boo* concert T-shirt?"

Lori grinned. "Her friend is wearing one too. It's really cool. I never noticed that little pocket before."

"That's how you can tell it's original," Syd told her. "We only printed two hundred of them with pockets. Those ladies must be hardcore fans and you just lied to them."

"You'll talk to them after the show." Lori was not the least bit contrite.

"You're scaring me a little," Syd said, and snuck a look back at the women. *Deja Boo* was Ache and Bake's first album and Syd's personal favorite. The tour had been tiny and the T-shirt run even smaller. There was every chance Syd had personally handled the shirts worn by these women. Syd remembered staying up all night to screen print the two hundred T-shirts with the tiny breast pocket. She'd always been sorry there weren't more except that owners could easily be identified as early fans. "I should probably go talk to them."

"After the show," Lori said, so vehemently that Syd paused to tease her.

"So, you don't think I should talk to them now?"

"Absolutely not."

"You think later might be a better time?"

"Talk to them after the show."

Before Syd could reply, the girl with the phantom teeth gunk reappeared from the bathroom. "I couldn't find anything," she told Lori, who shrugged her shoulders.

"Must have got it with your tongue. Good for you."

"I really did try," the girl acknowledged, as if she deserved a prize.

"I should probably get going," Syd said quickly. "It was nice meeting you."

"I'd love to…" the girl started, but Syd had already made her escape.

The Third Pig's backstage area, located directly behind them, was an easy pivot to safety, but Syd chose a route that involved walking past the women at the bar. She still had half an hour before her set. It was nice of Lori to look out for her, but Syd didn't like the idea of lying to fans, especially pretty ones wearing original *Deja Boo* tees.

"I knew that was you," the blonde said, when Syd approached them. Alcohol sparkled in her eyes, but she seemed mostly in control. "Your niece Grace babysits for my twins," she said, and showed Syd a picture on her phone in case she didn't believe it.

"Adorable children. It's nice to meet you," Syd replied, and locked eyes with the redhead standing to the left. She couldn't help noticing that she wasn't wearing a bra, or a wedding ring.

"It's nice to meet you, too. I'm Beth, and this is Katie," the blonde said. She looked down the bar where Lori appeared to be glaring at them. "That bartender just lied to us. She told us you were out back on a bus."

"She's the bar owner," Syd clarified, and gave Lori a little wave. "And she's very protective."

"Well, we don't bite," Beth said, bristling a little. Her voice rose and Syd wondered how much she'd had to drink. "Did she tell you we were from Beaumont? We went to the same high school you did."

"Lori said you knew my niece," Syd said, and gave Beth her best magazine-cover smile. She didn't need this drama before her show, especially with a friend of the family.

Beth softened. "Grace is the best. We love her to pieces. She's the one who made the connection with the ZAP chairs." She gestured to the cute redhead. "Katie's the woman who wants to buy them."

Syd smiled at Katie. "I can't believe you really want those crazy things."

"Those crazy things are saving my job," Katie said and her green eyes shone with humor. "You've no idea how excited I was when Grace showed me the pictures."

Syd felt a small zing. "I can't wait to hear about your project. Tomorrow at three, right? You've got my address?"

"Yes, good luck with the show tonight."

"Thanks," Syd said, smiling and, even though it was really time to get backstage, asked the question at the forefront of her mind. "I've been admiring your *Deja Boo* T-shirts." She smiled shyly. "I haven't seen an original one in a long time. Did you buy them online?"

Katie pretended to be insulted. "We were at the shows," she said, and then returned Syd's smile. "You blew that club away."

"How old were you?" Syd popped the second question on her most wanted-to-know list.

"Sixteen," Beth answered for both of them. "Katie went all three nights. She used her babysitting money to pay for the tickets and had nothing left over to buy Christmas presents."

"I had to knit everyone hats," Katie reminisced, causing Beth to giggle.

"We pretended they were potholders," she said, laughing at the memory.

"You really went all three nights?" Syd asked Katie. It was really time to go backstage, but she couldn't make herself pull away.

Katie shrugged, and her curls caught the light. "Your music was important to me. I was struggling with my sexuality back then. *Deja Boo* explained every secret crush I'd ever had."

"That makes me really happy," Syd said, and didn't resist when Katie opened her arms for a hug. Pressing against her, she felt Katie's nipples against her stomach and had to pretend it didn't affect her.

"Thanks for sharing your music," Katie said. Pulling away, she cast a worried eye over her shoulder.

Syd didn't have to turn around to know who was standing behind her. The Aqua Velva announced Joe's presence like the town crier.

"I look forward to seeing you tomorrow," she told Katie, who nodded.

"Me too," she said.

Beth giggled. "Why don't y'all get a drink together after the show tonight?"

*Thank God for drunk friends.* Syd nodded at the same time as Joe's hand landed on her shoulder. "I'd like that," she said.

Katie's eyes lit up. "Yeah?" she asked.

"Text me," Syd said, and turned to face the music.

# CHAPTER NINE

## Deja Boo

*In my waking dreams*
*I like to stage a scene*
*That begins and ends with you*
*Your essence is so fine*
*That mostly I don't mind*
*That none of this is true*
*You're just my Deja Boo*

Katie sang the lyrics of her favorite Ache and Bake song at the top of her voice. Standing next to Beth watching Syd Collins light the room on fire, she almost felt as if she'd gone back in time. One stunning detail kept her mind firmly fixed on the present. Less than ninety minutes ago, the sexy rock goddess prowling the stage before them had suggested Katie meet her after the show for a drink. It was a fantasy come to life that Katie still couldn't quite believe. Syd Collins possessed that intangible *it factor* people wrote about in magazines but she was also a real person. Katie could still feel Syd's arms, wrapped lightly around her waist, and tingled at the possibility of more contact. Never before had Katie wished a Syd Collins performance would finish more quickly, but Syd was halfway through the encore and Katie wasn't sorry.

*I've seen this room before*
*Walked through that open door*
*And all I find is you*
*None of it is true*
*And there's nothing I can do*
*But live these dreams of you*
*You're just my Deja Boo*

Everyone in the jam-packed, twelve-hundred-person venue had their faces tipped to the stage, basking in Syd's radiance. Stripped down to a white tank top and tight black jeans, Syd appeared every inch the rock star. It was hard to believe how friendly Syd was in person, or how beautiful. Who had skin like that? Once or twice during the show she'd seemed to purposefully glance in Katie's direction, causing Katie's already warm body to heat to an even higher degree. Was it possible Syd Collins was checking her out? Katie wasn't sure, until the last verse of the song when Syd turned and looked directly into her eyes.

*Nothing I can do*
*But dream my dreams of you*
*My secret Deja Boo*

Katie dared not make eye contact with Beth for fear that Syd would see them geeking out. All around her fans had noticed something was going on and were sneaking glimpses in Katie's direction. The attention only amped Katie's adrenaline rush. Music pulsed in her ears. Squeezing Beth's hand, she tried to relish the moment.

"I'm having a great time," Katie yelled into the din created as Syd exited the stage.

Somehow, Beth heard her. "Me too," she shouted, giving Katie hope that one day they'd truly be friends again. The small strides they'd made in the last week were encouraging if not miraculous. Katie had finally met Beth's three-year-old twins and her husband, Jimmy. They still hadn't engaged on the topic of their eight-year estrangement, but Katie knew it was coming soon. Why else would Beth agree to come to Atlanta, if she didn't want to clear the air?

"Do you want another drink?" Katie asked her now.

Beth giggled. "Yes, please." Linking her arm through Katie's, she pulled her through throngs of fans screaming for another song.

They found the bartender handing out cups of water like it was snack time at soccer practice. Katie was suddenly incredibly thirsty and wondered how Syd made it through a ninety-minute show. She thought of the singer with a cup tipped to her perfect lips and felt a surge of heat. Would they really meet up later? Katie took a cup and noticed Beth fuming beside her.

"There's that lying bitch," Beth said. Her speech slurred a little and Katie wondered if she was drunk.

"Syd said that Lori was just being protective," Katie reminded her, and inventoried what they'd had to drink that night. The second shot of bourbon probably hadn't been a good idea after the bottle of wine they'd shared at dinner. Katie grabbed another cup of water from the bar.

"She's still a liar," Beth said, loud enough for people around them to turn their heads. If the bar owner heard, she didn't react.

"Let's get some air," Katie said, and steered Beth toward the back exit.

"What about the second encore?" Beth asked, and Katie hesitated. She hated to miss a minute of a Syd Collins performance, but Beth really looked like she needed some air. Katie shoved a cup of water into her hands. "I don't think Syd's playing another encore tonight," she said, and then blinked when the lights came on indicating she was correct.

Beth's look of disappointment matched the murmuring of the crowd. She stuck out her bottom lip. "Text Syd about getting a drink," she commanded and somehow splashed Katie with her cup of water.

"Hey, be careful," Katie said, and put a hand in her hair which had grown in volume during the evening. Pulling it off her shoulders, Katie twisted the mass of red curls into a bun at the back of her neck. The night air felt good on her skin though it was unseasonably hot for April.

"Text her!" Beth said, again, and water hit Katie's foot. "Let's all go get a drink."

"Why don't we invite Syd to get food with us, instead?" Katie suggested. "I know it's Syd Fucking Collins, but she still has to eat."

"Syd Fucking Collins," Beth repeated reverently.

Before she could lose her nerve, Katie took out her phone and typed in a quick message to Syd. Since getting the number from Grace last week, Katie had used it exactly four times. Each instance, her message had been carefully thought out, edited by Beth, and then edited again. This time, Katie held her breath, and pressed send.

*Want to grab dinner?*

"Did you text her?" Beth squealed, and splashed Katie's foot again.

"Yes," Katie said, and shook off her boot. A return message came in, and she showed it to Beth.

*Do you like Middle Eastern food?*

"Syd likes you," Beth yelled, and clapped her hands together. The noise echoed loudly in the alleyway, and she lowered her voice. "She really likes you," she whispered. Though Beth was clearly impaired and increasingly slurring her words, Katie tended to agree. Syd Collins was almost certainly sending a vibe.

"What should I say?" she asked, happy for any advice.

"Tell Syd, yes! Tell her we eat anything," Beth said, and pushed the phone back into Katie's hands like it was a live grenade. "This is so much fun. What if Syd Fucking Collins kisses you?"

"That would be really fucking nice," Katie said, not joking at all. She hadn't kissed a woman since leaving Brooklyn almost three months ago and her body craved affection. If, by some miracle, Syd Collins wanted to get close to her tonight, Katie would be hard pressed to shut it down.

Beth gripped Katie's shoulder as the three dialogue dots turned into Syd's answer.

*4324 Prospect Place - See you in an hour?*

She let out a shout and spun Katie around. "It's a date. We're kebabbing with Syd Fucking Collins."

"I know," Katie said, and then immediately began to second-guess the plan.

Was it smart for Katie to hang out with Syd before she'd officially purchased the ZAP chairs? What if something went wrong? Just because there was a sexy vibe between them, didn't mean Katie had to act on it tonight. Syd's two chairs represented one fourth of Katie's exhibit. If there was any chance of sabotaging the deal, Katie needed to wait. Of course, she needed to wait. Too much was on the line. Maybe after the papers had been signed, Katie and Beth could take Syd to dinner. Right now, they needed to go back to their Airbnb, so Katie could wake up tomorrow and be an adult.

"I hope the restaurant has grape leaves," Beth said and looked so happy that Katie began to waver. Surely, she could keep her hands to herself in a restaurant? Beth would certainly benefit from a meal.

"I bet it does," Katie said, and resolved to hold it together for Beth who was now staring glumly at her phone. "What's wrong?" she asked her.

"What are we going to do for an hour? Prospect Place is really close."

"Oh." Katie saw her chance. "How about we take a walk? I'll map a loop back to this spot. I've been hoping to talk to you anyway."

Beth looked suspicious. "About what?"

"About what happened the night I left," Katie said quickly and then swallowed hard. The time had finally come to unravel the knot of tension between them. "Every time I try to talk to you about what happened, you shut me down."

Beth's gave her head a small shake. "This isn't necessary. I'm over that night." She tossed her water cup in a graffiti-covered dumpster and started to weave down the alley. "I thought we were moving past it."

"What are you over?" Katie asked, confused as she watched Beth's retreating figure. "And where are you going?"

"You said you wanted to take a walk," Beth shouted, and Katie hurried to catch up with her.

"Do you even know where we're going?" Katie asked. She'd spent little time in Atlanta and had no idea if the neighborhood was safe.

"Actually, I do." Beth gave Katie a sad look. "I dated a guy named Scooter French my junior year in college. Scooter went to Emory. Oh, that's right, you never met him."

"You dated someone named Scooter?" Katie joked, but Beth was beyond teasing.

"What the hell happened to you?" she asked, now shouting. The words echoed off the alley walls, magnifying their force. "You ghosted me with no explanation. I was your best friend and you kicked me aside like I was a piece of dirt."

Katie looked for the right words to explain. "I never felt that way. You're not dirt, Beth. I never wanted to lose touch with you. I didn't mean for it to happen. After our kiss, I just thought…"

"You thought what? That we weren't friends anymore? That I didn't want to see you again?"

"It was hard for me, I was so embarrassed," Katie said, but Beth shook her head.

"How do you think I felt?" Beth yelled. "You kissed me, and then never called me again. That was it. Eight whole years."

"I didn't come back because I was in love with you," Katie screamed. "After the kiss, I knew you didn't feel the same way about me. It was mortifying. I couldn't face you."

Onlookers streaming out of the club shot worried looks in their direction, but no one intervened. Katie regretted the public nature of the exchange but not the exchange itself. Already there was a thaw in Beth's reserve. The disappointed look had been replaced by one of fury.

"I didn't even know you were gay," she said. "Why didn't you say anything? Why didn't you tell me?"

"Because I didn't know, myself," Katie answered, truthfully. They turned a corner onto a main street, and she saw a bustling sidewalk café. "Can we sit down a minute? Please?"

"Okay," Beth said. She followed her across the street and sat down. "Say what you need to say."

Katie sank into a chair. "I'm sorry I was such a coward. Bailing on our friendship was such a lame thing to do…"

Beth looked defeated. "You didn't even come to my wedding."

"I know, I'm sorry," Katie said, feeling a deep sense of shame. "I wanted to come, but I couldn't face it. I understood by then that my feelings for you were just puppy love but I'd behaved so badly that I was embarrassed. I rationalized that you didn't need to deal with me and my stupidity at your wedding. So, I just didn't go."

"I thought I'd done something to make you angry with me," Beth said.

Katie took her hand across the table. "You didn't do anything. It was all me. I wanted to explain it all to you. I just didn't know how."

Beth frowned. "Be honest, would you have reached out to me if you hadn't landed the job in Beaumont?"

Katie wished she had a different answer. "Probably not, but I'm glad it's happening now. I've really missed you and we're about to party with Syd Fucking Collins."

"Good answer," Beth said, and her face softened. "Jimmy thought you were hilarious and now my mom's dying to see you."

"Really?"

"She even asked me to give you a hug."

"Your mom sent me a hug?" Katie asked, not bothering to hide her smile.

Beth opened her arms and she leaned forward.

# CHAPTER TEN

## *Bolting*

Syd pried the plastic top off the container of hummus and put it on the table next to the tzatziki and baba ghanoush. The freshly made, all-organic condiments would support the main meal of either falafel or kebbe. Syd didn't know if Katie and Beth were vegetarian, so she had ordered both. Syd preferred the kebbe. Deep-fried ground beef with a crispy, bulgur wheat coating, the Middle Eastern delicacy looked like a small meatball. Syd, a regular at Taste of Lebanon, had ordered the takeout before leaving the Third Pig. It was easier than hassling with the public, especially after a show when her fans were out in force.

The guests were due any moment. Katie, the adorable, braless redhead had texted moments ago to check the address. Syd wondered if the sparks she'd felt earlier in the bar would continue to ignite. There was something about Katie that had her curious. Syd couldn't put her finger on what it was and was excited to see if it persisted. Women tried to get her attention all the time. They knitted her sweaters and baked her cakes. One gal wrote her graduate dissertation on the effect Ache and Bake had on modern lesbian culture. Syd couldn't be bothered to read it. Why had she suddenly developed an interest in Katie? Was it the T-shirt? Could she hang the attraction on a perky pair of nipples?

The timer sounded on the toaster oven and she pulled out three slightly puffed rounds of whole-wheat pita bread. Wrapping them in aluminum foil to keep warm, she added the package to the buffet just as the doorbell rang. Syd looked at her watch and congratulated herself for taking a sponge bath before dinner had been delivered. There had been no time for a proper shower, so she'd made sure to cover the essentials.

*Pits, tits and naughty bits*
*Clean my whistle, lickety-clit*
*Taking a love bath for you*

Syd snorted at the silly lyrics. One hazard of being a songwriter was that phrases were always popping into her head. It was the inherent power of her muse and there was no turning it off. It was also the basis of Syd's artistic success. The reason Ache and Bake's songs of mischief and lust resonated so well with her fan base was because Syd had the ability to make them feel what was in her heart. If she was experiencing a genuine emotion, she was usually able to capture it in her music. That's why her last album had been particularly vicious and the birthday song for Emma so sweet.

The doorbell rang again, and she took off her apron. Though it was past midnight, Syd was full of energy and bounced with anticipation as she made her way through the foyer. She'd yet to entertain anyone in her home besides Lori, Joe, Colette, and her family. Katie was especially cute. Syd had found her in the audience minutes into the show and had had a hard time looking away. It wasn't just that she wasn't wearing a bra, though her bouncing breasts were so distracting Syd had missed a chord transition. Katie had a look in her eye that made Syd feel seen. It was entirely possible that it was all preshow adrenaline or a trick of the light. Still, Syd hoped it was something more.

She opened the door and found the two women whispering quietly on the front porch. "Welcome, ladies," she said, and stepped forward to great them but Beth screamed, surprising her.

"Oh my God, it's really you!" she said, and would have fallen off the porch if Syd hadn't grabbed her arm.

"Watch out," she said, pulling her back to a standing position. "Are you okay?"

"I think she may need to use your restroom." Katie smiled, apologetically.

"Of course," Syd said, now worried the impromptu invitation had been a mistake. What was she thinking giving drunk groupies her home address? Colette would have a fit if she found out. "Let me show you the bathroom."

Syd guided the weaving duo to the small bathroom off the downstairs guest room. Katie didn't seem nearly as drunk as her friend. A head shorter, she staggered under Beth's weight, nearly carrying her into the bathroom. Syd turned on the light and stepped aside to let them enter. A moment later, Katie came out and closed the door behind her.

"Beth was surprised to see you because she thought we were meeting you at a restaurant," she explained.

"That's right," Beth shouted from inside the bathroom. "When I saw it was a house, I thought that woman from the bar had lied to us again. I'm pretty familiar with Atlanta but I didn't know there was residential housing on Prospect Place. I thought it was all restaurants."

"I'm conveniently located right in the center of town," Syd said, making sure to speak loudly enough for Beth to hear her too. "Would y'all rather go out? We'd have to hurry." she glanced down at the oversized diver's watch on her left wrist. "Everything closes by two."

"Are you kidding?" Katie answered, as if Syd had suggested she eat a live mule. "I was promised Middle Eastern food." She pulled out her phone and showed Syd their text exchange from earlier in the evening. "This is you, right?"

"It's me," Syd said, charmed that Katie had taken the time to assign a sexy picture of her to the contact page. She tapped the screen. "Nice photo."

"Thank you." Katie said, looking adorably smug. "I took it myself."

"No way," Syd said and felt a little zing.

"Ache and Bake was playing the Trocadero in Philly," Katie replied. "It was maybe five years ago? I drove down for the show and stayed with a friend. Snapped this picture from the first row."

"Nice," Syd nodded, absurdly jealous of the unnamed friend. She tried to remember the Philly show and came up with an image of topless women dancing in the balcony. "It's a shame the Trocadero didn't make it."

"My friend in Philly was devastated," Katie agreed.

"Do you see a lot of live music?" Syd asked, pushing jealousy from her mind. This was getting silly. What was it about Katie that made Syd want to project romantic fantasies onto everything?

"Any chance I get," Katie replied. "New York has so many great venues." Listing them, she grew excited, and another curl slipped from her bun. "I also love theater, and book readings and museums, of course."

"Of course." Syd smiled. "I can't wait to hear more about the ZAP exhibit. The chairs are outside in the garage. We can see them any time you like."

Katie hesitated. "We should probably get some sober calories into Beth first. Otherwise, tomorrow's going to be over before it begins, you know?"

"We can't have that," Syd said, and then saw a flash of words in her head.

*Tomorrow's over before it begins.*

She paused a moment to turn the phrase over in her mind before storing it away to think about later. Now wasn't the time to start composing songs. Never mind that a two-part bridge was taking shape in her head. Drunk women needed food.

"I've got things laid out in the kitchen."

"Wonderful," Katie said, and then surprised Syd by laying a hand on her arm. "What happened just then? Did you go somewhere?"

Syd felt a blush creep into her cheeks. She rarely discussed her songwriting process with other people, but Katie's attention felt magnetic. "You just said something that made me think of an idea for a song."

"I did?" Katie put a hand to her chest, drawing Syd's eyes to her nipples which were still pushing pleasantly against the fabric of the old T-shirt.

Syd shrugged. "Why not you? I take my inspiration anywhere I can find it."

Katie nodded. "My grad-school advisor called our big ideas, brain bolts. She warned us not to take them for granted."

"Brain bolt is good way to describe it," Syd agreed. "Once I get an idea for a song, the rest of it comes together pretty quickly."

"Oh." Katie frowned. "I hate to interrupt if the juices are flowing. We can always come back tomorrow to see the chairs. That was the original plan, anyway." She glanced at the bathroom door. "I'm starting to worry Beth might be beyond dinner."

"What about you?" Syd asked quickly. The idea of Katie leaving right now made her inexplicably sad. She wanted her to stay, have dinner and talk some more. "Are you hungry? I've got a feast laid out in there and I'd love the company of a beautiful woman." Syd jerked her thumb toward the kitchen and winced at her lame line. It had been too long time since she'd flirted with any kind of real intent. Fortunately, Katie didn't seem put off. If anything, her eyes were flashing a green light.

*Green eyes, green light, flashing go, all night.*

Syd blinked. Okay, wow, maybe she needed to start writing these down. Katie's advisor hadn't been joking about the tricky nature of inspiration. Syd's muse, a frequent visitor before the divorce, now only showed up after she'd had a couple of bourbons. It was not a method to be relied upon.

"Did it just happen again?" Katie called her out. "Did you go to that place?"

"Maybe," Syd admitted, thrilled at the thought of Katie watching her so intently.

"Another brain bolt, this soon?" Katie asked. "Is that normal?" She looked so serious Syd wanted to kiss her.

"I think you're the one inspiring them," Syd said.

"Really?"

"I do."

"Well, I think you're really fucking hot," Katie said and winked at her.

They walked into the kitchen to the buffet on the granite countertop. The encounter was beginning to feel like a date, and she was beginning to hope Beth never came out of the bathroom. Reintroducing the third wheel would almost certainly throw their flirty conversation off track. A moment later, Syd's wish was answered, when Katie received a text.

"Beth is lying down in the bedroom," she said, and looked up from her phone uncertainly.

Syd was quick to put her at ease. "That's okay," she assured her, and hoped Beth had found the guest room, where the sheets were clean, and not the master suite where Syd's sweaty stage-clothes still littered the floor. "I hope she had a good time tonight. I saw y'all singing in the audience."

"Are you kidding?" Katie said. "We had a great time. Beth just had too much to drink." She popped a Kalamata olive into her mouth. "I should probably check on her before fixing my plate."

"No problem," Syd replied. "Want to take her a glass of water?"

"Great idea," Katie said. She waited for Syd to pour a glass from the stoneware pitcher on the counter and then disappeared down the hallway.

Syd took cutlery from the drawer. She hoped Beth wasn't so sick that she required tending but just unwell enough to leave Syd and Katie alone. A few minutes later, Katie returned with the verdict.

"She's snoring," she said, and grabbed another olive.

"She's welcome to sleep here. You both are," Syd replied quickly, and then embarrassed by the possible innuendo of the invitation, ducked behind the cabinet door to get dinner plates.

"Thanks, we've booked an Airbnb close by," Katie said. "Beth is supposed to take me out to the suburbs tomorrow to get a truck from a ZAP Board member."

"You're going to pick up a pickup?" Syd asked, playfully.

"Unless I get picked up," Katie shot back, making Syd blush.

"Will you use the truck to take Honey's chairs back to Beaumont?"

"That's the plan," Katie said, and took a piece of pita from the foil wrapper. "I couldn't believe it when Grace told me your grandmother had them."

"Honey had eclectic tastes," Syd replied.

"The ZAP Foundation is eternally grateful, and I plan to name my first child after her," Katie said. "Your grandmother has made my job so much easier. I only have two chairs left to find."

Syd put a piece of pita on her plate. "I'm still not clear how Grace put this all together. How did you two meet?"

Katie gave a little laugh. "Your niece…um…is friends with Arthur, the ZAP houseboy. Beth and I…um…ran into them one day, onsite. That's when Grace made the connection about the chairs."

Syd chuckled. "Why do I feel like there is more to this story?"

"I have no idea what you're talking about." Katie shrugged, innocently, and loaded her plate with a dollop of hummus.

"Can I pour you a glass of wine?"

"Water, please," Katie replied and added two falafel to her plate. "Beth isn't the only one who drank too much tonight. We were having such a good time."

"I'm glad you enjoyed the show."

"Are you kidding? Your show was amazing, I mean, you're amazing." Katie paused mid tabbouleh scoop to point the spoon at Syd. "But how can you still be standing after that performance? Aren't you exhausted?"

"I don't get up until noon," Syd said, and Katie made a tsking noise.

"I'm not talking about being sleepy tired," she said, and helped herself to the pickled turnips. "The energy you give off on stage, it's incredible. It must feel like you've run a marathon every night." she finished loading her plate and stood waiting for Syd to fix her own.

"Thanks for saying that," Syd replied. She pushed a piece of kebbe into a warm pita pocket and thought of how to respond. "It's definitely a workout. There's no doubt I burn a ton of calories on stage but it's not like I'm thinking about my girlish figure when I'm up there."

"The rest of us are," Katie teased her.

Syd smiled. "When the weather's warm, I almost always go swimming after the show."

"You have a pool?" Katie asked and looked out the dark kitchen window into the backyard.

Syd put down her plate and walked over to the wall. A series of light switches illuminated the backyard and a large rectangular swimming pool that was her favorite thing about her new home. Colette had tried to talk Syd into buying a smaller house on the next block but her arguments had fallen on deaf ears. Through the fog of her heartbreak, Syd had only seen the water.

"Amazing," Katie exclaimed and gave her head a little shake. "Can we really go in? I haven't been swimming in ages, and it's so hot tonight."

"We can," Syd said, charmed by her enthusiasm. "Should we eat dinner first?"

"Oh right," Katie said and looked down at her plate. "This looks delicious, by the way. I love Middle Eastern food. Did you make it?"

"I wish." Syd made a face. "I tried to make hummus one time and my sister declared it a chick-tastro-pea."

"That's really punny," Katie laughed. "Are you close with your sister?"

"I'm very close with Deb and very bad in the kitchen," Syd replied, touched Katie had asked about her family. "I know my

way around the grill but rely mostly on takeout for my meals."
She opened the back door and they stepped onto the patio
where an all-weather awning spanned the back of the house and
created the effect of an outdoor living room.

"So, you only eat pizza, barbecue and fried chicken?" Katie
teased and Syd wondered at the small edge in her voice.

She put down her plate on the patio table and settled into
a chair. "Maybe those were the only takeout options twenty
years ago, but Atlanta has any cuisine you can imagine. I've
been driving around a lot and discovered all sorts of things.
Tonight's dinner came from a place only a few blocks away. Next
door to that is a *pupuseria*, and next door to that, an Ethiopian
restaurant."

"*Pupuseria* is a great word," Katie acknowledged. She sat
down at the table, choosing the chair next to Syd. Even with
her mouth twisted into a suspicious frown, Syd thought she
looked adorable. "When I lived in Beaumont, cuisine choices
were limited."

"Beaumont's come a long way, too," Syd assured her. "Sorry
if I've gotten the wrong impression, but you don't seem to be a
huge fan of the South."

Katie dipped her head. "Is it that obvious?"

Syd was curious to know more. "How long did you live in
Beaumont?"

"Just in high school," Katie told her. "After my mom died,
Dad needed time to get himself together, so they shipped me
down to live with my grandmother."

"Reason enough for a negative association," Syd replied.

Katie looked thoughtful. "I never thought of it that way. I
mean, I know I suffered culture shock. Everything down here
was so different from what I was used to in Ohio. Before I met
Beth, I was truly miserable. I missed my mom so much."

"That must have been really hard," Syd empathized. She
tried to imagine navigating high school without the guidance of
her parents, Honey, or Deb and was overcome with loneliness.
"No wonder you hate the South."

"Well, right now," Katie said, and gave Syd an adorable little wink, "I don't think I hate the South at all."

"No?"

"I've actually just met the most interesting person."

"Oh, really?" Syd said and hid her smile behind a sip of water.

"It's true." Katie nodded. "The only thing I don't like about the South right now is the humidity." She pointed to her unruly bun. "My hair is driving me crazy."

"That makes two of us," Syd replied and felt her face color. "I mean, I think your hair is gorgeous."

"I like yours too," Katie replied, sweetly. "I'd never have the courage to cut mine so short."

Syd ran a hand through her closely cropped, dark brown hair. "I think it's way more courageous to deal with routine hair maintenance." She shuddered thinking of Carrie's endless trips to the salon, and constant monitoring of the weather. There were so many other dragons Syd would rather slay.

"Good thing you're so pretty," Katie said, and took a bite of falafel.

"Well, it's good you think so," Syd said, enjoying their banter. For the first time since the divorce, she felt as if she was firing on all cylinders. Everywhere she looked she saw words and music. Syd didn't know if Katie was having an effect on her or if it was simply the passage of time. She did know she didn't want the feeling to end.

# CHAPTER ELEVEN

## *Syd Fucking Collins*

"Do we have to wait thirty minutes before getting in the water?" Katie teased Syd and handed her a dirty dish.

Despite the earlier vow not to act on the strong sexual vibe swirling around them, Katie knew she'd been flirting outrageously all evening. It was a ridiculous situation. Risking the sale of two ZAP chairs for sex was a bad idea, potential job suicide. But Syd Collins was almost impossible for Katie to resist. Standing at the sink, apron tied around her lean body, she looked like a sexy short-order cook. Katie wanted to gobble up everything on the menu.

"We can do anything you want," Syd said, and gave Katie a shy smile.

"Options are nice," Katie replied, and put her cup in the sink. Making matters infinitely more complicated was that Syd seemed to be into Katie too. Surprisingly self-deprecating, she'd blushed more than once during the last two hours and even called Katie an inspiration. It was beyond flattering but didn't change the fact that Katie needed to secure the ZAP chairs before anything physical happened between them. Surely, she could keep it in her pants another day.

"There are extra bathing suits in the pool house," Syd said, rinsing Katie's cup.

"Do I have to wear one?" Katie heard herself reply and wanted to kick herself. Seriously, what was the matter with her? Just because she believed in honesty did not mean she had to spill every thought in her head.

Syd put the plates in the dishwasher. The small blush staining her cheeks was the only giveaway that she might be feeling nervous. "There's no rule. I mean, there are plenty of suits in the pool house, if you'd like to wear one," she said.

"What would you like?" Katie asked.

Syd's blush deepened. "I'd like you for you to know that I'm having a wonderful time tonight," she said, and picked up another dish.

Katie felt a wave of tenderness. Who knew Syd Collins was so sweet? Katie was finding it more and more difficult not to touch her. Syd was only standing a few feet away, her interest in Katie abundantly clear. The only thing that stood between them were two enormous chairs.

"I'm having fun too," she said, and watched Syd's mouth slip into a smile. "I'm sorry Beth isn't feeling well, but I'm not sorry to be spending time alone with you."

"I feel the same way," Syd replied, and removed the apron. "Are you seeing anyone?"

"Um…no," Katie replied, and just managed to cover her surprise. She hadn't been wrong. Syd Collins was feeling the same vibes she was. Was there a way to put hot pants on ice? "Currently, I live with my grandmother," Katie said, and it seemed to have the desired effect.

Syd's smile faltered. "In Beaumont?" she asked.

Katie nodded. "Flora lives in one of those big, brick houses off the main square."

"The ones with the window boxes?" Syd asked, politely.

"And the giant magnolias," Katie prattled on, now worried her moment with Syd was forever lost. What if she only got one chance? "It's close to campus but Flora has a garage so we don't have to worry about street parking." *Street parking? Who the fuck cared about street parking?*

"I grew up outside of town," Syd replied. "Both my parents were math professors at the university and didn't care to live near campus."

"Math professors?" Katie asked. The information was not part of the standard Syd Collins bio. "Are they musical?"

Syd nodded. "Dad used to play guitar. They live in Florida now and he mostly plays golf."

"My dad and stepmom live in upstate New York," Katie told her. "They never come south. Flora goes up there for a few weeks every summer and then again at Christmas. I was living in Brooklyn until recently."

"And now you live with your grandmother," Syd said, and seemed to deflate even further. "My grandmother just died. Well, we called her Honey. That's why I have the chairs."

"I'm so sorry," Katie replied. If there was a colder bucket of water than a recently dead adored grandmother, she'd yet to hear about it. "Did you pick the name Honey? Or did she choose her grandmother name, like Flora did?"

"I don't really know." Syd looked thoughtful. "I think Deb may have picked the name. She's a little older than me."

"Flora decided to pick her own name after a friend of hers got saddled with Gee-Gaw," Katie told her and teased out a smile. "It became a cautionary tale in her bridge group. After that, everyone picked their own grandmother name as a preemptive strike."

"The whole bridge club?" Syd was now laughing.

"Yes," Katie replied, and ticked the names off on her fingers. "Candace chose Mimi, Faye chose BeBe, and Pam chose Grandy."

"That's really smart."

"My grandmother is firmly in charge of her own narrative," Katie explained.

"I envy her that," Syd said, wistfully. "People have made up some wild stuff about me."

"That must be difficult," Katie said, and felt a pang of guilt for clicking on any and every article with Syd's name attached to it. She wanted to know the things not reported in the tabloids. "What did you study in college?"

"The original plan was to be a veterinarian, but I got a little sidetracked."

"Tripping over Grammy awards?" Katie joked.

Syd laughed. "Something like that."

"A vet, huh, do you have any pets?" Katie asked. She looked around but saw no evidence of a domestic companion.

"I did, but Carrie kept Annapurna in the divorce," Syd said. "That cat was the great love of my life."

"Oh, no," Katie said, horrified at the thought of Syd losing a pet. "What happened?"

"Carrie's mother originally adopted Annapurna, so my name wasn't on any of her paperwork. I hired a lawyer, but there was nothing I could do." Syd wiped her hands on a dish towel, taking time to rub each finger individually dry. Katie didn't know if she was being purposefully provocative or perhaps just had OCD. The effect on Katie was the same. She wanted Syd's hands on her body. She pushed the thought from her mind and made a joke instead.

"Did you consider cat-napping?" Katie asked.

Syd shook her head. "The divorce was hard enough. In the end, I found that the only things I could control were my own actions," she sighed. "I certainly couldn't control Carrie."

"Do you miss her?"

"I did for a while. Now, I feel lucky to be out of her way." She was quiet for a moment and then gave Katie a shy smile. "Hey, do you still want to get in the pool?"

"Yes!" Katie said, with more energy than she intended. "Let me check on Beth again first?"

"Good idea," Syd replied. "Meet you outside?"

"I'll be fast," Katie told her.

"Take your time," Syd said. Giving Katie a little salute, she walked out the sliding glass doors into the night.

Katie ran quickly through the quiet house, back toward the bedroom where she'd left Beth sleeping in the guest room. She needed to make sure her friend was okay before diving into either Syd Collins or her pool. It was important for Beth to know that Katie put her wellbeing first. Katie also needed to pee and fix her hair.

She found Beth sitting up in the bed watching television on her phone.

"What are you doing?" Katie couldn't believe what she was seeing. Comatose only an hour ago, Beth was now propped against Syd's starched white pillowcases wearing a fluffy white bathrobe.

"Shh, I've never seen this episode before," Beth said and patted her hand on the queen-sized bed indicating Katie should join her.

"What episode? What are you watching?" Katie asked and perched on the edge of the mattress. She looked at Beth's phone and saw a group of attractive men surrounding a tiny blond woman who was wearing a ball gown and holding a bouquet of roses. "Is this *The Bachelor*?" Katie asked, pretty sure she was correct.

Beth shook her head. "It's *The Bachelorette*. I'm an episode behind and I'm worried I'll hear something on social media before I find out who doesn't get a rose."

"That would be the end of the world," Katie joked.

Beth paused the video. "I live with three men, please don't tease me about my one guilty pleasure," she said, and turned back to the screen.

"I won't tease you," Katie agreed, "if you can explain the appeal. Everyone on this show is just faking it." She shook her head. "No one is really in love. It drives me crazy."

"So now you're taking the high road on love and honesty?" Beth asked and gave Katie a gentle push.

Katie winced. "I like to think I'm a work in progress," she said and was relieved when Beth smiled.

"You've never been able to hide what you think. Remember when you told Mr. Hall in anatomy class he had halitosis?"

"I was demonstrating accurate usage of a clinical term," Katie said, defending herself.

Beth nodded. "Well, you know he's dead now?"

"Maybe he should have brushed his teeth," Katie replied, making Beth laugh. She remembered the original reason she'd come back to the bedroom. "Hey, are you feeling better?"

Beth's mouth slid into a familiar-looking grin. "Don't be angry but I was never really sick," she said and then started to giggle.

"You're kidding," Katie said, wondering what was going on. "I was worried about you."

"I was a little buzzed," Beth admitted, still laughing. "But mostly I wanted to give you a fantasy night."

"You did?" Katie asked but knew she shouldn't be surprised. This was exactly the kind of thing Beth would do. "That's unbelievably sneaky and really nice."

Beth's smile softened. "You were obsessed with Syd Collins in high school. Pretending to pass out in her bed was the least I could do."

"This isn't Syd's bed."

"Have you seen her bed?" Beth dropped the phone.

"No," Katie said, though she wondered if the answer might be different in the morning. "She told me this was a guest room. Her bedroom is across the hall and there are three more upstairs."

"Syd gave you a tour?" Beth said and sat up straighter.

Katie shook her head. "Nothing like that. We ate dinner on the back patio. It's really nice. So is Syd."

Beth touched the luxurious duvet. "Her house is so much better than the Airbnb."

"You mean the Scare-bnb?" Katie asked, laughing.

"I would have booked a yurt to have a break from the twins." Beth looked defiant.

Katie laughed. "Syd says it's fine if we want to stay over."

"Syd Fucking Collins invited us to stay at her new house?" Beth exclaimed. "What exactly did she say? How did you manage an invitation? Tell me. Don't leave out a single word."

Katie smiled. "She's just really nice, and down-to-earth. We're mostly talking about song lyrics and grandmothers."

"No, no, no," Beth howled. "Song lyrics and grandmothers are not sexy. That's what we talk about at Gymboree. I want to hear juicy stuff. Didn't you talk about anything hot? How did Syd come to invite you to spend the night?"

"I think maybe because you were already sleeping in one of the beds?" Katie said, and Beth snorted.

"I take full credit."

"I told you, Syd is really nice," Katie said, wondering if Syd was in the pool yet and if she was wearing a bathing suit. "I'm also being really flirty," she admitted, and shook her head. "I may have invited myself swimming."

Beth looked excited. "Does she have a pool?"

"Yes, she's waiting for me right now."

"Now?" Beth slapped Katie's leg. "Syd Fucking Collins is waiting for you in a pool, right now?"

"As we speak," Katie confirmed, blushing a little. She knew she'd be enjoying Beth's reactions more if she wasn't so nervous herself. The conflict with the ZAP chairs aside, the possibility of hooking up with a celebrity crush was a mindfuck. Yes, Syd seemed really sweet. She also came loaded with Katie's adolescent projections. Katie worried it might be an impossible load to carry. Beth brought her back to earth with another slap.

"What are you doing back here?"

"I came to check on you."

"Why?" Beth was horrified.

"I just got you back," Katie told her, and Beth slapped her again.

"Stop hitting me."

"I'm not going anywhere," Beth said. Shucking off the fluffy white robe, she stuffed it into Katie's arms. "Go, have fun and don't worry about me."

"Really?" Katie asked.

"Really," Beth repeated, picking up her phone and snuggling into the covers. "I'm not going anywhere. Syd Collins has invited me to stay."

# CHAPTER TWELVE

## *Down to Business*

Syd adjusted the strap of her bikini top and scanned the back of the house for what felt like the hundredth time. She'd left her watch on top of her clothes in the converted garage, so she didn't know how long Katie had been gone. Maybe minutes, maybe longer. Syd had swum laps to calm her nerves and lost track of time. She hoped everything was okay with Beth. Too much alcohol was always problematic. If Beth had been sleeping before, she might be unwell now or, worse still, maudlin and weepy. Was that what was keeping Katie? Earlier, she'd said they'd been catching up. Maybe the two old friends were having a heart-to-heart and Syd was the third wheel.

She stood on her tiptoes and tried to get a better look into the back of the house. There was still no sign of life. Maybe Katie had called a Lyft and taken Beth back to the Airbnb. Syd's phone was currently streaming Dina Washington through an outdoor speaker, so she couldn't see her texts. She glanced up at the fairy strings her nieces had woven into the trees behind the pool and wondered if it was overkill. Grace and Emma had spent hours threading the delicate lighting through the dense natural screen of Leland cypress and crepe myrtle that hid the six-foot safety fence required by the city of Atlanta. The effect was dazzling, romantic, and totally wasted on Dina Washington who'd been dead now since 1963.

Syd suddenly felt silly standing all by herself in the pool listening to sexy love songs. Of course, Katie had taken Beth back to the Airbnb. Who wanted to be in a stranger's home when they didn't feel well? The longer Syd thought about it, the more she was convinced it was true.

She pulled at the bikini strap wondering why she'd worn a bathing suit in the first place. Katie had been quite clear about her intentions to swim naked. Was that why she bailed on their swim date? Had Katie gotten cold feet?

Perhaps tomorrow after they'd finished the business with the ZAP chairs, Syd could ask Katie on a proper date. Tonight had been a good beginning. She could feel something taking root beyond fandom and perky nipples. They'd had several conversations Syd wanted to pursue further. She wanted to know what other bands Katie liked, what books she read. Maybe they could have dinner in the revolving sundial room on top of the Peachtree Plaza Hotel. Syd already knew that Katie didn't have any food allergies. Was she afraid of heights?

Untying her bikini top, she flung it on a lounge chair. Now that she and Dina had the pool to themselves, she may as well get comfortable. Stepping out of the water she checked her phone and found a text from Colette chastising her for not playing more songs from the *Florida Man* album. Syd replied with a scared-cat-face emoji. They both knew this was a joke. Syd was happy to take Colette's advice, but the final decisions were hers alone. This way, if she was unhappy with an outcome, she'd only herself to blame. There were also texts from Deb and Grace who'd watched the livestream of the show in Beaumont. There was nothing from Katie.

"What happened to the music?"

Possibly because Katie was still here.

Syd turned to see that Katie was wearing the fluffy white bathrobe Honey had bought on her last spa vacation to Arizona. It was unclear what, if anything, she was wearing beneath it, but her smile suggested it wasn't much. Their eyes met for an instant, and then Katie dropped her gaze to Syd's bare chest, causing Syd's nipples, already rock hard, to begin throbbing. She cleared her throat. There were many things she wanted to say. First, she needed to make sure her voiced worked. "Um…I thought you'd left."

"Nope," Katie said, simply, and Syd thought she heard a smile in her voice. "I told you I was checking on Beth, remember?"

"How is she?" Syd asked and got worried when Katie made a face.

"We may have a problem there."

"What's wrong? Is Beth sick?" Syd beat back the compulsion to cover her chest. Katie's eyes on her naked skin felt like a caress. She wanted to know what was beneath the fluffy white robe, and behind the smile in her voice. Also, and this was possibly the most important question, was she still planning to get in the pool?

"Beth's not sick," Katie replied, and dangled a bare toe over the water's edge.

"What's wrong?" Syd asked, willing her to drop the robe.

"She's in love with your sheets."

"Oh," Syd said, happy to hear it was a joke. "You're both invited to stay. I told you that."

Katie's smile betrayed her answer. "You may never get us to leave," she said, and twisted the robe closed around her neck.

"I'll consider myself warned," Syd replied, and tried not to stare at Katie's hands. Why was she holding the robe so tightly? Was she nervous about getting in the pool? What had happened to the bravado from earlier in the evening?

"I was wondering something…"

"Yes?" Syd said, eager to know why Katie suddenly look so serious.

"Is there any chance I can see the chairs before we get in the pool?" Katie asked. "I can't believe I'm saying this, but I need to deal with the business part of the evening before we can move on to the…" She seemed to search for the right word so Syd stepped in.

"Swimming?" she answered, and Katie twinkled.

"Yes, I'm really looking forward to…um…swimming with you, but I'm trying to be more responsible in my life." She wrinkled her nose, as if the word was distasteful.

Syd was aware Katie had just started a new job in Beaumont. She didn't know what she'd previously done in New York but the look on her face suggested her professional life hadn't been as successful as she'd hoped. If signing the papers helped her in any way Syd was in favor. More and more she was beginning to understand the value of personal achievement. Perhaps if Carrie hadn't been so insecure about her abilities, she wouldn't have fucked the drummer. "You'll definitely feel better, um… swimming, once I've sold you the chairs," Syd said. "It'll only take a minute."

"Once you're transferred ownership to the ZAP Foundation," Katie corrected her. "I can't afford to mess this up. My grandmother got me the job."

"Well, my grandmother got me the chairs," Syd replied. She wondered what mess-ups Katie had suffered in the past. "The chairs are in the pool house." She gestured to the converted garage space, stuffed from floor to ceiling with Honey's furniture. "You want to check them out?"

"I want to buy them," Katie replied, and then looked intently back at Syd's breasts. "And then I want to go swimming."

"Deal," Syd said. She entered the pool house ahead of Katie and pulled on a sweatshirt to cover her throbbing nipples. Katie's bold stare had upped Syd's desire to an embarrassing degree, and she needed a moment to recover. Joe was right. It had been too long since Syd had let anyone touch her. Carrie's very public betrayal had left her too fragile to let another woman get close. Hooking up with a stranger was outside Syd's experience but nothing about Katie seemed strange.

She switched on the overhead light and walked farther into the room. The ZAP founders' chairs dominated the small space though other oddities and knickknacks vied for attention. Honey's taste wasn't for everyone. Syd personally hated the stuffed fox and hall tree made from deer antlers. Syd wasn't sure why Deb was so hellbent on keeping Honey's things away from her Aunt Arlene. It was true that Honey's sister had never been part of their lives growing up. Was that a reason to withhold a stuffed fox? Their mother thought Arlene's bitterness was a result of never getting married or having children of her own. Syd was inclined to agree but Deb, angry at the disdainful way Arlene had treated Honey, continued to hold a grudge and resented every item she took from the estate.

Katie entered the garage and her face clouded over. "Oh, no," she said, looking utterly distressed.

Syd felt a moment of panic and stepped over to inspect the chairs. The garage had a new roof but mice sometimes got inside and Syd couldn't bring herself to trap them. Thankfully, nothing seemed amiss. The chairs were exactly the way Syd remembered them: giant and ugly. "What's wrong?" she asked Katie.

"You put on a shirt."

"Oh." Syd looked down at the well-worn Beaumont University hoodie. "Technically, it's a sweatshirt," she laughed, and jammed her hands in the pockets to keep them still. Katie was so close she wanted to reach out and pull the tie on the bathrobe.

"Technically,"—Katie held Syd's gaze—"your body is beautiful."

"Thank you," Syd said, and wondered if Katie might try to kiss her. Two minutes ago, she'd been all business. Now she was looking at Syd like she was a popsicle on a hot day. "The chairs are over here," she said, and pointed to the thrones she and Joe had wrestled into the garage a few weeks ago.

"Oh, wow, these certainly look like ZAP chairs. Mind if I take a look?"

"That's why we're here," Syd said and moved behind a chair to allow Katie access.

"I love the Hummingbird Chair," she said, stepping eagerly over Honey's needle-point poodle ottoman to get a better look.

"It's my favorite of the two," Syd said, and traced a finger through the carved line of a hummingbird beak. Honey's other chair depicted a plump bird Syd didn't recognize. It was possibly a pheasant or some type of game bird.

"This is the Brown Thrasher Chair," Katie said as if reading Syd's mind.

"Are you a bird expert?" Syd asked and Katie shook her head.

"Not at all. I'm not even a furniture expert."

"Then how do you know these chairs are the real deal? No offense, I'm just curious."

"No offense taken," Katie said and took her phone from the pocket of the bathrobe. "It's actually an excellent question. You can help me authenticate them."

"Me?" Syd asked, now wary. She wanted to make sure Katie wasn't making a mistake but she'd no idea what she might do to help.

"Yes, help me compare this photo with the carvings," Katie said and showed Syd a picture of what looked like model drawings of the chairs. "I found a business ledger from a nineteenth-century Beaumont furniture maker."

"It was just lying around somewhere?" Syd asked, making Katie laugh.

Holding her phone next to the Hummingbird Chair, she told Syd about the ledger in the Beaumont University Library. Her face shone with excitement as she described the moment of her discovery. It was clear that despite whatever professional disappointment Katie had suffered in the past, she loved this job. "Thomas Graham and Sons made all eight chairs," she said, running her hand over the wood. "See how these carvings are identical to the picture? There's no doubt this chair is authentic."

Syd had little interest in artisan wood carving, but Katie was so enthusiastic she searched for a follow-up question just to keep her talking. "How many sons did Thomas Graham have?"

"Three, that I'm aware of," Katie answered, immediately. "Two definitely would have worked on the chairs. I plan to make the furniture makers part of my exhibit. I'm hoping to find some descendants and invite them to the opening."

"What a great idea," Syd replied, happy to see Katie so engaged. "When is the opening?"

Katie moved over to the Brown Thrasher Chair and began to examine its back. "It's a little premature to be planning a grand opening. I've got to find the rest of the exhibit first."

"Need help?" Syd asked, surprised at the words coming from her mouth. She'd no idea how to track down oversized nineteenth-century furniture and no idea where to begin.

"You want to help me find the last two chairs?" Katie repeated, as if she too, couldn't believe what Syd had just offered.

"Yes, I do," Syd said, and searched for a reason that wouldn't make her seem like a stalker. "I know the state of Georgia pretty well from touring with the band but I haven't been back for a while. I'd planned on doing a little sightseeing. If you need to drive somewhere out-of-the-way, I'd be happy to go with you."

"That would be amazing," Katie said, now looking flirty again. "But you must have better things to do. I mean, you're Syd Fucking Collins."

Syd laughed out loud, "Is that who I am?" She'd been given many nicknames in the past. This was the first she'd heard of this one.

"Yes," Katie replied, nearly shouting. "I've had a crush on you since I was sixteen. I can't believe I just told you that, and I can't believe that you want to go furniture hunting with me."

"I used to go to antique stores with my grandmother, maybe I'm feeling nostalgic," Syd replied, trying to play it cool. God, she was bad at flirting. "Her chairs are a fourth of your exhibit. I'd like to see how it plays out."

"I'd love your company," Katie said, "thank you."

Syd watched her hand travel down the bathrobe. For one, delicious moment, she thought Katie might unfasten the tie, but instead, she slipped her hand inside the pocket and pulled out a piece of paper. Syd recognized it as a check. "After careful inspection I'd like to formally authenticate these two national treasures and give you a check so we can go swimming."

"So, they're real?" Syd asked.

"You saw it yourself, the carvings are identical," Katie said and fluttered the check.

"Then I formally accept," Syd said. Taking the check, she put it carefully into the pocket of her hoodie and waited to see what Katie would do next. Syd hoped the business end of the evening was complete but Katie still looked pensive. "Is there anything else?"

"Is it okay if I post about this on social media?" Katie replied, hesitantly. "I understand if you don't want to do it, but I have to ask. I'm trying to get the public involved in the search for the last two chairs. Your involvement would give us a huge boost."

Syd considered the request. Most of the press she'd generated in the last year concerned her divorce and the controversial lyrics on *Florida Man*. Attaching her name to the quest for antique chairs would be a nice change from all the acrimony and revenge. She knew Colette would be thrilled. Any kind of publicity generated sales. If Syd's participation helped Katie find the chairs, then all the better.

"Absolutely," she said, and sat down in the Hummingbird Chair. "Why don't you take a picture?"

# CHAPTER THIRTEEN

## *Night Swimming*

Katie didn't consider herself an exhibitionist, her job notwithstanding, but she never missed an opportunity to go skinny-dipping. She couldn't remember the last time she'd been, which was a shame, and probably added to the pleasure she was feeling now. Moving though the shallow end of Syd's pool, water on her naked skin, it was as if she'd been enveloped in a cloud.

"This water is amazing," she told Syd. "Being here is a real treat. Thank you."

"I do it almost every night," Syd said, from a corner of the deep end.

"Lucky you," Katie said, and swam a little nearer.

They'd been in the pool for nearly fifteen minutes and, so far, had given each other a wide berth. Katie knew they'd come together eventually, and was relishing the anticipation, which felt almost as delicious as the water. Swimming naked on a starry night was a natural recipe for romance and Katie was not shy about making the first move. She wondered if it was a byproduct of the brutal-honesty gene and the reason she'd been so successful finding women to share her bed. Most of the time, all you needed was the courage to ask.

"I feel lucky," Syd said. Shadows dancing on the water obscured her facial expression but Katie thought she heard a smile in her voice. "My grandmother swam naked in the lake behind her house every morning."

"In Beaumont?" Katie asked and swam a little nearer. The Beaumont of her memory was not a place where grown women swam nude.

"Absolutely," Syd replied. "Thankfully Honey's closest neighbor was blind as a bat."

"Did you ever swim naked with her?" Katie asked. She couldn't imagine her own grandmother skinny-dipping. Flora loved the ocean but on their annual beach vacations she wore a coverup that came down to her knees.

"Oh, yeah," Syd said, and ran a hand over her head, making Katie wonder if she was nervous. They were now only six feet apart. Katie could see Syd's rosy nipples bobbing on the surface of the water and her wistful smile of remembrance. "When my sister and I were little, Honey took care of us. We went in that lake every day."

"Always naked?"

"Honey didn't own a bathing suit," Syd told her.

"Your grandmother wasn't a proper southern belle?" Katie asked, curious to know more about the woman who'd owned two of the ZAP chairs.

"No way," Syd said. "I think maybe she tried to be at first. Honey went to Beaumont University, pledged ZAP like all the hometown girls, but that's where her conformity ended. She was friends with all types of people. There was often a writer or artist staying in her house."

"Your grandfather didn't mind?" Katie asked.

"I never knew my grandfather." Syd shrugged. "He left town when my mom was only five."

"Oh, no," Katie said, worried she'd touched on a sensitive subject.

"It's okay," Syd replied. "He left Honey with enough Coke money that she never had to work."

"So your grandfather was a drug dealer?" Katie asked, trying to keep her face straight. She knew Syd was talking about Coca-Cola stock. Many local families had famously invested early, and the beverage was said to have built half the town.

Syd cracked up. "Pretty much."

"That must have been hard for your grandmother," Katie said, and silently congratulated herself for staying focused on the conversation. Syd's grandparents were interesting but no competition for Syd herself. Especially when she was naked and looking at Katie like she wanted to be kissed.

Syd shrugged. "Honey never talked about her husband. He was twenty years older and her psychology professor."

"Très scandal," Katie said. "That would never happen now without a lawsuit."

"That's what my sister says." Syd nodded, but then frowned. "I, for one, am glad my grandparents met."

"Me too," Katie said, laughing. "Without that Coke money, she wouldn't have bought the chairs. I'd have four more to find, instead of two."

"That's exactly what I was thinking," Syd said, and splashed water playfully in Katie's direction.

Katie dove out of the way but sent a wave of her own shooting back at Syd. Suddenly, it was as if a door opened, and all the pent-up sexual energy from the evening spilled out into the pool. They splashed each for few frenzied minutes. Syd's size gave her the literal upper hand but Katie's speed leveled the playing field. Katie took a wave in the face and pursued Syd to the shallow end of the pool and pinned her to the side wall. They were inches apart. Katie looked into Syd's eyes making sure the invitation to kiss her, present all night, was still there.

"Caught you."

"Yeah, you did," Syd said, and her voice cracked, reminding Katie of a track from Ache and Bake's second album where Syd whispered a lullaby, a capella.

"You caught me too," Katie said, and pressed their lips together, gently. Keeping the pressure light, she moved her mouth against Syd's, and then slipped her tongue inside.

"Mm," Syd murmured, which Katie interpreted as encouragement and increased the pressure. Making out with Syd was even better than Katie's fantasies and as the kiss continued, Katie slipped her hands from the pool deck and put them around Syd's neck. Her body felt supple and strong. Katie wanted to get as close to her as possible. Everything, everywhere was deliciously wet. Brazen with desire, Katie pushed a thigh between Syd's legs and was surprised when she pulled her mouth away.

"This is so intense. I can't seem to get enough of you," she whispered shyly and buried her face in Katie's neck.

"Uh-huh," Katie responded, her mind a wordless fog. She slid her hands down Syd's back, touching each vertebra until she reached her ass. Syd's lips were now tracking south, down Katie's collarbone toward her nipples which throbbed painfully with anticipation. Syd did not disappoint. Closing her mouth over Katie's left breast, her fingers found the other. "So good," Katie said, urging her on.

Their bodies moved together in a slow rhythm that increased to frenzied motion when Katie shifted her weight, aligning their centers. Syd was still working Katie's breast and she cried out.

Katie knew she wouldn't last long. It had been months since she'd let another woman touch her like this, and her body was shifting into overdrive. She rocked harder against Syd's body, the sense of urgency so strong, that she'd no thought of embarrassment. Incredibly, Syd was responding with equal intensity. The energy swirling around them felt raw, primal. They didn't speak. Mouths fused together they rode the miraculous wave of mutual release.

When it was over, Syd rested her head on Katie's shoulder. "That was...that was...just, wow," she said, and kissed Katie's neck.

"You're, wow," Katie said, still enjoying small aftershocks. Her hands remained firmly cupped around Syd's ass, and she pulled her closer. "You're also an amazing kisser."

"I concur," Syd said, and then giggled. Shyly, she looked up and met Katie's eye. "I mean, you're a good kisser too," She said, and pecked Katie's lips again, before teasing her mouth open with her tongue.

Katie was soon lost in another languid kiss. But the urgency of a few moments before had settled into something more intimate. Gone was the question of whether or not they'd become lovers. It was on, happening right now. Katie slid her hands from Syd's ass, up her body, to find her breasts. She'd nearly swooned when she'd stepped on the patio and seen Syd topless in the twinkling fairy lights. There was something about Syd's long, lean body that lit Katie on fire. It went beyond the teen fantasy. This was a woman in Katie's arms, not a poster and not a poser. Syd Fucking Collins was a flesh and blood human. She had a dead grandmother and a sister named Deb. There were nieces and a guest room and a woman at the bar, who lied to protect her from fans. She was also kind and generous and had volunteered to help Katie to find the additional ZAP chairs.

Katie moved her thumbs in small circle across Syd's breasts and smiled at the resulting growl. "You like that?" she murmured against Syd's lips and felt her mouth twist into a smile.

"I'm kind of sensitive," Syd replied, and then hissed when Katie slipped down to take a nipple in her mouth. "That's so good, really good," she said, arching forward.

Katie found Syd's passion thrilling and gently pulled at her other breast with a thumb and forefinger. Syd groaned and rocked her hips against Katie's, stirring her ardor even further.

"Are we doing this again?" Katie asked, giggling, and Syd stopped short.

"Don't you want to?" she asked, and the look in her eye was so uncertain that Katie's heart melted.

"Are you kidding?" she asked and pecked Syd on the lips. "I'm fucking Syd Fucking Collins. I could go all night."

# CHAPTER FOURTEEN

*Greasy-spooned*

Syd woke late morning to the sound of soft calypso music playing on her phone alarm. She'd never understood why, given the choice, people chose blaring buzzes or beeps when there were so many more pleasant ways to wake up.

Earlier that morning she'd been roused in an extremely pleasing fashion that had had nothing to do with noise. Katie had left to get the truck an hour ago and Syd was still tingling from her touch. Allowing herself a private smile, she pressed the snooze button and scrolled through her texts.

Colette had forwarded a screenshot of Katie's Instagram post with Syd sitting in the Hummingbird Chair. Syd was surprised to see how many times the image had been shared but not that her manager had been delighted with the exposure. Publicity-shy after her split with Carrie, Syd had been less inclined to show her face. Something about Katie made her feel confident. She sent Colette a happy-face emoji and then answered Deb's proof-of-life check-in with a cross-eyed selfie. Lori and Joe wanted Syd to come over for a brunch debrief but she talked them into pizza later in the day. Syd's last text was an itinerary from Katie indicating that Beth had taken her out to the board member's farm to get the truck and that she'd be back within the hour to collect the chairs.

Springing from bed, Syd took a quick shower and slipped into a low-slung pair of cargo pants and a black tank top. She wanted to find something to cover the chairs before Katie returned with the truck. It was better left unsaid the harum-scarum way the antiques had found their way to Syd's garage a few weeks ago. She'd been thankful to have Joe's help getting them out of the U-Haul and into the garage. Big and unwieldy, they weren't impossible to move alone but much easier managed with a cohort. Syd texted Katie to pull the truck all the way up the driveway so they'd only have to carry the chairs a few feet once they got them outside. A few minutes later she received a reply.

*I remember exactly where your garage is*

Syd blushed at the double entendre. Katie was as sassy as she was cute and unabashedly sexual. She wondered if the magic she'd felt the night before would still be present in the light of day or if sobriety and sunshine would reveal smoke and mirrors as it often did. The lyrics spinning in Syd's head were real enough. Whether inspired by Katie or the rush of a successful performance, Syd was full of a bright new energy. It was thrilling.

Out in the garage Syd pulled a couple of old quilts from a trunk and carefully wrapped the bird chairs, binding them with duct tape. Idly, she wondered if Katie had eaten breakfast and what time she was expected back in Beaumont that day. Did Katie's grandmother keep tabs on her whereabouts? Was anyone else tracking her movements? Syd found that she was intensely curious about every aspect of Katie's life. They hadn't made plans past Katie returning to collect the chairs, but Syd hoped to spend more time with her. Maybe she would invite Katie to be her guest at the benefit for the Beaumont Humane Society. She wondered what her family would say if out of the blue she turned up with a date.

Nervous energy flooded her body when Syd saw Katie turn the corner onto her block. Frantically, she looked around for a place to check her reflection and then caught herself. What was going on? Syd rarely thought about her appearance. Why the sudden need to be pretty? Was it because she was thirty-three and recently divorced? Was it because Katie had told Syd she was attractive? Was Syd really that needy, or did Syd just need Katie? A lyric began to take shape in her head and she decided to stop questioning things. Walking outside she went to meet the truck.

Katie hadn't said if Beth was also coming back to the house but Syd saw no sign of the Mini Cooper behind the green pickup. Katie looked like a doll sitting behind the wheel and Syd gave her a shy wave.

"Welcome back," she called and started down the driveway. She wondered why Katie wasn't driving up to the garage and if she might be nervous navigating the borrowed vehicle. "Do you want me to pull the truck up the hill?"

"Not yet," Katie said and opened the door. She was dressed in a pair of perfectly fitted denim overalls and a green shirt that matched her eyes. Syd knew she must have stopped by the Airbnb to collect her things and that Beth had continued on to Beaumont. "I want to take you out to breakfast," she told Syd. Closing the distance between them, she wrapped her arms around Syd's waist and pulled her into an easy hug.

"Breakfast sounds great," Syd replied. She couldn't help noticing that their height difference made for a nice fit. With Katie's head tucked beneath her chin, Syd melted into her warmth and closed her eyes.

After a tender moment Katie spoke again. "Sorry if this hug is presumptuous but you looked so gorgeous standing there. I couldn't resist."

"You look pretty too," Syd replied, inhaling the sweet smell of Katie's hair. "I love your overalls."

"Thank you," Katie said, and pulled back to smile into Syd's eyes. "I dressed for a country breakfast. Can we please go somewhere that serves grits? I haven't had them since I moved back to Georgia."

"There's nothing more southern than grits," Syd pointed out.

"I think I told you last night that I'm coming around on the southern issue," Katie replied, making Syd laugh.

"I'm so glad," she said, and searched her mind for a restaurant. "There's a twenty-four-hour greasy spoon not far from the Atlanta Zoo that's bound to have grits. Let me get a couple of things from the house."

"Meet you in the truck," Katie said and brushed Syd's mouth quickly with her own.

Lips tingling, Syd went back to her house and grabbed a pair of dark sunglasses and a black Nike baseball cap. She never knew when she might be recognized and took precautions when she didn't care to be. She'd given her public everything she had the night before at the Third Pig. Perhaps she was being selfish, but today Syd only wanted an audience of one.

"Which way to the restaurant?" Katie asked, when Syd climbed into the truck. "Beth and I grabbed a croissant near the Airbnb, but I'm still starving," she said, looking comically serious.

"The place I'm thinking of is only about a mile away," Syd said, her body humming in response to Katie's proximity. She wanted to reach over and take her hand and was relieved when Katie acted first. Her fingers closed easily over Syd's wrist and then slid up her arm before retaking the steering wheel. Syd blushed, happily. Whatever was happening between them, Katie was feeling it too. "I don't remember the name of the diner," she told her. "But I know exactly where it is." She pointed a finger up the road. "There's a mermaid on the sign."

Katie gave Syd an odd look. "Um, does it start with a star and end with too many bucks?" she asked, her nose wrinkling adorably.

Syd laughed. It hadn't occurred to her that the diner shared a mascot with the ubiquitous coffee chain. "Have you heard of it?" she deadpanned.

Katie didn't miss a beat. "People say it's *grande*."

Irma's Diner did indeed have a mermaid on the sign, but any resemblance to the Seattle-based coffee franchise stopped there. It was the type of place where the menus were cleaned with Lysol and cigarettes were still sold from a vending machine in the lobby. Syd loved Irma's lack of pretention and hoped Katie liked the grits.

They parked on a side street near the restaurant and requested a table near the back by the kitchen door. It was another precaution Syd took to protect her anonymity. Getting star treatment didn't always mean you'd had a positive experience. The minute someone recognized Syd the whole vibe of their outing would change. Syd would be obliged to turn on her public persona which meant she wouldn't be able to focus on Katie. It wasn't what she wanted today. Keeping her head down, Syd removed the sunglasses and set them on the Formica table. Wearing glasses inside would only invite more attention. The hat was protection enough if Syd kept the brim pulled low. So far, no one in the half-capacity establishment had given them a second look, including the waitress.

Katie called to the harried-looking woman walking past their table, "Excuse me? Can we get some coffee, please?"

"I'll be right with y'all," the woman said and flashed them a scattered smile.

"Thank you," Katie said. Turning back to Syd she pretended to take a bite of the menu.

Syd noticed the table next to them was also waiting to be served and worried it may be a while before they actually got any food. "We can try somewhere else. There's a Waffle House close by."

Katie shook her head. "I'm a big girl," she said and took a packet of crayons from the stainless-steel table caddy. "Distract me with stories. I'll be fine."

Syd nodded thoughtfully. "Okay, my manager liked the picture you posted on Instagram last night," she said and shivered when she felt Katie's leg press against hers beneath the table.

"Really? I'm so glad," Katie said. She drew a smiley face on a paper napkin and held it up in front of her face.

Syd laughed. "Colette liked the picture so much she shared it to my private account."

"That's so cool," Katie said and pulled out her phone. "The last time I checked, the photo had ten thousand likes and twenty-five shares. I looked at the other posts on the ZAP national site and you're threatening to take the lead over last year's rush results when a Bush cousin pledged at the University of Texas."

"I'm honored," Syd laughed.

The waitress walked by again without glancing their way and Katie buried her face in the crook of her arm. "I need another story."

"Okay," Syd said, trying to think of something interesting. "Has anyone ever told you why Lori and Joe named their bar the Third Pig?"

Katie looked up. "No, but Beth and I were wondering about that last night. What's the story?"

"According to Joe, the bar is named after a stunt Lori and her friends pulled when they were teenagers," Syd told Katie.

"What happened?" Katie asked and started fiddling with sugar packets.

Syd wondered if she was hungry enough to eat one. "Lori and her friends let three pigs loose in their high school but numbered them one, two, and four."

Katie thought for a moment, and then laughed. "That's inspired! Is Lori the woman who lied to us last night?" she asked.

Syd nodded. "Lori and Joe are very protective of me. I mostly appreciate it. I knew them pretty well before moving to LA and now we're neighbors." The waitress went by again and Syd lifted her hand.

"It may take an act of God to get her to notice us," Katie said. Her phone beeped and she glanced at the screen. "Hey, look at this!"

Syd smiled at the happiness in her voice. She'd no idea why Katie was excited but found her joy infectious. Syd's grin only grew wider when she learned the reason Katie was pleased. A ZAP alumnus named Pish-Posh had private messaged the ZAP Instagram account a photo of a woman sitting in big wooden chair. The message said the chair had been spotted at Scott's Antique Market earlier that morning in South Atlanta. Syd couldn't make out any carvings but it looked to be the right size.

"Do you think it's a founders' chair?" she asked Katie. Syd had attended the famous antique show held bi-monthly at the Atlanta Exposition Center countless times with Honey. Without traffic it would be a thirty-minute drive from where they were now.

Katie studied the picture for several moments. "Unfortunately, no," she said and pointed to the screen. "See the finials? None of the ZAP Chairs have that detail." Katie swiped through the ZAP National posts and showed Syd the post of the Graham and Sons renderings of the chairs.

"I see what you mean," Syd agreed. "But it's still cool Pish-Posh reached out."

"That's the Syd Collins effect," Katie said, giving her credit. "I can't thank you enough for letting me post that picture. Though I'd like to. You know, thank you again, sometime very soon." She tilted her head, flirtatiously.

"I'd like to see you again, too," Syd said and seized the opportunity to make a plan. "I'm playing a benefit for the Beaumont Humane Society in a couple of weeks. I could put you on the guest list," she offered.

"I actually already have tickets," Katie said shrugging adorably. A strap on her overalls slipped from her shoulder and she pushed it back into place. "My grandmother hooked me up."

"That's great, can we spend time after the show?" Syd asked. "I've got another gig at the Third Pig that Friday so I won't be in Beaumont until midday Saturday."

"Sure, are you free Sunday too?" Katie wanted to know and Syd felt an absurd surge of happiness. Coupled with Carrie since high school, she'd never experienced courtship with another woman. Having the freedom to explore the magic brewing with Katie felt like a gift. Katie also seemed interested which was a good thing because Syd kept conspiring new ways to spend time with her.

"I'm free Sunday," she said and then wondered where she and Katie might go in Beaumont to be alone. It was hard for Syd to think of being with Katie without also considering *being with Katie*. The knowing way she looked at Syd only fueled the fire.

"Two weeks suddenly seems like a long time," Katie said, and made a face like something smelled bad.

"I'm free the rest of today," Syd said and watched Katie's expression change.

"You just said rest," she said, slyly. "And I'd like to second that motion. If we ever get served, we could go back to your house and take a nap." She made a big show of stretching her arms into the air. "I had a pretty late night."

"I wouldn't say no to a nap," Syd replied, calmly, though the thought of being alone with Katie again made her giddy. She searched the restaurant for the waitress and found her chatting with a butch woman wearing an Ani DiFranco T-shirt. The butch glanced Syd's way and did a double take.

Syd nodded back intently.

"Who is that?" Katie asked.

"Maybe our meal ticket," Syd replied.

"I don't understand."

"Wait and see," Syd told her. As much as she hated to blow their cover, a nap was in the offering. Maintaining direct eye contact with the butch, Syd took off her hat.

# CHAPTER FIFTEEN

## *Rare Bird*

Katie drove the pickup back to Syd's feeling light-headed. She still couldn't believe the last twenty-four hours had really happened. What were the odds that in a span of just one day, Katie would reconcile with Beth, score two ZAP chairs and have sex with her long-time celebrity crush? If it wasn't for Syd Fucking Collins sitting next to her in the truck, Katie might be convinced it had all been a dream.

Once Syd had taken off her cap, service at Irma's Diner had been solicitous and swift. Katie was fairly certain they'd been given someone else's breakfast. Not two minutes after they'd ordered, a steaming bowl of grits had appeared on their table alongside coffee and cinnamon rolls the waitress said were on the house. Katie wondered if the woman was being nice or just trying to hasten Syd's departure. The presence of a celebrity in the diner certainly hadn't made her job any easier. Among the many people who'd begged a photo were the cook, manager and cashier. Syd had taken time to chat with each person, leaving the poor waitress scrambling and Katie to eat all the food.

Taking a hand from the steering wheel Katie placed it on her stomach. "I think I over-grit it," she said and felt a jolt of happiness when Syd laughed.

"I wanted to help with the cinnamon rolls, believe me," Syd said and put her hand on top of Katie's as if she were expecting a baby.

Katie felt guilty until she remembered the waitress had given them six more to take home. "I didn't realize I'd eaten both cinnamon rolls until the plate was empty. Why didn't you eat anything?"

"I've got to be careful when cameras are out," Syd replied and opened her mouth comically wide. "Tonsil shots aren't the most becoming."

"There *were* a lot of people in your face," Katie agreed. She'd been impressed with how Syd had taken the time to talk to each fan who'd approached the table. Syd had missed breakfast, but she'd given everyone a moment. "Does that kind of thing happen a lot?" Katie asked.

"Not so much." Syd shook her head. "It's the day after a show. There were bound to still be a few fans around."

"That was more than just a few fans," Katie replied. "People were shooting video like you were a zoo attraction. It must be hard having strangers come at you like that."

"It's part of the job." Syd shrugged it off. "And I promise you, it doesn't happen very often."

"Maybe not in LA, where every third person is famous." Katie shook her head. "I'm beginning to understand why Lori lied about your identity last night. I thought that one lady was going to sit in your lap."

"If I hadn't taken my cap off, we'd still be sitting in that booth," Syd reminded Katie.

"That's true." she nodded thoughtfully. "The grits were delicious but I'm not sure they were worth risking your life for, especially when you didn't even get to taste them."

"I didn't take off my hat to score grits," Syd said and smiled sweetly.

"No?"

"I did it for the nap."

"Oh, the nap," Katie said, completely charmed. "A nap is a different story. A nap could be worth risking your life for."

"That was my thought," Syd said and indicated for Katie to turn left.

Katie spun the wheel. The more time she spent with Syd the less she thought of her as the celebrity singer from the poster above her bed. It was almost as if Syd Collins were two people. The down-to-earth woman sitting next to Katie in the truck looked identical to the hard-edged performer, but the resemblance stopped there. Off stage, Syd Collins was a total sweetheart.

"When do you need to be back in Beaumont?" Syd asked, and Katie hid a smile. Each time Syd indicated she'd like to spend more time together, Katie felt like she'd been given a gift.

"No time in particular," Katie said. "I just told my grandmother I'd be home sometime later today. She's excited to see the chairs."

"I'll bet," Syd said. "I'm glad this is all working out."

"Me too," Katie replied, unclear if Syd was referencing the chairs or what was happening between them. Katie was happy about both.

They pulled in front of Syd's house and switched places in the cab. Katie was comfortable driving the truck on the open road but glad to let Syd reverse the old Ford up the steep driveway. Watching the dark eyes in the rearview mirror she found herself stirred by Syd's confidence. There was something so sexy about a woman in command of a machine.

Syd put the truck in park. "Should we load the chairs now?" she asked and looked so earnest Katie wanted to kiss her.

"That depends," Katie replied. "Do you think you'll have more energy after our nap or less?"

"Good point." Syd blushed. "We should probably move them now."

"I agree."

They carried the chairs out of the garage and placed them carefully onto a tarp in the back of the truck. Katie was touched

Syd had taken the time to wrap them in blankets but worried the quilts she'd chosen were too valuable to use for packing material.

She raised the issue with Syd who didn't seem concerned. "A two-hour road trip won't hurt these quilts," she said, fingering the fabric. "If you think they're worth saving you can give them back to me next week after the benefit."

"I'm looking forward to that," Katie said and took Syd's hand. "Seeing you perform twice in two weeks will be a treat."

"I'm glad you think so," Syd replied and glanced back over her shoulder toward the street. It occurred to Katie that Syd might be worried about cameras and she let go of her hand. Syd had been beyond nice posing for Instagram and downright heroic removing her cap at the restaurant. It wasn't fair to risk additional exposure just because Katie was feeling handsy.

"Should we go inside?" Katie asked already thinking of the bed she'd crawled out of a few hours earlier.

Syd looked hesitant. "I thought we might nap on the patio. I just installed a turntable back there so we could listen to albums. It's private and the daybed is really comfortable."

"I love that idea," Katie said, intrigued Syd had thought out a nap scenario. "Have you chosen the first record?"

"I've got it narrowed down to five possibilities," Syd said and Katie smiled because she knew she wasn't kidding.

They grabbed the box of cinnamon rolls from the truck and walked around the house to the awning-covered patio. Stepping into the cozy space Katie took in the details she'd missed the night before. Caught up in the moonlight she hadn't noticed the whimsical French poster art or rack of well-tended succulents.

"It's so nice back here," she said and sank gratefully into the soft, white cushions of the daybed. Despite her interest in the salacious opportunities presented by the nap, Katie was also genuinely tired. The evening had been physically taxing and hadn't allowed for much sleep. Beth had needed to be on the road early so they'd left Syd's only a few hours after Katie's head had hit the pillow.

"I'm glad you like it," Syd said. "Pretty soon it'll be too hot to spend time outside." She pulled the cord to the ceiling fan and Katie heard a whirling noise followed by a soft breeze.

"I'm already beginning to feel a little warm," she said and unhooked the bib of her overalls.

Syd's eyes widened a bit but a smile played at her lips. "I'm going to put the cinnamon rolls inside and grab the music," she said and turned the knob on the back door. Katie was surprised to see it open without a key.

"Don't you lock your back door?" she asked, worried for Syd's safety. It would be so easy to sneak through the gate and gain access inside.

Syd looked sheepish. "Yeah, I know I should probably lock it," she said, pausing on the threshold. "Being back in Georgia has lulled me into a sense of security. We always left the doors unlocked growing up. I'll do better."

"Thank you," Katie said, feeling validated. Being with Syd was so easy. Normally, after spending eighteen hours with a woman, Katie would be looking for an exit. Right now, Katie only had a desire to know Syd better. She wondered what albums Syd would choose and how long it would take her to return from the house. Sinking farther into the daybed Katie watched the blades of the ceiling fan and thought about sliding the rest of the way out of the overalls. How would Syd react if she came back and found Katie completely naked? Thinking of the dark eyes on her skin caused pleasant shivers to erupt across her body. Katie couldn't remember the last time she'd been this excited about a woman. Beth had urged her to live in the moment but Katie kept catching herself fantasizing about something more. Part of her thought the idea preposterous; the other part was squirming against the cushions.

The back door opened and Syd came back out on the patio whistling something Katie didn't recognize. She opened an armoire housing the entertainment center and propped a small stack of record albums inside against the turntable.

"What's that song?" Katie asked and Syd turned to look at her.

"I'm not sure yet," she said and slid a record from its sleeve and placed it on the stereo. "What do you think? Do you like it so far?"

"You mean it's not a real song?" Katie asked, surprised.

Syd dropped the needle onto a spinning disc. "Oh, the song definitely exists," she said, looking thoughtful. "It just takes time to tease it through." She came to join Katie on the bed.

Katie recognized the iconic vocals of Billie Holiday and felt herself relax. Opening her arms, she pulled Syd against her body and slipped a knee between her thighs. "Is it crazy to say that I've missed you?" she asked, nuzzling her neck.

Syd made a murmuring noise and lifted her head. "It's not crazy, because I've missed you too," she whispered and claimed Katie's lips.

They traded kisses for several heated minutes, Katie letting her hands wander freely beneath Syd's T-shirt and down the back of her jeans. She tasted of fresh toothpaste, leading Katie to suspect she'd taken a moment to brush her teeth while inside the house. "You feel so good," she said, her hand lingering on Syd's ass. "I'm glad we're here."

Syd slid onto her side, turning Katie with her. "Are you sleepy?" she asked and kissed Katie's eyelids.

"I'm a lot of things," Katie said, and laid her head on Syd's shoulder.

It may have been the three orgasms she'd had the night before or a sugar crash from the two cinnamon rolls at breakfast but Katie began to drift. What felt like minutes later she opened her eyes to find the sun had set and Syd had fallen asleep against her shoulder. She took a moment to relish the visual and then realized they were not alone. Later, she understood that it was the voices that must have woken her. Katie had just enough time to rouse Syd and refasten her overalls before an older-looking couple appeared on the patio holding a takeout pizza and a six-pack of beer.

Syd was adorably disheveled but took great pains to make everyone comfortable. "Katie, I'd like you to meet Lori and Joe," she said, rising to a sitting position and swinging her long legs to the floor. "I invited them to bring me dinner tonight and totally lost track of time. Sorry, guys."

"It's okay with me," Joe chuckled and put the beer down on the café table. "Nice to meet you, Katie. Were you at the show last night?"

"Lori and Joe own the Third Pig," Syd explained but Katie had already made the connection.

Standing, she offered her hand. "I met Lori at the bar," she said and then tilted her head, skeptically. "If that's her real name."

Lori laughed. "I deserve that. Can I apologize with a beer?"

"Thanks, but I've got to drive home soon," Katie said, and must have let her eyes linger too long on the pizza box because minutes later she was seated at the table eating a steaming slice of mushroom and pepperoni. If Joe and Lori were phased by her unexplained presence on Syd's patio, they didn't show it. Lori was interested in the search for the founders' chairs and asked to see both the photos and renderings on Katie's phone.

"Syd's grandmother had two of the eight?" she asked astutely.

Katie nodded. "And there are two more out there," she said smiling. "The quest is on."

"Do you have any leads?" Lori narrowed her eyes at Syd. "Where did your grandmother get hers?"

"We're not sure," Syd said. "Honey was a prolific antique shopper. She might have gotten the chairs anywhere." She shrugged at Katie.

"I'm hoping to flush them out with a social media campaign," Katie explained to Lori and Joe. "Syd let me post a picture of her on Instagram last night. We got a lot of attention."

"That's smart," Joe said and picked up a slice of pizza. "I guess you've reached out to antique stores already?"

"There's a whole network of Zeta Alpha Pi's searching every thrift shop and estate sale," Katie assured him.

"What about auctions?" Lori wanted to know.

Katie frowned. "I haven't targeted auctions specifically," she said and made a note to check into it.

"There are auction houses all over Georgia," Lori said. "The firm who decorated the Pig took me to a big place in Augusta. Everything was one of a kind."

"I need two very specific chairs," Katie said and showed them the updated wanted poster where everything but the Snowy Egret Chair and the Robin Chair was crossed out.

Joe looked dubious. "Good luck with the search," he said and raised his beer in Syd's direction. "At least if you don't find them you still got to meet the rarest bird in the state."

# CHAPTER SIXTEEN

## *Gnat Line*

"I can't believe you're actually doing this," Syd told Deb, and then dove to the ground when a tennis ball came whizzing at her head, followed by a Labrador retriever. "Watch out, Ray," Syd yelled, but the dog was long gone, streaking across Deb's lawn after the ball.

Deb looked pleased. "This should get me to ten thousand steps," she said, her eyes tracking the black wristband attached to the dog's harness.

"How long has this been going on?" Syd asked, rising to her feet. She swiped at the cloud of tiny black bugs buzzing her face. It was gnat season in Beaumont and being outside meant dealing with swarms of insects whose sole purpose in life seemed to be to fly up Syd's nose.

"It was Ray's idea, actually," Deb said, digging a bug out of her eye.

"Don't pin this on Raymond," Syd said, spitting out a gnat. Syd loved her hometown but did not miss living below the invisible geographical boundary that divided the state. It was one of the reasons she'd chosen to move to Atlanta and not the college town where she'd grown up. Syd was already in a mild state of annoyance, and the bugs did not improve her mood. The Georgia Gnat Line, or GGL, started in the middle of the state, on the western side, and tracked northeast on a sweeping diagonal. On one side of the GGL, gnats were a huge nuisance, on the other side, they were barely noticeable. The farther south you went, the worse they became. May in Beaumont was ground zero.

"I promise, it was Ray," Deb assured her. The dog came bounding back into view and Deb bent to one knee.

"No way," Syd said, refusing to believe it. "Putting your step counter on the dog to increase your numbers is too devious. If you'd told me Toby thought of it," she said, referencing Deb's eight-year-old tabby cat, "I might believe you."

"It was Ray," Deb assured her, and slapped at a bug. "You know how he chews socks."

"Yeah." Syd nodded. The pet was a notorious fabric thief, known to steal any scrap of cloth that smelled like the family. Syd had learned the hard way always to keep her suitcase closed. Owen still referenced the time he'd found Syd's briefs under the dining room table and thought they were a dinner napkin. "Sock chewing doesn't explain how it was Ray's idea to cheat the step counter," Syd said and picked another gnat out of her eye.

"If you'll just be patient, I'll explain everything," Deb said. She pressed a button on the step counter and frowned. "I need him to fetch one more."

"Can we please go inside?" Syd asked. "The gnats are driving me crazy."

"Calm down, and listen to my story," Deb said, and threw the ball again. Ray went racing after it, and she looked pleased. "A few weeks ago, I needed to shower at the gym, so I put the step counter in my sock."

"Okay," Syd said, picturing the narrative.

"Ray found it when I got home." Deb shrugged. "I started to chase him but I was down on my steps that day, so I just let him go."

"So, you're cheating yourself?" Syd asked, and a gnat hit the back of her throat. She spat it into her hand. "I've got to go inside. It's time to get ready for the show."

"No, I'm cheating Owen," Deb explained.

"What does Owen have to do with your step counter?" Syd asked, confused.

"I'm sick of cleaning the cat box," Deb said, as if this were a connection Syd should have made on her own.

Ray came trotting back, and Deb bent to greet him with her squeaky dog voice. "Good boy, Ray-Ray. Who's the best boy? Let's see that collar," she said. Checking the readout, she punched a triumphant fist into the air. "Eleven thousand one hundred and five steps, bitches!"

"Am I bitches?" Syd touched a hand to her chest.

"You are," Deb said. "Now let's go. The gnats are horrible."

"Ya think?" Syd replied, and happily started walking back toward the house. "Now, will you please explain about the cat box?"

"Owen and I have a bet," Deb said, walking quickly to keep up with Syd. "Whoever gets the most steps, doesn't have to clean Toby's cat box for a week. Owen won for two months in a row until Ray started pitching in." Deb adopted her squeaky dog voice again. "Who's Mama's sneaky boy? Who's Mama's little accomplice?"

"Why don't you just make Emma clean the cat box?" Syd asked. "Isn't that the perfect job for a ten-year-old?"

Deb snorted. "Why don't you make Emma clean the cat box?"

"I'm not her mother," Syd said, and then immediately wished she could take back the comment. Picking a fight with Deb was not a great way to prepare before a performance. In a few hours, Syd would take the stage at a house concert benefitting the Beaumont Humane Society. She'd woken that morning excited about the event. After a series of texts from Katie, she was less enthusiastic. It wasn't fair to vent her disappointment on Deb. Fortunately, her big sister wasn't shy about calling out Syd's uncharacteristic behavior.

"What crawled up your butt and died?" she asked, and her eyes narrowed. "Something go wrong with your new crush?"

"Katie can't make it to the show tonight," Syd admitted. It was annoying Deb could read her so well, though it saved everyone time in the long run. Stepping onto the front porch, Syd kicked off her boots and reported the bad news that was only a few hours old. "I didn't realize how much I was looking forward to seeing Katie again until she canceled."

"Well, I knew," Deb said and unlaced her tennis shoes. "I mean, it's all you've been talking about these last two weeks."

"I haven't been that bad," Syd protested, and Deb laughed.

"I'm pretty sure that Owen and Emma knew how much you were looking forward to seeing Katie tonight. Oh, and Grace," Deb added. Removing her shoes, she put them in a large wicker chest by the front door. Syd tossed her boots in after them and Deb dropped the lid.

"How do Owen and Emma know about Katie?" Syd asked.

"Maybe it was that picture of you on Instagram?" Deb suggested, reminding Syd of the photo Katie had taken of her in the garage. "Every Zeta Alpha Pi in the country knows about you and Katie."

"Just that I'm helping her find the founders' chairs," Syd protested and Deb snorted.

"Don't take this the wrong way, but that picture of you is sexy as fuck. Did you see how many people shared it?" she asked and walked into the kitchen, Ray at her heels.

"Colette may have mentioned it," Syd called after her, annoyed they were getting off the subject. She was happy Katie's post had generated so much attention for the chairs but still bummed she couldn't make the benefit.

"Even Owen said you looked hot in that picture," Deb shouted back.

"Great," Syd said, and plopped down on the sofa. I'm glad to have the family's support."

"The girls are taking full credit for your night in the pool," Deb replied, her voice getting nearer. "They claim it was the fairy lights."

"The fairy lights certainly didn't hurt," Syd acknowledged, and thought of Katie in the twinkling glow. Their night together had been close to perfect. Katie had been just the right amount of assertive. If not for her confidence, Syd wasn't sure anything physical would have happened between them. Not that Syd wouldn't have wanted it to. She just wouldn't have known how. Her game was literally games. If Katie hadn't chased her down in the shallow end, Syd might have initiated a round of frisbee golf.

"Why isn't Katie coming to the benefit?" Deb asked. Walking back into the living room, she handed Syd a glass of sun-brewed iced tea, and then sat down in one of two oversized leather chairs next to the fireplace.

"She has a work thing," Syd said. She took a sip and was instantly transported to Honey's patio. "This tea is perfect," she told her sister who nodded.

"You can taste the sunshine," they said, at the same time, and then smiled at each other.

Whether hosting her book club or a visiting poet, Virginia Clairmont had always had sweet tea in her refrigerator. Syd could still see the orange plastic container, bottom left next to the skim milk and homemade yogurt. Honey had believed in leaving tea in the sun to steep, considering vitamin D the second most important ingredient after the sugar. Sweet, but not overly so, her special recipe was the perfect remedy for Syd's afternoon blahs. Relaxing into the couch, she told her sister about Katie's change of plan for the evening.

"There's an auction tonight in Dothan, Alabama. Katie found it online when she was taking a bath."

"Katie told you she was in the bathtub?" Deb asked.

Syd nodded. "I don't know why she mentioned that part, but, yeah, she did say it," she replied, annoyed with herself for including the gratuitous detail.

Deb sipped her tea. "Katie mentioned the bathtub because she wanted you to picture her naked."

"Yeah, I caught that," Syd agreed. She couldn't quantify exactly what was going on with Katie, but the physical part was not in question. Katie's total lack of self-consciousness was thrilling and more than a little contagious. Syd loved that she'd come braless to the concert and their night together in the pool had been one of the most prolonged, intense sexual encounters of Syd's life. "I was really looking forward to seeing her tonight," she told Deb. "I'd kind of built it up in my head."

"Katie's not coming to your show?" a voice said behind them.

Syd turned to see Grace enter the room followed by Emma who was holding a small shopping bag. Ray ran to greet them and Emma dropped to the floor to hug the dog. Opening the bag, she removed a blue sequined bow tie, and clipped it around Ray's neck.

"Look what we got for you to wear to the party, buddy," she said, and sat back on her heels, to survey her handiwork. "What do y'all think? Doesn't Ray look handsome?"

"We got Dad one, too," Grace told Deb, and plopped down on the couch next to Syd.

"He'll love it," Deb said.

"Dogs are invited tonight?" Syd asked, perking up. She hadn't known that pets were included in the evening.

"Only if you adopted the animal at the Beaumont shelter, and only if they're house-trained," Deb said, looking for the invitation on her phone.

"That sounds like Jennifer." Syd nodded. She'd only spoken briefly to her childhood friend earlier that morning but was looking forward to catching up.

"What if the dogs start to fight?" Grace asked, and summoned Ray to adjust his bow tie. "It's all fun and games until someone loses a tail."

"I don't want Ray to fight," Emma said from the floor.

"Ray will be fine," Deb assured her.

"Why isn't Katie coming?" Grace asked.

"She has to work," Syd told them, and felt the sting of the letdown once more.

"On a Friday night?" Grace asked.

"I work on Friday nights," Syd reminded her, and gave her niece a little shove.

"When was the last time you saw Katie?" Emma asked, now looking worried.

"It's only been two weeks," Syd said, trying not to feel defensive. She didn't think Katie was blowing her off, they just had a scheduling conflict. But her nieces didn't look convinced, so she prattled on. "One of the chairs is going up for auction tonight in Dothan. Katie needs to go down there and bid on it."

Grace looked doubtful. "Doesn't the auction house have a remote option?" she asked, like Syd had just woken up in a cabbage field. "Daddy sells signed footballs at the Sugar Bowl every year, but he never actually goes to New Orleans. Mom won't let him."

"It's true, I won't." Deb nodded her head.

"Katie did bid online for the chairs," Syd explained. "It's actually me who's insisting she go to Dothan."

"Really?" Deb looked impressed. "You didn't tell me that part."

"I wouldn't forgive myself if something glitched with the auction website and she lost it," Syd said. "There are only eight ZAP chairs, total. I'll play a lot more concerts."

"You've got it really bad, Aunt Syd," Grace said, smiling. "I wondered if something was up when I saw that picture of you she posted on Instagram."

"Why is everyone talking about that picture?" Syd asked.

"Because you look so happy," Grace replied, as if this were obvious. "Katie's really cute, by the way. I totally get the attraction."

"I can't believe Grace met your new girlfriend before I did," Deb said, looking annoyed. "When am I going to meet Katie?"

"Me too," Emma echoed. "I want to meet Katie, too."

"If I hadn't recognized Honey's chairs, she wouldn't be dating Aunt Syd right now," Grace gloated.

"We're not dating...yet," Syd reminded her niece. "Please don't jinx my chances."

"Okay," Grace agreed. "I'll chill. Which bird is carved on the Dothan chair?"

"It's a snowy egret," Syd told them. "Katie found the chair-maker's ledger in the Beaumont University Library. The book has intricate sketches of all the chairs. That's how Katie was sure Honey's chairs were part of the ZAP collection."

"Do you think Honey had the chairs because she knew they were associated with ZAP house?" Grace asked.

Syd shrugged. "Katie asked me the same question. Honey never told me anything about her years in the sorority. It never seemed like a big deal."

"Were you in ZAP when you were at Beaumont, Aunt Syd?" Emma asked, drawing a laugh from Grace.

"No, I wasn't," Syd answered. "I was too busy with music to think about pledging a sorority. Greek life is a big commitment."

"Aunt Syd was a GDI, like me," Grace told her younger sister. "A god-damned independent."

Syd heard a tinge of pride in her voice and didn't bother to correct her. To consider yourself GDI, the Greek system had to occupy some territory in your brain. Aside from being attracted to pretty houses stuffed with prettier girls, Syd had never given the Greeks enough thought to subscribe to any brand within their system.

"Were you a GDI too, Mom?" Emma asked Deb.

"No, your mother was a traitor." Syd cackled.

"I pledged Beta," Deb clarified, "and it's not against the law."

"It is if you're from Beaumont," Grace said, correcting her. She ran a hand through her long, dark hair, looking thoughtful. "All the local girls join ZAP. It must have been a huge deal when you bucked the system and chose Beta instead."

"Your Aunt Arlene was not happy," Deb acknowledged. She looked at Syd. "Do you remember that? Honey and Mom were supportive."

"I was at band camp," Syd reminded her.

"Aunt Arlene lost her mind," Deb told her daughters. "Didn't talk to me for two months. You'd think I'd gotten the f-word tattooed on my neck."

"Why did she care so much?" Syd asked. Never before had she had any curiosity about sororities. Katie made a previously boring subject very interesting.

"Arlene accused me of shaming the family." Deb rolled her eyes. "I felt horrible, for about five minutes, and then Honey set her straight."

"What did Honey say?" Syd asked, though she had a good idea of what the answer might be. Their grandmother had a special way of phrasing things that came right to the point.

"I think the exact words she used were: *mind your damn business, Arlene,*" she admitted, smiling.

Grace howled with laughter. "I love that! *Mind your damn business, Arlene.* Can we put it on a T-shirt? Or, better yet." Grace turned gleefully to Syd. "You can write a song!"

"No way," Syd said. Rising from the couch, she looked down at her niece. "I never use my gift for evil."

"What about "Florida Man"?" Grace challenged her. "Isn't that song about Uncl...I mean Paul. Didn't you write "Florida Man" about Paul?"

"The Florida man is universal," Syd replied, enigmatically. She'd never acknowledged that the most popular song on the new album was based on the man who'd stolen her wife, not even to her family. "You read about him in the newspaper all the time. If you ever read one, you'd know."

"The song is universally about Paul," Grace persisted.

"Paul's in there somewhere, sure," Syd said and kneeled to rub Ray's head. "But you can't give him full credit. That asshole only did half the things in the lyrics." She winked at Emma.

"Did he really smoke crack in a cop car?" Grace asked eagerly. "Were you there?"

Syd held up a hand. "I've said all I plan to say on this subject."

"Of course, "Florida Man" is about Paul," Deb said, looking at Syd as if she'd grown a second head. "I read a whole article about it in *Atlanta Magazine.*"

"That was an opinion piece," Syd said, and ran for the stairs. Revenge was dark energy she didn't want to revisit. The lyrics to "Florida Man," no matter how catchy, tasted bitter in her mouth. Before she'd learned of Paul's affair with Carrie, Syd had considered him a friend.

"It's our opinion that you're lying to us," Grace called after her.

Syd didn't bother replying. Dwelling on the origins of "Florida Man" wasn't how she wanted to spend her time before the show. She still had to wash her hair and make the set list. The fact that Katie wasn't coming tonight was making these tasks seem more difficult than they actually were. Syd couldn't believe the level of her disappointment. It bordered on pathetic. When Katie had suggested that they might meet the following day, it had alleviated the letdown, but only just a little. Dothan was a five-hour drive from Beaumont. It was likely Katie would spend the night, which meant it wouldn't be until late tomorrow until Syd saw her again, kissed her lips. Syd was also sad to miss the adventure. Katie's quest for the chairs was romantic in ways that did not involve her perfect nipples. Syd was interested to see how it played out.

Trudging up the stairs, she resolved to put on her game face. People had paid a lot of money to attend tonight's performance. Tickets had sold for two hundred and fifty dollars a head, mostly to friends who were coming out to support the Beaumont Humane Society. Syd couldn't let them down. She also couldn't let down Jennifer who, in addition to engineering the entire event and apparently letting rescue pets roam freely about her house, was putting up Colette in her guest cottage. As usual, Syd's old friend was going the extra mile.

Jennifer had spent most of her childhood in boarding school, but anytime she was in town she'd appear at Honey's back door looking for Syd as if she'd just seen her the day before. Her parents had lived on the other side of the lake and mostly ignored their only daughter, preferring to focus on their art collection. Honey was the only one who wasn't shocked when Jennifer wed a local boy and settled nearby. Not because she thought the marriage would last, and it hadn't, but because Jennifer craved domesticity. She'd had four daughters in five years before divorcing her husband and getting her real estate license.

An hour later, Syd was standing on a small stage in Jennifer's cavernous living room, with her Portuguese water dog, Sinclair Chewis, sitting on her foot.

"Are you ready?" Colette asked and handed Syd a mug of hot tea with a dash of bourbon.

"As I'll ever be," Syd said, shifting her weight. Sinclair yawned but didn't move.

"You want me to take the beast?" Colette said, though she looked dubious about being able to accomplish the task.

"Sinclair's okay," Syd said. She took a sip of tea and handed the mug back to Colette. Three months post-partum, Colette looked like a twelve-year-old who'd stuffed her bra. Syd wasn't sure the tiny woman was capable of managing a house plant, much less a giant dog.

"As long as you're comfortable," Colette said. Looking relieved, she handed Syd her guitar. "Remember what we talked about?"

"I do," Syd assured her, and strummed the first chords of "Florida Man". Someone in the crowd hooted, and Colette scurried off to stand next to Jennifer, looking ravishing in a pair of white linen capri pants and matching tank top.

One by one, faces in the audience lit with recognition upon hearing the popular song. To appease Colette, who'd driven down from Atlanta to escape her new baby, Syd agreed to play "Florida Man" in the set. Getting it over with allowed her some semblance of control, as no one could ask her to play it later. It wasn't much but, as Honey had often said, *something was more than nothing, and usually often more than enough.*

"Florida Man" wasn't just about the man who'd taken Syd's wife. It was about the breakdown of society playing out in local headlines. The reason it struck a nerve with the public wasn't due to Syd's hatred of Paul, but because it illustrated another one of Honey's platitudes: *people were going to do what they were going to do.* The world was more disappointing each day. It was as she had told Katie, there was nothing Syd could do to control anyone's actions but her own. Closing her eyes, she blocked out all the noise in her head, and began to sing.

*I saw you on the news at four, spanking the monkey on the maternity ward,*

*Life with you is never a bore. It's all just great.*

*Mama always said look out for the loser, toking crack in the back
of a police cruiser,*
*Guess she hoped I might be choosier, now it's too late*
*So, meet me beneath the underpass, you bring the weed and we'll
spilt the gas.*
*I'm reaching out to take your hand, Florida Man.*

Syd heard the crowd singing along and smiled in spite of
herself. It was uncanny how much her fans loved the vengeful
lyrics. She opened her eyes and took a peek at those in the front
row. Everyone seemed to be having a great time. Winking at
Jennifer, who was dancing with a small Pomeranian, Syd sang
the chorus.

*Florida Man, what is your plan? Are you running away? Are you
taking a stand?*
*What I really need to know, is there room in your
van? Florida Man?*
*I'm coming down to you, we're all coming down, Florida Man.*

The crowd was singing so loudly, that Syd let them take
over the second verse. Unhooking the microphone from the
stand, she held it out over the front row who seemed to know
the words better than she did.

*Let's steal shit from the lost and found*
*Wrestle alligators, and walk naked round town.*
*Always stay high, you'll never come down, Florida Man.*

Syd sang the final chorus and the song was blessedly over.
The crowd responded enthusiastically, and she took a moment
to allow the applause to wash over her. Everywhere she looked
people seemed to be having a marvelous time. Even the dogs
looked happy. Perhaps tonight wouldn't be a total loss. She
looked for Deb and found her next to Owen, who was talking to
a woman with red hair. Syd did a double take. It couldn't be true,
but there she was. Standing in Jennifer's living room, chatting
with Syd's family and snuggling their dog was Katie.

# CHAPTER SEVENTEEN

## *BOLD*

With growing apprehension, Katie watched Syd walk across the crowded living room. Stopping to greet guests along the way, posing for pictures with dogs and signing autographs, Syd's progress seemed slow. Katie caught her eye and noticed a hint of hesitation. Could Syd be having second thoughts about a second date? Earlier in the day when Katie had called to cancel their evening plans, Syd had seemed truly disappointed. It was one of the reasons Katie had decided to stay in town for the event. Had something happened to change Syd's mind? Part of Katie worried she was angry about the Instagram post which was still generating a significant amount of publicity. Syd hadn't said anything but it was possible she found the attention annoying.

Katie searched her mind for another reason Syd might be upset. It couldn't be the performance. Although less provocative than her show at the Third Pig, tonight's concert had only served to highlight Syd's flawless pitch. The hometown crowd had responded with hometown love, demanding and receiving four encores, before allowing Syd to leave the stage. There was no way Syd could be concerned about the show.

"Baby sister doesn't look happy," Deb said, confirming Katie's suspicions that something was wrong. Seated on the couch to Katie's right, a shorter, shapelier version of her famous younger sister, Deb was in the mood to chat. "See that little pout?" she narrowed her eyes. "Syd's panties are in a wad for sure."

"I hope everything is okay," Katie said, trying in vain not to imagine Syd's panties. Sadly, their patio make-out session had never reached the point of reveal but Katie was pretty sure Syd had been wearing boy shorts.

"Me too," Deb said, and stroked the large, yellow Labrador retriever lying on the carpet by her feet.

Katie had met Syd's sister when they'd both arrived a few minutes late to the benefit and Grace had introduced them in the driveway. Deb was Katie's favorite kind of southern woman. Outgoing and funny, she was full of both observations and questions. They'd chatted nearly twenty minutes before joining the party. When they'd finally made it into the living room, Syd had already begun her set.

"Do you think Syd could be angry that I showed up tonight without letting her know?" Katie asked and hugged her arms to her chest. May in Georgia meant central air-conditioning systems were already set to all systems blow. Katie was close to freezing in the sleeveless dress she'd unwisely chosen for the party. Syd's frosty look was not helping matters. "I wanted to surprise her."

"Syd's not big on surprises," Deb said, and tugged a napkin out of her dog's mouth. The big Labrador, who'd been introduced to Katie as Ray, did not seem interested in the rawhide bones provided for the canine guests. Katie thought it an ingenious way of keeping the dogs busy. Not one had made a noise during the event. Deb rubbed Ray behind the ears. "You need to be careful with Syd. My sister has PTCD—post-traumatic Carrie disorder."

"I may have read about that," Katie replied, carefully. She knew better than to gossip about Syd's ex-wife—even to her lovely, likable sister. She could, however, provide assurances that her own intentions were honorable. "I really like Syd," she started but Deb cut her off.

"Just don't hurt her," she said, with a sad smile. "You're the first woman that's sparked her interest since the divorce. Syd's vulnerable. So please, be straight with her."

"Okay," Katie agreed, quashing the impulse to make a joke. The look on Deb's face did not invite humor. "I'd never intentionally hurt Syd."

"Then we're on the same page," Deb said. Her husband approached holding two frosty glasses and she frowned. "What happened to my margarita?"

"The machine froze," Owen said, and handed her the glass. Katie had only exchanged brief pleasantries with the Beaumont football legend in the foyer, but she liked his smile and thought anyone willing to wear matching bow ties with their dog a safe bet.

Deb took a cautious taste. "What's this?"

Owen shrugged. "Jennifer's calling it Bold Punch." He handed the other glass to Katie. "I'm drinking beer."

"Bold as in *big ole liquor drink*?" Deb asked. She took a deeper sip of the drink and smiled. "Jennifer got this recipe from Honey. She used to make it on poker night."

"That doesn't surprise me at all." Owen knocked his beer against Katie's tumbler. "Cheers to Deb's very bold grandmother."

"I'll drink to Deb's grandmother," Katie said, and lifted her glass.

"That's right, you bought Honey's chairs," Owen said, making the connection.

"I certainly did," Katie replied. "Deb's grandmother has made me very popular at work."

"I'm the one who made you popular at work," Deb informed her. "If it wasn't for me, Great Aunt Arlene would have given the whole estate to her church."

"I had no idea," Katie said, and lifted her glass again. "Here's to Deb." She clinked glasses with Syd's sister and took a tentative sip of the drink which tasted mostly of vodka and lime. It was much too strong to imbibe with the auction only minutes away but rude to put it down when Owen had gone to such trouble procuring it. Katie knew she had no choice but to hold the glass no matter how cold it was making her hand.

Deb smacked her lips. "What happened to the auction? Did y'all get the Snowy Egret Chair?"

"Oh, no. Not yet," Katie said, and tried to hide her surprise. The idea that Syd had repeated a detail of Katie's life to her sister seemed surreal. Then again, the idea that Katie had seen Syd naked, fucked her in a pool, also seemed surreal. It was an unreality that she hoped to continue.

Syd was now halfway across the room posing with a pair of French bulldogs. A tiny woman with giant breasts took their photo and she moved on.

"When will you know that you've got the chair?" Deb pressed, and Katie dragged her attention away.

"Online bidding closes at nine," she explained, and took her phone from the hip pocket to check the time. "The live auction won't start until seven p.m."

Deb looked alarmed. "It's already seven thirty."

"The auction is in Alabama," Katie explained, calmly. The hour time zone difference between the states meant it was only six thirty in Dothan. Katie still had thirty minutes before the live auction began.

"When did the bidding start?" Owen wanted to know.

"Last week," Katie replied. "But I didn't find out about the auction until yesterday." She smiled remembering the moment of discovery. Miraculously, Lori's advice to investigate auction houses had borne fruit. Following the weekend in Atlanta, Katie had returned to Beaumont and called every auction house in Georgia.

"What happened yesterday?" Owen asked.

"I expanded my search to Alabama and found an auction called Bama Birds," Katie explained.

"No way," Owen laughed.

"You could have knocked me over with an egret feather," Katie replied, enjoying the conversation. Deb and Owen were nice people. Besides Beth, who couldn't attend the benefit because there'd been a last-minute crisis at the print shop, Katie didn't know many people in Beaumont. There were probably other members of her high school class still living in town, but as Katie hadn't been friends with them as a teenager, there was nothing to rekindle now. Forgetting her vow not to drink, she took another sip of the BOLD cocktail and shivered.

"Are you cold?" Deb asked, and pulled a soft-looking, gray cardigan sweater out of her bag.

"A little," Katie admitted, eying the garment longingly. It looked warm and the color wouldn't fight with her white dress. "Are you sure you don't need it yourself? It's freezing in here."

Deb shook her head. "Hormones have my thermostat out of whack. I'm hotter than a black dog in a sunspot," she said, and handed Katie the sweater. "Just touching this thing makes my body go up a degree."

"If you're sure," Katie said, and gratefully accepted the cardigan. Her arms had been goose bumped all night. The big ole liquor drink had only made it worse.

"Hold our drinks, honey," Deb told her husband, and helped Katie into the cardigan. "How's that?" she asked.

"Much better," Katie said, "thank you." She looked across the room where Syd was now hugging an older woman with beautiful salt-and-pepper hair. Tiny big-boobed woman approached, and they posed for a picture. Katie wondered at the older woman's identity. Syd looked genuinely pleased to see her and was now whispering something in her ear.

"That's no one to worry about," Deb said, following Katie's gaze. "Syd worked for Jane in high school. She's director of the Beaumont Humane Society and married to a woman named Frieda who is our local fire chief."

"Frieda would kick Syd's ass," Owen agreed.

"Syd mentioned she'd considered being a veterinarian," Katie said. She wasn't worried about Syd fucking her old boss and getting her ass kicked by the Beaumont fire chief. She was worried about Syd's inscrutable expression. Katie checked the time and then slipped her phone into the pocket of the cardigan.

There were twenty minutes left before the live auction began. Plenty of time to find out what was bothering Syd.

"Syd told me you were driving to Dothan to attend the live auction," Deb said, as if reading Katie's mind.

"Syd *thought* I should be there, but I assure you, it isn't necessary," Katie said, and explained how she'd made the opening bid of two hundred dollars, with an escalation bid of up to twenty-five hundred.

"Don't count your egrets before they hatch," Owen teased, causing Deb to laugh.

"There's a good chance I'll get the chair for two hundred," Katie told them, confidently. She pulled her phone from the pocket of the cardigan and scrolled through photos on the auction site until she found a picture of the Snowy Egret Chair. The Graham's ledger indicated there were six life-sized egrets carved into the high back of the chair, though it was hard to determine the number from the photo. Beaks pointed out in all directions. Katie wondered if some were meant as coat hooks and worried about founder Bernice Wolfe Calhoun getting poked in the head.

"That doesn't look comfortable," Owen said. "It's even stranger than the chairs Honey had."

"It's been up for almost a week and no one else has bid on it," Katie told them and pocketed the phone once more.

Deb made a tsking noise. "I bet that's why Syd's worried. She's scared that you're going to lose the chair."

"You think Syd's scared?" Katie asked. She turned to look for Syd and found her standing in front of the couch and staring down at them.

"Who's scared?" Syd asked.

Katie hesitated. So many times in the past her straightforward nature had gotten her into trouble. Not everyone wanted to hear the truth, certainly not all the time. But, looking into Syd's eyes, Katie saw only trust and vulnerability so she didn't hold back. "Are you scared that I'm going to lose the chair?" she asked. "You know, because I'm not at the live auction?"

"Scared is a strong word," Syd said, and her gaze dropped to Katie's lips.

Katie felt a strange stirring in her chest. She felt compelled to stand and press her body against Syd's, but kept herself in check. Just because it suddenly felt as if they were the only two people in the room didn't mean it was true. Katie knew other party guests were watching them. Some had cameras out and were shooting video. Syd was a nationally recognized celebrity and the details of her private life had been bought and sold a million times over. Katie did not wish to provide additional product to peddle.

Owen stepped in to break the spell. "That was a great show, Spud," he said. Rising from the couch, he rested his bear-sized hand on Syd's shoulder. "You're a gifted entertainer. The dogs loved you. Only one was barfing, but I think he ate too much kibble. That's not on you, Stud."

"Thanks, bro," Syd said, and Katie saw the first genuine smile of the evening.

"You really were wonderful," Deb agreed, and then exchanged a look with her husband. "Do we need to go check on that thing?"

"Yes, that thing," Owen responded, robotically. "It does indeed, require checking. We'll see you out back." Taking Deb's arm, he left Katie and Syd alone with the dog.

Syd sat down on the couch and took Katie's hand. "Hi," she said, smiling intently into her eyes.

"Hi," Katie replied, marveling at the sudden butterflies in her stomach. She hoped Syd was only worried about the chair and not concerned they were moving too fast. Auction anxiety was an easy fix. There was no unlicking someone's areola.

"I'm glad you're here," Syd said, and squeezed Katie's fingers. The butterflies melted magically away, leaving a warm feeling behind. "I'm glad to be here," she replied, wondering how soon they might be alone. The benefit wasn't scheduled to be over until nine, but surely Syd had more than fulfilled her obligation. Katie could see a couple of women approaching in her peripheral vision and willed them to disappear.

Syd squeezed her fingers again. "I've been looking forward to seeing you since you drove off in the pickup truck."

"Thanks for driving it back down the hill for me," Katie said.

"Anytime," Syd replied. "I wish we'd been able to say a proper goodbye."

The words warmed Katie even further. As much as she'd enjoyed Syd's texts, it didn't compare to being in her presence. Guileless and sweet, a huge part of Syd's appeal was that she didn't seem to be aware of her own magnetism. No wonder Deb and Lori were so protective. "I wanted to see you too," Katie told her. "That's the reason I didn't go to Dothan, tonight."

"Yeah, about that," Syd said, and looked hesitant. "It makes me happy that you want to be with me, it really does, but I'd feel responsible if something went wrong and you didn't get the chair."

Katie felt another surge of heat. She couldn't remember the last time someone had shown her this much consideration. "Please don't worry about the auction," she said, and pushed up the sleeve of the cardigan.

"Only if you're sure," Syd said, now eyeing the sweater. "Is that my sister's cardigan?" she asked.

"Yes." Katie nodded, and pushed up the other sleeve. "It *was* freezing in here a few minutes ago. I bought a cute new dress, just for you, but it was so cold, I had to borrow Deb's sweater."

Something changed in Syd's eyes. Her gaze to dropped to Katie's neckline. "You bought that dress for me?" she asked.

"Yes," Katie admitted. "I dragged Beth all the way to Beaumont Plaza Mall."

Syd cocked her head to one side. "You went to the *Mall*, for me?"

"I did," Katie said, feeling warmer than ever. "The crossed straps are the best part." Standing, she slipped off the sweater and let it drop to the couch.

"You found that dress at Beaumont Plaza Mall?" Syd whistled, and looked up at Katie with undisguised appreciation.

"Technically, I think this is supposed to be a beach cover-up," Katie admitted, and told Syd about how Beth had discovered the garment on the sale rack.

"So, it's okay to get it wet?" Syd said, and then blushed adorably. She rose from the couch and stood just inches away from Katie.

The women who'd been lurking in Katie's periphery took the opportunity to approach and ask Syd for a photograph. A mother-daughter duo wearing the same color lipstick, they were so starstruck in Syd's presence they could barely speak. When Katie offered to take their picture, the older woman pushed her phone into Katie's hands as if she were being robbed at knifepoint. She posed the trio next to the fireplace.

"Do you want Ray in the picture?" Katie asked, and turned to look for the dog.

"Where did he go?" Syd asked.

Because the Labrador retriever was nowhere in sight. Also missing, from where Katie had left it on the couch, her cell phone deep in the pocket, was Deb's cardigan.

# CHAPTER EIGHTEEN

## *Early Dazed*

"Is it possible Deb's dog took her sweater?" Katie asked, and ran a hand nervously through her hair. Freshly washed, it looked to Syd like spun red-gold in the light.

Syd wanted to call out the likeness but first needed to put Katie at ease. She glanced at the spot next to the couch, where Ray had been only a moment before. There was every chance the dog had taken Deb's cardigan, but no chance Deb would be angry about it. Syd tried to explain this to Katie. "Ray loves anything that smells like family," she said. "It's the price of admission for riding the Ray train."

Katie only looked more stricken. "Can you please help me find him?" she asked, and stood on her toes to scan the room.

Syd tried not to get distracted by the bare flesh peeking through the straps on the back of the dress. "Of course, I'll help, but I swear, Deb won't care," Syd assured her. "Ray does this kind of thing all the time."

Katie shook her off. "I need to find that dog," she muttered. Handing the phone back to the women who'd requested the picture with Syd, she disappeared into the crowd.

"What just happened?" the woman asked.

"My dog took her sweater," Syd explained, looking for glimpses of Katie's red hair in the crowd.

The teenage daughter nodded, as if this type of thing happened to her all the time. "Was her phone in the pocket?" she asked, alerting Syd to the real problem.

"Yeah, I think that might be it," Syd told the girl and started after Katie. It was worse than she'd thought. Katie wasn't worried about losing Deb's sweater—she was worried about losing her job.

Jennifer's house was enormous but built all on one level. The open floor plan allowed each room to flow graciously into the next. All had views of the lake, but there was no sign of Katie. Syd moved through the crowd avoiding eye contact with fans and looking for red hair. A guy she remembered from high school tried to say hello and she pretended not to see him. Until she knew that Katie's bid was secure, there was no time to be polite. Where was she? Syd pulled out her phone to call her, and then stopped herself, remembering, the dog had Katie's phone.

Suspiciously also missing, were the rest of Syd's family and Colette. It couldn't be a coincidence. Most likely they'd all followed Ray to the same destination. But where had they gone? Syd walked the length of the house, looking in every room until she got to the front foyer where Jennifer was saying goodbye to some guests. A tiny frown appeared on her face when she noticed Syd.

"What's wrong, Siddhartha?" she drawled, looking beautiful and bemused. Syd had spoken briefly to her old friend upon arriving at the party, but they hadn't had a proper conversation in weeks. Jennifer knew nothing about Katie, the ZAP founders' chairs or the impending auction. There was not time to explain it all now, so Syd addressed the problem at hand.

"Ray took Deb's sweater," Syd said. "I really need to find it."

Jennifer's intelligent blue eyes widened with concern. "Who is Ray?" she asked, looking back into the dwindling party.

"Ray, the dog," Syd explained. "He's wearing a blue bow tie," she said, and checked her watch. The live auction began in fifteen minutes. She hoped it was enough time to find the sweater, the dog and the phone.

"Oh, that Ray," Jennifer snorted. "I just saw him a few minutes ago. He was running around in the yard with your sister and a cute redhead."

"That's Katie," Syd said, and ducked back into the party.

"Katie?" Jennifer asked, close at her heels. "Who's Katie?"

"A woman I met," Syd called over her shoulder. Moving quickly past the remaining guests, Syd grew cautiously optimistic. If Katie was with Ray and Deb, that meant they'd found the sweater and the missing phone. There was a chance Katie had already logged into the auction website. She could be babysitting the bid on the Snowy Egret Chair right now. Maybe everyone was outside waiting for Syd to find them. She opened the closest door to the deck just as Jennifer caught up with her.

"You met someone?" she asked, her voice full of surprise. "When? What happened?" Grabbing Syd by the arm, she yanked her back inside the house.

Syd looked through the glass door, but saw no sign of Katie. Sighing, she turned back to Jennifer. "It's a long story."

"Well, start at the beginning and don't leave anything out," Jennifer said, sounding irritated. "I can't believe this is the first I'm hearing of a new woman in your life. Why didn't you tell me?" Jennifer didn't subscribe to social media so wouldn't have seen the Instagram post.

"Because it's early days and I'm early dazed," Syd said, and then shook her head. "See that? What just happened?"

Jennifer frowned "See what?" she asked.

"My head is exploding with lyrics," Syd answered. She pulled her phone from her hip pocket and texted the clever phrase to herself for safekeeping. Syd had already incorporated some of the Katie-inspired ideas into new material. It was fascinating how she'd reopened Syd's creative channels but hard to articulate why. Syd did her best to explain the situation to Jennifer. "Katie inspires my songwriting. I'm seeing whole bridges. Lyrics are coming out of nowhere."

"A new muse?" Jennifer asked, her blue eyes narrowed.

"I think so, maybe," Syd said. It was premature to make such a declaration after only a few, magical encounters but Syd's reaction to Katie didn't feel like a fluke.

Jennifer scrunched up her nose like there was a bad smell in the room. "I don't love the sound of that. You used to say Carrie was your muse, remember?"

"Because she was," Syd said, and then took a moment to discuss her new crush with her best friend. It was only fair. Jennifer had been there in Syd's darkest hour of need and deserved to know Syd wasn't rushing into another mess. "Katie isn't like Carrie at all, I promise. She's funny and sweet and sexy."

Jennifer looked unconvinced. "But she's got red hair."

"Okay, fine, her hair is red, yes," Syd admitted. "But it's much curlier. Katie is wonderful, you'll see. She's the polar opposite of Carrie. I promise."

"If you say so," Jennifer said, skeptically. "I'd hate to see you make the same mistake."

"Me too," Syd said, holding her tongue because she knew Jennifer always had her best interest at heart. The day after the news of Carrie's betrayal went public, she'd sent Syd a case of pinot noir and the keys to her cabin in Colorado. The respite had been key to Syd's recovery. Living in unfamiliar surroundings among unfamiliar people allowed Syd to dole out the pain of her heartbreak in measured quantities. If she'd had to face it all at the same time, she wasn't sure she would have survived.

"Is she butch?" Jennifer challenged. "You said Katie wasn't like Carrie, does that mean she's butch?"

"No." Syd frowned. She didn't like to think of herself as someone who was attracted to a particular type. Yes, Katie and Carrie were both small, feminine women with red hair, but the similarities stopped there. "Katie is nothing like Carrie," she told Jennifer. "Help me find her, and you'll see for yourself."

"Deal," Jennifer said, and took out her phone. "I'll text Deb, and you text Katie."

"That's the problem, I can't text Katie," Syd said, and explained her theory about the stolen sweater and Katie's missing cell phone.

Jennifer put a hand over her eyes. "This sounds like a movie my children would love to watch, but I'd need a bottle of wine to sit through," she said. "Text your sister. We can grab a drink while we wait for her reply."

"Okay," Syd said, and followed Jennifer outside. "I'll send a group text, but I don't want a drink. I can't stop looking until I find Katie or her phone."

"We'll find both more quickly this way," Jennifer insisted and walked toward the bar. The deck was vacant, except for a bartender who was fiddling with the broken margarita machine. Noticing them, he stood back at attention. Tall and broad with a handsome, movie-star face, he reminded Syd of a cartoon she'd once seen of a Canadian Mountie.

"I finally got it working, ma'am," he told Jennifer, and sheepishly held out two perfect margaritas. "Sorry I didn't have the machine up and running for the party. Your punch was… um…really popular."

"It was Syd's grandmother's recipe," Jennifer said in her flirty voice, alerting Syd to the existence of a possible attraction. Though always outwardly charming, Jennifer loathed inefficiency. Syd knew if the bartender weren't gorgeous, the frozen margarita machine would have resulted in an even more frozen hostess. His chiseled features seemed to thaw Jennifer and her standards. She took the drinks and handed one to Syd.

The bartender did a double take. "Hey, Syd Collins! Great set," he said, and then looked nervously at Jennifer. "I only heard it through the door, but she sounded great."

"Thanks, man," Syd said, and took a moment to take a picture with him. Next, she sent a group text. Maybe everyone was together, collected around the dog somewhere. But where?

"Tell me how you met this new woman," Jennifer demanded, and took a sip of her margarita.

"Her name is Katie," Syd said, not loving Jennifer's tone. Her friend was allowed to be protective, but only to a point.

"Right, Katie, how did you meet?" Jennifer asked.

"I met Katie at the Third Pig. She was wearing an original *Deja Boo* concert T-shirt," Syd said and checked her phone. Finding no response, she continued her story.

"The T-shirt with the tiny pocket?" Jennifer asked, looking impressed.

Syd nodded. Sparing the intimate details, she described meeting Katie at the bar, the sale of the ZAP chairs, and the invitation to dinner.

"You invited strange women to your house?" Jennifer looked horrified. "Does Colette know?"

"Katie and Beth are not strange women," Syd corrected her. "They went to Beaumont Central a few years behind Carrie and I. Grace babysits for Beth's twins. It's small-town Georgia stuff and I kind of love it." She smiled. "This kind of thing never happened to me in California."

"What did Colette say?" Jennifer persisted.

"Are you kidding?" Syd replied. "Katie posted a picture of me on ZAP National's Instagram account that got lots of attention so Colette is thrilled."

"No one tells me anything."

"I'm telling you now."

Syd had also told her manager about the offer to help Katie find the chairs, though hadn't mentioned tender feelings were developing between them. Something exciting was happening with Katie. Syd wanted to see how it played out before letting her overprotective friends weigh in. Her phone buzzed and she checked the screen. It was from Deb.

*We're at Grandfather Cottage with the dog.*

There was no mention of Katie so Syd texted back.

*Is Katie with you? Did you find her phone?*

"Who is that?" Jennifer asked over her shoulder. "Did they find the phone?"

Syd moved the phone so Jennifer could see Deb's return message.

*Yes Katie. No phone.*

*Colette and Grace are walking back from the main road to help search.*

"Oh, shit," Syd said and looked out toward the shore.

Grandfather Cottage was sited directly on the water, about two hundred yards from Jennifer's main house. Named for the clause that allowed it to exist, the cottage pre-dated the law preventing residents building within fifty feet of the water. Jennifer used the small residence mostly for house guests but often entertained on the back porch, which commanded amazing views of the lake.

"Call her," Jennifer said.

Seconds later Deb's voice was coming out of the phone speaker. "Hey, y'all. We chased Ray all the way to the cottage. He had the sweater but not the phone. Katie thinks it fell out somewhere in the yard. We're going to walk back toward the house now. Grace and Colette are all the way up at the main road. They're walking back, but it may take a while."

"Is Katie with you?" Syd asked. "Can I talk to her?"

"You're on speaker, Squid," she heard Owen say. "You're talking to all of us."

"Hi, Syd," Katie said, sounding calmer than Syd expected. "Sorry for all the drama."

Syd couldn't tell if Katie was truly unconcerned or just playing it cool. The only thing she knew for certain was that the auction had already begun. She'd never forgive herself if Katie lost the Snowy Egret Chair due to Ray's bad manners. "I'm so sorry the dog took your phone," she said and threw an elbow at Jennifer who was smirking into her hand.

"We're sorry, too," Deb echoed, through the speaker. "Aren't we sorry, Owen?"

"Mortified," Owen agreed.

"How can I help? What do you want me to do?" Syd asked, ready for instructions.

"I can't use anyone else's phone because the auction house gave me a special log-in number," Katie said. "So, keep calling my cell. We're going to walk back up the road now. I'm hoping we'll hear the ringer."

"Okay," Syd said, and Jennifer nodded. "We'll start walking and meet you guys somewhere in the middle."

"Okay," Katie agreed, "see you soon."

Syd ended the call and pulled up Katie's information. She hovered her finger above the call button but did not start dialing. Until they were out of earshot of the gnat fans there was no point. Syd turned to Jennifer. "You in?"

"Who could refuse such an invitation?" Jennifer asked, and took a deep sip of the margarita. "Watch this for me?" she asked the bartender.

"I'll be right here," he promised.

A minute later, Jennifer and Syd were running away from the house toward the narrow driveway leading to the cottage. Syd put Katie's number on redial and strained her ears for a ringtone. The only noise was Jennifer's heels tapping against the asphalt. Syd wasn't sure how Jennifer managed to keep pace with her own sure-footed Doc Martens, but there was no time to ask questions. The auction was well underway. They needed to find Katie's phone.

"Wait a second," Jennifer said. She grabbed at Syd's arm, pulling them to a stop. "Did you hear something?"

Syd strained to listen, but heard nothing but the faint sound of voices approaching from the other direction. She slapped at a gnat. "I don't hear a phone," she said, wishing she'd asked Katie what her ringtone was.

"Listen!" Jennifer insisted, and clutched at Syd's arm more tightly.

Syd shook her head. "I still can't hear anything."

"Your ears are shot from standing in front of an amplifier for the last ten years," Jennifer informed her, and blew a bug out of her eye. "Call the number again. You can be the big hero and kiss the girl and I can go finish my margarita and…"

"Tend the bartender?" Syd suggested.

"Exactly," Jennifer replied. Slipping out of her heels, she stepped off the road.

"Where are you going?" Syd asked. "Did you hear it again?" Even though Jennifer was suspicious of Katie, Syd was grateful to have her there.

"I thought I heard something," Jennifer said, and stopped short. "Call the number again, and be really quiet."

"Okay," Syd replied and pressed the call button.

"I can hear it!" Jennifer exclaimed and fell to the ground. Seconds later she handed Syd a cell phone. "Nice ringtone," she said, smirking.

"Isn't it?" Syd agreed. She'd only caught the last fragment, but the opening chords of "Deja Boo" were iconic. Syd felt a small thrill. Whatever was happening between them, Katie was feeling it too.

# CHAPTER NINETEEN

## *Grandfather Cottage*

Watching Syd emerge from the woods, cell phone in hand, Katie felt relief wash over her. The last twenty minutes had been an anxiety dream come to life. Chasing the bow-tied Labrador retriever through the fancy party, Katie had felt like an utter fool. It was now clear to her that she'd been far too cavalier about the auction. It had been one thing not to travel to Dothan, but Katie should have made tending the bid her priority. She hadn't even checked to make sure there would be cellular service at the party. You never knew in rural areas. Not to check had been an unconscionable oversight. If Katie lost the Snowy Egret Chair because of a preventable error, there'd be no excuse to give the board of directors, or herself.

"You found it," Deb squealed, and rushed forward to yank Syd up the small incline to the road. "Bring it over here so Katie can log on to the auction," she insisted.

"I'm coming," Syd said, looking adorably ruffled.

"Good job, Squid," Owen said, and clapped her on the back. He held his other arm high in the air to distract the gnats from his face. He'd taught Katie the trick when they'd left the cottage and she'd walked down the road like a student vying for attention.

"Thanks, but it was all Jennifer," Syd said and handed Katie the phone. Their eyes met in the dim light and Katie felt a jolt of happiness.

A woman Katie recognized from the party stepped out of the woods holding a pair of shoes. "Syd's right. You can make the reward check out to me. That's Jennifer with two ns."

"Will do," Katie replied, and forced a smile. "Thank you, so much." Katie was thrilled to have the phone back but there wasn't time to celebrate. She chanced a look at the screen. The phone still had power but there was no cell service. If Katie was going to sign in for the auction, she needed to get back to the house. Her expression must have betrayed her consternation as Syd stepped forward and took her arm.

"Is everything okay?" she asked, and looked expectantly at the screen cradled in Katie's hand. "Is something the matter with your phone?"

"The 'Deja Boo' ringtone came through loud and clear," Jennifer said, and Katie wondered at the challenge in her tone.

"Thanks, 'Deja Boo' is my favorite song," Katie said, meeting Jennifer's eye. Whatever point her hostess was trying to make, it would have to wait until after the she'd secured the Snowy Egret Chair. Katie turned to Syd. "My phone is fine, but I need Wi-Fi to sign in to the auction. I need to get closer to the house."

"The signal is better at the cottage," Jennifer replied before Syd could answer.

Katie looked hesitantly down the unlit road in the direction she'd just come. The thought of monitoring the auction in the spooky lake shack did not appeal to her. "I'll be fine in my car. I've troubled you too much already."

Jennifer wouldn't take no for an answer. "I promise, the signal's better at the cottage. My mother needs perfect Wi-Fi to stream The Home Shopping Network and I need my mother to stay in the guesthouse."

"If you're sure," Katie said, and checked the time. The auction had been live for twenty minutes. There were thirty-seven items ahead of the Snowy Egret Chair. If the auctioneer went in the order they were listed in the catalogue, he wouldn't reach the chair for another hour. But Katie couldn't leave it to chance. She'd left enough to chance already.

"I'm positive," Jennifer said. "When you're done, walk back to the house and we'll all have a margarita."

"Okay," Katie said, and glanced down the road again. "I should get going." She'd stupidly allowed Flora to tell the other board members about tonight's auction. Some of the women had registered and planned to follow along. Katie wondered if they'd be able to tell that she hadn't signed in yet.

"Wait for me," Syd said, and took her hand.

Katie didn't play hard to get, and clasped Syd's fingers in her own. "Thank you," she said, already feeling better. Maybe when she logged in everything would be okay. Maybe the dog-in-the-bow tie screwball comedy scene had all been for nothing. Whatever happened, Katie was holding hands with Syd Collins on a beautiful spring night. Things could be worse. She squashed a gnat against her forehead. "Let's go."

No one seemed to think Syd accompanying Katie to Grandfather Cottage was a bad idea and no one offered to come with them.

"The Wi-Fi password is on the fridge," Jennifer said, and hooked her arm through Deb's. "It's either, *purchase more purses*, or *purses to purchase*. I can never remember which. You'll figure it out."

"Thanks, buddy," Syd said, and gave Jennifer a tight salute.

"Yes, thanks," Katie echoed, and wondered if anything romantic had ever existed between the two old friends. Could that be the reason Jennifer seemed suspicious? Deb had divulged many details of Syd's life tonight, but she'd said nothing about Syd having a past with her beautiful hostess. Katie pushed the image away and focused on the current problem.

"See you two back at the house," Jennifer said, and spun Deb in the other direction where the road was still visible.

"Yes, good luck to you, ladies," Owen said, following behind them. "It's been fun but I'm done with the Scooby-Doo portion of the night. I heard a rumor the margarita machine was working."

"Yes, and I'm working the margarita machinist," Jennifer joked, and the trio started walking back toward the house.

Katie squeezed Syd's hand. "I can't believe I've caused so much drama tonight. I'm beginning to think I should have just driven to Alabama."

"Alabama is never the answer," Syd said and squeezed Katie's hand in return. "And I'm sorry about the drama, too. The dog is not to be trusted in polite company."

"I won't argue with that," Katie replied. Matching her stride, Katie told Syd about cornering Ray on the deck only to be tripped up by a pair of Pekingese in matching hats. "I almost had him," she said.

Syd made a sympathetic noise. "How did you know your phone was still in the pocket?" she wanted to know. "It could have fallen out in the house."

"I could see it through the pocket of the sweater," Katie told her. "I was hoping it would fall out, believe me."

"Then what happened?" Syd asked. "How did Deb and Owen get involved?"

"They found us in the yard," Katie told her. "Owen went streaking by me like a rocket. Deb was right behind him. They were both screaming for Ray."

"I can totally picture this." Syd giggled.

"Your sister is surprisingly fast."

"She really is," Syd agreed.

"The dog was faster than both of them" Katie shook her head. "I'm pretty sure Ray thought they were playing a game."

Syd scoffed. "It's called the I'm-being-a-pain-in-the-ass game. I'm sorry he pulled this stunt on you. There should be a warning label on his back."

"Ray's okay," Katie replied. "I never should have let the phone out of my sight."

Syd neither agreed or disagreed with the statement. She simply squeezed Katie's hand.

They turned a corner and the cottage came into view. Katie picked up the pace. The sooner they got within Wi-Fi range, the sooner they'd know if there was a problem with the auction. Syd was being unbelievably sweet. Katie would've understood had she chosen not to come to the cottage with her. Playing a solo set and then smiling through the meet and greet had to be exhausting. Syd should be relaxing with a margarita right now, not slapping at gnats on a dark country road. Nevertheless, Katie was glad to have her company. They neared the house and Syd let go of her hand.

"Jennifer keeps the key in a turtle shell on the back porch. I can go around and get in the house through the kitchen door. You wait here on the front porch. I'll let you in."

"Or, I could just come with you," Katie replied. As much as she appreciated Syd's gallantry, she didn't love the idea of being left alone on the dark road. She also didn't like losing contact with Syd's body.

Syd chuckled. "Okay, come with me."

Together, they walked around to the back of the cabin. It was still light enough for Katie to see to the lake, but she barely registered the view as she followed Syd through a screened door onto the porch.

"Let me grab the key," Syd said, and let go of Katie's hand. Katie watched her turn over an object and heard a rattling noise. Moments later the back door opened and they stepped inside the house. They passed through a small living room into the kitchen where Syd flipped on the overhead light and took a piece of paper off the refrigerator. She handed it to Katie and, together, they sat down at the kitchen table. Syd remained silent while Katie logged in. The signal activated almost immediately.

"It works," Katie said, glancing up at Syd.

"Purchase more purses." Syd grinned, and pushed back from the table. "Do you want something to drink?" she asked, and gestured to a wall of cabinets. "Jennifer usually has tea."

Katie nodded without answering. The auction site had come up and she needed to find the Snowy Egret Chair. Scrolling through the catalogue, she stopped at the listing and exhaled.

"Here it is," she said, and heard Syd shut the cabinet door and walk across the small kitchen. Katie felt a hand on her shoulder.

"It doesn't look like they've reached it yet," she said.

"We've got plenty of time," Katie assured her, feeling a deep sense of relief. "It won't go up for at least an hour."

"An hour?" Syd looked surprised.

"Yeah," Katie replied, feeling ridiculous for the unnecessary drama. She cringed to think of what Syd's friend must think of her. "I'm really sorry," she said, and looked up to see Syd's face only inches away.

"Don't worry about it," she said, smiling into Katie's eyes. "Anyone would be freaked out to lose their phone. If one of my nieces lost their phones, they'd call in the National Guard."

"That's funny," Katie said, desperately wanting to kiss her.

"It's true," Syd assured her. "Also, none of this was your fault. All you did was borrow a sweater."

"Okay, thanks for saying that," Katie murmured. She couldn't wait any longer and pulled Syd into a heated kiss. She'd been thinking of Syd's lips for two weeks. Tasting them again was even better than she remembered.

After a blissful moment, Syd broke contact and her lips slid to Katie's ear. "I'll make the tea."

Reluctantly, Katie let her go. "I'm glad one of us is an adult," she joked, and turned back to her phone. What was wrong with her? Not two minutes ago the ugly-chair gods had granted Katie a reprieve. Why couldn't she honor them and pay attention to the auction?

"I am a few years older than you," Syd pointed out, and filled the kettle with water.

"Are you saying there's hope for me to mature?" Katie asked.

"There always hope," Syd said, and lit the stove. "What's going on with the auction, now?"

"You've got thirty seconds to make an offer on a walking stick with the state bird of Alabama on the top," Katie told her.

"Pass," Syd said. "What's up next?"

"Let me see," Katie said. She clicked on the arrow and a brooch with an ornate golden eagle came on the screen. She flashed her phone at Syd. "Want me to bid on it for you?"

"Pass," Syd said and walked closer to the table. "What's after that?"

Katie clicked the advance arrow. "Another brooch," she said, and forced herself to concentrate. Syd was, once again, dangerously within reach. "There are several brooches in the catalogue. Some of them are quite pretty."

"May I see the others?" Syd asked, and sat back down in a chair.

"Sure, but it's your last chance for the walking stick," Katie said. "M. Stapp is about to win it for forty-five dollars."

"Why do they say you've won something at an auction when you're actually buying it?" Syd asked, looking adorably confused. "I've never understood that."

"Bidding can be a very competitive thing," Katie explained.

Syd looked concerned. "Do you have any competition for the Snowy Egret Chair?"

"No, I don't," Katie said, and clicked back to lot twenty-three. "Let me show you." Just as suspected, the only bid on the Snowy Egret Chair was her earlier one for two hundred dollars. "It's still just me."

Syd looked relieved. "That's good," she said, rising to brew the tea. "Do you have any leads on the last chair? Which bird is it?"

"The Robin Chair," Katie said. "It originally belonged to one of the founders, named Alethea Albright Buchannan. She was from Washington County, Georgia."

"A place too small to be called a town?" Syd asked and Katie knew she was spinning lyrics again. It was fun watching Syd's mind work. Katie could almost see the gears moving in her brain. Something seemed to occur to her and she paused. "Is Alethea a pretty name or just Alicia said with a lisp?"

"Both," Katie laughed. "And I have no idea where her chair is. The truth ith alluthive," she joked and heard Syd laugh. "Right now, Instagram is our best publicity. Your picture is almost up to one hundred thousand likes. I'll post again tomorrow if I get the Snowy Egret Chair. Maybe it will flush the Robin Chair out of the bushes."

"*When* you get the Snowy Egret Chair," Syd corrected her, sweetly. "And I'm happy to have been of service."

"Thank you, for everything," Katie said and her eyes wandered to the living room where she assumed there was a couch. "You don't have to sit here and watch people buy bird brooches. Why don't you take a nap? You must be exhausted after performing. I'll wake you when I win the chair."

Syd looked torn. "Maybe, but only because Jennifer's sectional is made of memory foam and extremely comfortable."

"You don't say?" Katie said, and pretended to get up from the table.

Syd laughed, and handed her a steaming mug of tea. "Wake me before the chair comes up? Please? I want to be there in your moment of glory."

"I promise," Katie said, and accepted a chaste kiss.

A moment later she heard Syd put her cup on the coffee table and settle onto the sofa. There was still another five minutes remaining on the eagle pin and an hour before they got to the Snowy Egret Chair.

Katie took a sip of tea, and hoped it was caffeinated.

# CHAPTER TWENTY

## *Auda-Bonnie*

"Cows! I see cows!" Katie yelled, and pointed her finger out of the truck window toward a pasture ahead on the left.

"Where? How many?" Syd asked, squinting at the horizon. The interstate highway was under construction, so she and Katie were driving back roads. The detour added an hour to their journey to retrieve the Snowy Egret Chair, but Syd didn't consider this a hardship. It gave her extra time in a confined space with Katie and allowed for Syd's favorite travel game of Highway Barnyard. "You have to count the animals, remember?" she said emphatically, though she hadn't played in years. "Every cow on your side of the road counts for one point. Dogs are two points. A horse is worth five points and a white horse is the most valuable at ten points. If there's a graveyard on your side of the road and I see it, all your animals die and you start again."

"There are too many rules," Katie protested, furiously counting the cows in the far-off pasture. She got to seventeen and lay exhausted against the passenger seat. "Am I winning? Did I win?"

"The game's not over until we reach our destination," Syd said. "The GPS says we have two more hours to go. You won't win until we pass the *Welcome to Dothan* sign."

"What if there isn't a *Welcome to Dothan* sign?" Katie asked skeptically.

Syd shook head. "There's always a welcome sign. This is the South, remember? We're polite."

"That wasn't always my experience." Katie snorted.

"I've been thinking about that," Syd said, and was met with a sweet look of surprise.

"You've been thinking about me?" Katie asked.

"I told you that yesterday." Syd fought off a blush. "What I've been thinking is, doesn't high school suck everywhere? It can't just be the South. Maybe you just hated high school."

Katie looked thoughtful. "That's true. I think part of my unhappiness came from the fact that I wasn't used to the culture. I'd come from Ohio. It made assimilating extra tricky," she said, frowning. "It's hard to know who's being genuine."

"You've got to be careful, that's for sure." Syd thought of the painful lessons she'd learned being married to Carrie. "But being friendly might be equally important."

"More important than being careful?" Katie wasn't convinced.

"Maybe." Syd shrugged. "Southerners forgive a lot of sins. Bad manners isn't one of them."

Katie laughed. "I'll keep that in mind," she said. "My grandmother tells me I'll catch more flies with honey but it seems so fake."

"You don't have to be fake to be friendly," Syd replied. "*My* grandmother used to say that if you listen to people carefully, they tell you who they are."

"You must miss her," Katie said, softly.

"I do," Syd said.

A herd of cows appeared over the horizon and she paused to count them. Syd's score was now higher than Katie's who began to question her again about winning.

"What if the *Welcome to Dothan* sign is missing?" she asked. "How do you know who wins the game if that happens? Surely there's a rule for that."

Syd didn't miss a beat. "If the welcome sign is missing, the driver wins. Everyone knows that."

"Cows!" Katie screamed, and began counting again.

She got all the way to thirty and Syd poked her playfully in the ribs. "You're really good at this game," she said, and was rewarded with a laugh.

"If the museum thing doesn't work out, I may go pro," Katie said, and shot Syd a sly look.

"Definitely, keep your options open," Syd agreed. Two mares came into view, and Katie screamed.

"Horses!"

They tallied livestock from central Georgia into southern Alabama, both women putting big numbers on the board. Twice Syd lost everything to country graveyards but won in the end when a Baptist cemetery claimed all of Katie's animals just outside of town.

They rolled into Dothan a few minutes before noon Alabama time and went directly to the auction house. Syd stepped out of the truck into the vacant parking lot. "Doesn't look like anyone's here."

Katie got out on the other side of the truck and frowned at the white, box-shaped building. A large sign above the awning read Boyd's Auction House. "I'm supposed to meet a woman named Wanda here at noon," she said, and checked her phone. "This is the address she gave me."

"Maybe she's late," Syd said, hating to see Katie looking uncertain. She'd been very candid about the importance of succeeding in this new job. Syd felt horrible for doubting her judgment about traveling to attend the live auction. The sale of the Snowy Egret Chair had gone through just as Katie had predicted. There'd been no additional bidders and Katie had won the lot for two hundred dollars. If you didn't include the knee-shaking celebratory kiss Katie had planted on Syd when it was all official, the event had almost been anticlimactic. "Why don't you just text?"

"Okay," Katie said, and sent off a quick message. A notification came back almost instantly. "Wanda's in there," she said, sounding relieved.

Syd followed Katie, across the parking lot to the front door of the building. Before they could knock, the door opened and a woman stepped out into the bright sunshine. Draped with pink feather boas, she looked like she might be on her way to Mardi Gras. "Welcome to Boyd's," she said, sweeping an arm dramatically inside the showroom.

Caught by surprise, Syd almost laughed, but Katie was all business.

"Thank you for meeting us, Wanda," she said and stuck out her hand. "I'm Katie Simmons."

"Wanda's inside," the woman said. "I'm Bonnie. Friends call me Auda-Bonnie."

"Bonnie Miller?" Katie asked, and the woman inflated.

"Have we met?"

"We haven't, but I'm familiar with your collection," Katie continued, smoothly. "I assume you're called Auda-Bonnie after Audubon, the famous nineteenth-century naturalist?" she asked, and Bonnie preened.

"I have an original in my collection," she said. "A small rendering of an American coot, painted in 1831."

Katie nodded, as this was something she'd expected. "You've a very eclectic eye."

"I have my grandmother to thank for the coot, but I like to think I've taken the collection to a new level," Auda-Bonnie said, and then placed a hand to her feathered chest. "I hate to sell any of my treasures but I need space in the aviary."

"You've more bird-themed art?" Katie asked, and Syd knew she was thinking about the last chair.

"Are you an avian art collector?" Auda-Bonnie grew excited.

"In a way," Katie said, and Syd wondered how much she'd divulge. If Auda-Bonnie had the last ZAP chair in her collection, it might not be wise to tell her its value. Katie bit her lip. "I was fortunate enough to win the Snowy Egret Chair in last night's auction."

"I bought that silly thing at an estate sale in Atlanta." Auda-Bonnie looked amused. "It's hard to sit in because the beaks poke you in the head."

"It's going to be part of an exhibit I'm curating for the ZAP Foundation," Katie told her, doubling down.

"The sorority?" Bonnie asked. "My cousin was a ZAP at Middle Tennessee College."

"Really? I was a ZAP at Colgate," Katie said, and filled Auda-Bonnie in on the project.

Syd's worry that Bonnie might be offended the Snowy Egret Chair hadn't sold for more money was unfounded. If anything, she seemed pleased. "My chair's going on display in Beaumont?"

"When I find the last one," Katie told her. "Syd's grandmother owned two." She turned to bring Syd into the conversation. "This is my friend Syd Collins," she said, and then paused expectantly as if Auda-Bonnie might be familiar with Syd's music.

"It's nice to meet you," Syd said, and shook the woman's hand. Syd was too famous to take her anonymity for granted but was fairly certain Auda-Bonnie wasn't interested in the alt-rock music scene. She was, however, very interested in the quest for the bird chairs of Zeta Alpha Pi.

"Tell me about the other chairs," she said, and Katie explained the carvings and the furniture maker's ledger she'd found in the Beaumont Library.

A smaller woman in a drab beige suit emerged from the building just as Katie was finishing her narrative. Auda-Bonnie pounced on her like she was a field mouse. "These women are hunting bird chairs!" she exclaimed, grabbing at the woman's frail shoulders.

"How interesting," the woman said from beneath a cloud of feathers. "You must be Katie."

"I am. It's nice to meet you, Wanda," Katie said, and gestured to Syd. "This is my friend Syd Collins."

Wanda extracted herself from Auda-Bonnie's bosom and assessed Syd's face as if she were a piece of art. "Isn't there a famous actress named Syd Collins?" she asked.

"I think maybe there's a singer?" Syd said, ignoring Katie's snort. "It's nice to meet you both."

"Come into the showroom, and we'll get you your chair," Wanda directed them. "I'm happy to say it's in excellent condition."

"Thanks."

They entered the building and Syd pulled Katie aside. "You're doing a great job," she whispered and was surprised when Katie's face sank.

"Did you expect me to fail?" she asked, and Syd remembered she was sensitive about her job.

"I'm talking about the southern charm initiative," she clarified, and took Katie's hand. "It's working."

"Oh, that," Katie said, and her expression lightened. "Do you really think so?"

"In the best possible way," Syd replied. "You're charming the feathers off Auda-Bonnie."

Katie glanced over her shoulder at Wanda and Auda-Bonnie who were safely inside the showroom. "She does seem to like me."

"You happen to be very likable," Syd said, resisting the urge to kiss her. It wouldn't do to both preach and breach professional etiquette in the same morning.

Two hours later they were counting cows, on the road back to Beaumont.

They'd had no information regarding the Robin Chair but Katie had posted a picture on Instagram of Syd standing back-to-back with Auda-Bonnie in front of the Snowy Egret Chair and the post already had twenty thousand likes. Driving back to Beaumont, they had the chair secure in the back of the truck and stomachs full of excellent BBQ. Syd thought the afternoon an unqualified success.

"I've had a great day," Katie said, as if reading Syd's mind. "Thanks for coming with me and thanks for posing with Auda-Bonnie. That was going above and beyond."

"Are you kidding? I've had a wonderful time," Syd replied. She couldn't remember the last time fun had felt so effortless. If you'd told her a month ago she'd be champing at the bit to drive an old pickup truck to Alabama to collect a giant bird chair, she'd have asked you for a sip of your drink. There was something about being with Katie that made Syd feel good. She knew both Jennifer and Colette questioned Katie's motivation but she didn't care. Her instinct was to keep Katie around. It was a simple feeling of heedless joy that she didn't want to question.

"I can't believe I've never played the cow game," Katie said, and sipped from a giant Styrofoam cup of sweet tea she'd held onto since lunch.

"I can't believe you're still drinking that sweet tea," Syd said. "I only finished half of mine and I'm about to jump out of my seat."

Katie looked at the cup as if it were a snake. "Is that why I feel so crazy?" she asked, and set it down in the holder.

"What did you think it was?" Syd asked.

"I thought it was being around you," Katie said, and put a hand on Syd's thigh.

"Are you trying to distract me so I won't notice the graveyard coming up on your side?" Syd sucked in a breath. "Because I know it's there, just after the place with the boiled peanuts and pickled pig's feet."

Katie moved her hand to boldly cover Syd's center. "Is it working?"

"Like a sinner on a Sunday morning." Syd gulped, using one of Honey's favorite phrases.

Katie spat out her tea. "Who's distracting who now?" she asked. Taking her hand from Syd's leg, she grabbed a napkin and wiped at the splatter on the dashboard.

"All is fair in love and Traveling Barnyard." Syd smirked, and began to count the cows to her left.

"I'd like to be with you tonight," Katie said, softly, and put her hand on Syd's leg again. "Last night was fun, but I was hoping for a little less drama and a lot more kissing."

"I like kissing," Syd said, wondering where they might go to find privacy. Beaumont held little appeal as Katie lived with her grandmother and the guest room at Deb's wasn't exactly suitable for overnight guests. If Colette wasn't hiding out at Grandfather Cottage, Syd would point the pickup toward the lake and not stop until she'd reached the sunset. But Colette was staying the weekend and Syd would not invade her hard-won sanctuary.

"How far is Atlanta?" Katie asked, and Syd realized she was a step ahead of her.

She did the calculations and ventured a guess. "Five hours? Is that too far?"

"Not for me," Katie said. "But I'm not driving."

"Atlanta it is." Syd grinned. Changing the destination on her GPS, she set the course for home.

# CHAPTER TWENTY-ONE

## *Annapurna*

"How are you doing? Still okay?" Syd asked.

"I'm okay," Katie lied, and felt like a five-year-old squirming in her seat. She never should have finished the sweet tea. Just because the BBQ place had given her a bucket-sized cup did not mean she'd been required to finish it. She shoved a hand between her legs. "I've no right to complain. You warned me there wouldn't be a place to stop after that last gas station."

"So, you'll believe me next time," Syd said.

"I certainly will," Katie replied, pleased that Syd had placed them in a future context. It was silly. Though wildly premature to discuss having a relationship, they were behaving as if one were already underway. "I'll never doubt you again," she promised, and willed her bladder to hold on.

"We're almost home," Syd promised, breathing even more life into Katie's domestic fantasies.

Syd pulled into the driveway, and ran ahead to unlock the door while Katie did a two-step on the front porch. When Syd finally flung open the front door, Katie was about to burst.

"The closest bathroom is the door on the left," Syd shouted, as Katie flew past her into the foyer. "The same one Beth used."

"Okay," Katie said. She ran down the hallway, turned left, and yanked open the door. But it was the wrong one. Instead of the apparatus she was hoping to see, she found a washer and dryer.

"That's not the room you want," Syd said, and opened the door across the hall.

"Thank you!"

Minutes later, feeling leagues more comfortable, Katie considered her reflection in the bathroom mirror. She almost didn't recognize the confident-looking woman smiling back at her. Was it possible she was making a fool of herself imagining a romance with Syd? It was hard to trust her own judgment, clouded as it was by serotonin and sweet tea. Historic artifacts required at least two sources for authentication. Katie decided to consult an expert and sent a message to Beth.

*Is it too soon for me to be smitten with Syd Collins?*

Beth's reply came back quicker than Katie imagined possible. *No.*

Katie smiled at the screen.

*But I just met her and I'm ready to move in.*

Beth sent back a house emoji and a heart.

*You've been crushing on the woman since tenth grade.*

*Now you've met her, and she's nice, and good at sex.*

*Would be strange if you were not smitten.*

Katie felt a rush of relief. Beth wasn't wrong about the crush. Maybe it wasn't weird to be falling so quickly. A fantasy version of Syd had occupied space in Katie's head for so long. Transferring those feelings to a flesh and blood woman, who made her writhe in ecstasy, hadn't taken much. The thing to consider was why Syd was so interested in Katie? The obvious, cringe-inducing answer was Katie's physical resemblance to Syd's ex-wife. Katie ran her fingers through her hair. She liked to think she was more than just freckles and follicles, but she had to consider the possibility that Syd had a type. Beth texted again.

*Where are you? How was the Humane Society benefit last night?*
*I'm home with children and starving for stories!*
Katie typed in a quick reply.
*I'm in Syd's guest bathroom*
*The one where you pretended to puke*
A second later, the phone buzzed in Katie's hand. Beth didn't bother with a greeting. "I thought Syd was coming to Beaumont this weekend."

"A lot has happened in the last two days," Katie replied. She filled Beth in on the auction, the dog chase and the drive to Dothan. "Everything has been so crazy. We came to Atlanta to be alone."

"Why didn't you just use the upstairs of Maguire House, like everyone else?" Beth joked.

Katie was surprised to feel a stab of annoyance. The idea was not unreasonable as Katie had discretionary usage over the space. Why shouldn't she use it for the same purpose as hundreds of other naughty ZAP girls?

"Because my friendship with Syd doesn't feel casual," Katie said, admitting her feelings to both Beth and herself. "When I said I was smitten, I may have been understating things."

"Oh, yeah?" Beth asked.

"I'm falling for her, Beth. Syd's too special for Maguire House. I want quality time with her, not a quickie."

"This sounds like a big deal for you," Beth said, but not unkindly.

Katie had to agree. She had lots of experience with women but little to none with relationships. "Things with Syd feel different," she admitted to Beth. "Normally when I get this close to a woman I cut and run before she can reject me."

"I kind of noticed that," Beth teased and Katie was reminded of who she was taking to.

"A therapist once said I bail on relationships because my mom died when I was so young," she admitted. "I've never had a real girlfriend because I always leave them before they can leave me."

"That makes sense," Beth said. "I can see how losing your mom might make you distrust the world. Don't be so hard on yourself."

"That's just the thing," Katie told her. "I've known this truth about myself for a long time and never bothered to address it. Syd makes me want to let down my guard."

"Where is she now?" Beth asked suddenly. "Did you leave her in bed?"

"No, but that's a good question," Katie replied, sparing Beth the details of the mad dash to the bathroom.

"Go find her," Beth commanded. "Call me tomorrow with a full report."

"I promise to text," Katie replied. She couldn't commit to anything further. If the next twenty-four hours went as envisioned, Katie would be too tired to talk. The more she got to know the real Syd Collins the more she craved her body. Katie had heard that emotional response could heighten a physical connection but had never personally experienced the phenomenon until now. Every time Katie touched Syd she felt as if there was an added jolt. "Good night, Sensei."

Beth hesitated just a moment, and then replied, "Goodnight, Grasshopper."

Pocketing the phone, Katie imagined she heard a smile in her voice.

She walked out of the bathroom and turned toward the kitchen. Katie didn't know exactly how long she'd been on the phone and wondered if Syd was in the backyard. In the truck she'd said something about needing to check the chlorine levels in the pool. Katie called her name, but got no answer. She turned the corner out of the bedroom wing and thought she heard voices. Was there someone else in the house? Was Syd on the phone? Quietly, she made her way down the central hallway toward the kitchen. Katie heard a second voice and knew someone else was there. But who? Outside the door, she paused to listen.

"I'm still not clear how you got inside my house," Syd was saying to someone. Her voice sounded so bitter Katie took a step back. What was going on?

"When have you ever locked the back door?" another woman replied harshly. "You've really got to learn how to use a key, Syd. Someone's going to break in here."

"What are you doing here?" Syd asked, holding her ground.

"From the weird posts I've been seeing on Instagram, I didn't expect to run into you," the woman replied, sounding annoyed. "Aren't you out looking for chairs?"

Katie felt a chill run down her spine. She couldn't be sure until she saw her, but this was almost certainly Syd's ex-wife, the infamous Carrie Outlaw. What was more certain was that Syd was not happy to see her.

"That's got nothing to do with you," Syd said, sounding enraged.

A large white cat poked its head out of the kitchen, and Katie missed the woman's reply. The cat confirmed her identity. Syd had been so sweet talking about Annapurna, the pet she'd shared with her ex-wife. What were they doing in Syd's house? Syd also seemed to be in the dark.

"I don't understand what you're doing here," she said, now almost yelling. "Are you giving me back Annapurna?"

"I know how much you loved the cat," Carrie replied, sounding exasperated. "You begged me for Annapurna when we divorced. I thought you'd be happy."

"A little notice would have been nice," Syd said more quietly and ran her fingers through her hair. Turning her head to look at the cat, she noticed Katie standing in the shadows and gave her a sad smile. "I do have a life, you know."

"You live alone," Carrie said, and Katie imagined she could hear a sneer in her voice. "Paul said gifting you Annapurna would be doing you a favor. I wasn't sure he was right until I saw those weird pictures of you on Instagram. That is some crazy, desperate shit. You are obviously lonely, Syd. I know our breakup was hard, but it's been more than a year. Don't you think it's time to move on?"

Katie watched Syd sink lower. She desperately wanted to come to her rescue but wasn't sure what was appropriate. Would Syd like it if Katie were to make her appearance known by drop-kicking her guttersnipe of an ex-wife into the next county? Because it was certainly an option. She clenched her fists and tried to think of a plan.

"I have moved on," Syd said, and chanced a glance back at Katie. "I've even met someone. It's still early, but I think she might be special."

Katie's heart swelled at Syd's words. What she heard next made her see red.

"You don't need to make up a phantom girlfriend to impress me," Carrie said. "You're better than that, Syd. One day someone will come around and rock your world. I promise."

"She's not lying," Katie said loudly from the other room. Slipping out of her dress, she walked into the kitchen wearing only a pair of tiny black briefs. "At least, I don't feel like a ghost."

"I can see you just fine," Syd said, grinning from ear to ear.

"Okay, good," Katie said, and kissed her softly on the cheek.

Syd slipped an arm around Katie's waist as if the moment had been scripted. "Katie, this is my ex-wife, Carrie."

Katie assessed the woman who'd so callously broken Syd's heart. A minor celebrity in her own right, Carrie Outlaw had caught the public's attention by dancing in Syd's spotlight.

"Sorry for my casual appearance," Katie told her, and looked down at her body as if she were wearing a lumpy sweat suit and not just a pair of underwear. The sight of her own bare breasts, nearly derailed her train of thought. "I…um…I didn't know we were expecting visitors," she said, recovering just in time.

"Carrie just popped in," Syd told her. Releasing Katie, she bent down and scooped up Annapurna. "She brought us a gift."

"Is this Annapurna?"

"She's half Syd's," Carrie said, now looking murderous. "It's only fair that she takes half the responsibility."

"Fair?" Syd asked, and Katie felt her body stiffen. Annapurna must have felt it too as she jumped from Syd's arms onto the floor. "How is it fair to drop a cat at my house without telling me?"

"I was going to leave a note," Carrie sneered. "I was trying to find a piece of paper when you surprised me."

"I surprised you?" Syd asked, and shook her head. "I need you to go."

Carrie made a face. "Don't worry, I was leaving anyway. I'll only leave Anna if you promise to take good care of her," she said, as if five minutes ago she hadn't been about to dump the cat and run. "Annapurna doesn't deserve to get caught in the crossfire."

"Get out," Syd said, again.

"Fine," Carrie spat, and started toward the back door.

"Wait," Syd called after her, and Katie worried she might say something she'd later regret. "Where's the litter box?"

"They don't travel well," Carrie said, and shrugged as if her low ick-threshold didn't have repercussions for Syd. She gestured to a half-used bag of generic cat food on the counter. "I brought food. Anna throws up a lot, but the vet says that's normal."

"Please leave."

"I'm going."

When the back door finally slammed shut, Syd closed her eyes. "She always has to have the last word."

"A friend from school calls that a bitch flex," Katie said, and pulled Syd into a hug.

"Bitch flex, describes Carrie perfectly," Syd lamented, and rested her head on Katie's shoulder. "The reason Carrie and I worked as a couple was that she needs to have the upper hand, and I don't give a shit. I always knew Carrie was a diva, but she was my diva. I loved her enough to let her have her way. Eventually, that drove her crazy too and she turned on me."

"Were you surprised when she started up with Paul?" Katie asked, hoping she wasn't overstepping. "Had they ever given you any inkling that something was happening between them?"

Syd let out a sigh. "I'd be lying if I said I'd never thought their relationship wasn't a little too touchy-feely," she said, softly. "Paul's aggressively macho—it's part of his bad-boy appeal. I know how much Carrie liked the attention so I let it go."

"Did you know she was bisexual?" Katie pressed.

"I didn't," Syd admitted. "It wasn't something we ever talked about so I was as shocked as everyone else. In hindsight, it doesn't seem so surprising. It's not about sex for Carrie, not really. It's about being in the spotlight. Leaving me for Paul put her in the headlines."

"For about five minutes." Katie scoffed.

Syd hugged her more tightly. "I feel like an idiot."

Katie tried to ignore the sensation of her naked breasts pressed into Syd's T-shirt. Now was not the time for seduction. Syd was discussing the dynamics of her failed marriage. Katie needed to pay attention and offer advice. "Strong emotions can blind us to what's happening right in front of us."

"My eyes are open, now," Syd said. "After we broke up, Jennifer said she'd always thought Carrie was a narcissist and a bit of an exhibitionist to boot. I'm mortified that I didn't see it."

"I'm the one who walked into your kitchen topless," Katie said, trying to lighten the mood. She pulled away to meet Syd's eye.

"Are you kidding?" Syd asked, raking her gaze across Katie's bare torso. "That may have been the single most favorite moment of my life. You shocked the unshockable Carrie Outlaw. She couldn't pull her jaw off the floor."

"She was bugging me," Katie said, and then gasped when Syd dropped her head and took a nipple into her mouth. "God, that feels good," she said, and cradled Syd's head against her chest. Heat shot to her groin and she groaned.

"God, you're sexy," Syd said, moving over to nuzzle Katie's other breast.

Katie allowed the torture to continue for several moments and then pulled away. She hadn't driven halfway across the state of Georgia to have sex on the kitchen floor. There was the added issue of getting the cat settled before they could properly relax. "What are we going to do about Annapurna?" she asked, and Syd look startled.

"Oh, shit, Annapurna. Where are you, baby?" Syd said. Letting Katie go, she searched for the cat.

"What are we going to do about a litter box?" Katie asked.

Syd look up from where she was crouching next to the kitchen table. "I love that you said we."

"Well, it's my problem, too. *Mais oui*?" Katie replied, pretending she wasn't thrilled with Syd's reaction. "Cat pee smells horrible."

"We'll need to get a box ASAP," Syd agreed. She threw a disdainful look at the kibble on the counter. "I'll need to get some better food, too. Look at that crap Carrie has her eating." The cat chose that moment to walk back into the kitchen. "Hey, baby," Syd cooed, and scooped her into her arms. "You going to be my new roommate?"

Katie smiled at the reunion. Yes, Anna was imposing on Katie's personal time with Syd, but it was impossible not to be moved by what was happening in front of her. "How long has it been since you've seen her?"

"Almost a year," Syd replied, and buried her face into the cat's neck. "I had Anna when she was a kitten. I can't believe she's back. It's going to take me a minute to get used to this."

A thought occurred to Katie. "Why don't I go pick up the cat supplies, and let you two get reacquainted," she said.

Syd's face softened. "Really, are you sure?" she asked.

"I'd probably need to get dressed first," Katie laughed, and looked down at her still-swollen nipples.

"That feels like an unnecessary tragedy," Syd said, following Katie's gaze. She bit her lip. "Here's an idea. How about we put Anna in my bathroom with some of this crap food for an hour while we take a nap?"

Syd looked so earnest Katie wanted to kiss her. "I like that plan," she agreed.

"You're supposed to put cats into a smaller, confined place when you first bring them to a new house, anyway," Syd continued, warming to the idea.

"I've heard that, too," Katie said, liking very much where the conversation was leading. "Should I bring the cat food?"

Syd nodded. "Grab a bowl from the cabinet next to the sink and follow me."

Katie did as she was told. A few minutes later she was padding barefoot towards the bedrooms. She'd stopped to collect her dress along the way but she didn't bother to put it back on. Once they got the cat settled, Katie imagined she'd be wearing less clothing, not more.

Syd walked a few steps ahead, murmuring sweetly against Annapurna's neck. Eavesdropping, Katie wondered if Syd would be able to leave the cat in the bathroom after all. She'd never had a pet, but imagined it might be devastating to lose one in a custody battle. They got to the bedroom and she made a decision.

"Do you want to snuggle the kitty in the bed for a minute, before we put her in the bathroom?" she asked.

"Could we?" Syd replied, and looked so hopeful Katie had to smile.

"Of course, we can."

The evening wasn't going the way Katie had expected but that didn't mean she wasn't enjoying herself. Being in Syd's company was thrilling in ways she couldn't yet articulate. The rush of being with a celebrity crush had faded against the backdrop of something even shinier emerging on the horizon. Katie could almost see it if she squinted. The way Syd looked at her, eyes full of intensity and hope, made Katie feel special. She wanted to dive into the dark pools and live in the image of herself she saw there.

"We can do anything we want," Katie assured her. Taking her by the hand, they sank down on the bed.

# CHAPTER TWENTY-TWO

## *Timbuk-three*

"Do you like that? Does it feel good?" Syd said, and scratched Annapurna behind the ear. The cat opened her mouth in a wide yawn, and Syd smiled. "Oh, are you tired from a long night climbing the drapes? Do you need some caffeine?"

It was six thirty in the morning and the rising sun cast an orange glow through the back windows of the house. Settled comfortably in the kitchen banquette, Syd continued to reacquaint herself with Annapurna. Though heavier than the last time Syd had seen her, the cat was the same intelligent creature who needed to know every inch of her environment. Unable to sleep, Syd had stayed up watching her explore her bedroom and replaying the scene in the kitchen.

She still couldn't believe Carrie had snuck into her house. Had her ex-wife always been this person? So many questions came to mind. How was it possible Syd had been married to someone this selfish and never noticed? Why hadn't Carrie just given Annapurna to Syd in the divorce? Was it purely out of spite? And what did loving a narcissist say about Syd's self-esteem? If it hadn't been for Katie's grand entrance, Carrie would have succeeded in robbing Syd of her dignity. Again.

It was a moment Syd would never forget. Katie had literally shielded Syd with her naked body. It was beyond touching and a stroke of genius beating Carrie Outlaw at her own game. The look on her face when she'd seen Katie's perfect breasts was worth Syd's five-a.m. trip to the hardware store to get a cat box. She'd also stopped by a local bakery for an assortment of pastries to thank Katie for coming to her rescue. Syd hoped to thank her in other ways as well.

Annapurna tilted her head toward the door, letting Syd know they were no longer alone. "What is it, girl? Is it my phantom girlfriend?"

"It is I," Katie said, and zombie-walked into the kitchen, wearing the fluffy white bath robe.

"Good morning," Syd said. She started to get up, but Annapurna made a noise, deep in her throat, suggesting the idea might be unwise.

Katie laughed. "She really missed you."

"Don't worry, Anna and I had plenty of quality time last night," Syd assured her, and rubbed the cat's back.

Katie lifted her arms into a languorous stretch, causing the belt to slip on the bathrobe. She gave Syd a flirty look. "I crashed hard from the sweet tea."

"That was some hard-core stuff," Syd said. Eyeing the bathrobe, she wondered what, if anything, was underneath.

"I might need some hair of the dog," Katie said, and mimed tipping a tea cup.

Syd did a quick mental inventory of her tea cabinet. "I have Earl Grey. Let me get it," she said, and started to rise. The cat growled again and she sat back down.

Katie laughed. "I'll do it," she said, and picked up the kettle. "Would you like some too?"

Syd held up a mug. "I've got coffee. There's more in the pot if you'd like some." she pointed to the coffeemaker.

Katie's eyes lit up. "Why didn't you say so?" She next noticed the white baker's box on the counter. "What's that?"

"A box of happiness," Syd said, and watched, tickled, as Katie picked through the offerings so thoughtfully, she might be choosing an engagement ring. "You can have more than one, you know," she told her.

"Oh, I plan to," Katie said, still studying the contents of the box. She looked up. "When exactly did you get these?"

"I went out about hour ago," Syd told her.

"On a Sunday morning?" Katie asked, skeptically.

"This is Atlanta, not Timbuktu," Syd laughed. "They have both hardware stores and bakeries. I've been exploring a lot since moving back. I even found a bookstore."

"What is the world coming to?" Katie mused, and poured herself some coffee. "I bet Timbuktu isn't even Timbuktu anymore."

"Timbuk-three?" Syd suggested, and Katie giggled.

Katie removed a raspberry-jelly donut from the box. "I can't believe you left here at five. I thought you liked to sleep in. Did you get any sleep, at all?"

"Not really," Syd admitted.

Katie's eyes widened. "None?" she asked, and spun the donut as if looking for the best place to mount a frontal assault. "As in, nothing?"

Syd shook her head. "It's not unusual for me to stay up into the wee hours. But I usually go to bed a little earlier than this." She looked out at the sunrise. "You'd be surprised how much you can get done in the middle of night."

"What did you accomplish last night?" Katie asked, and gave the donut another spin.

"I mostly played with AP," Syd admitted, and fluffed the cat's tail.

"Why didn't you wake me?" Katie asked, looking flirty again. "I thought we had plans."

"You were too peaceful," Syd said, feeling a rush of heat at Katie's suggestion. She loved how unapologetically sexual she was. Carrie, for all her prancing exhibitionism, had been a pillow princess when she and Syd were alone. The energy was completely different from Katie, who actually got a hungry look in her eye when she looked at Syd. There was nothing hotter than someone who wanted to fuck you.

"Dead people look peaceful," Katie joked. "I want to look sexy."

"I didn't say it was easy, not touching you," Syd said, and let her eyes linger where Katie's bathrobe parted at the neck. "Sleep isn't something I take for granted," she explained. "I'd never wake you, unless it was some kind of emergency."

"It might be an emergency soon," Katie said, and finally sank her teeth into the donut. Jelly appeared at the corners of her mouth and she hummed with pleasure. "Hmm."

For the first time in her life, Syd was jealous of a pastry. She wanted to lick the jelly off Katie's face, plunge her tongue deeply into her mouth and lick her until she screamed. Something about Katie ignited a fire in her. Was it a harbinger of something important? Was it just lust? Did Syd care?

"Thanks for getting these," Katie said, and took another bite of the donut. "Raspberry is my favorite."

"I might have remembered you mentioning that in a text," Syd replied. It was the beautiful thing about archiving messages. Unlike spoken conversations, you could always go back and reference specific information. Of the many things they'd discussed, donuts had come up more than once. Syd knew that Katie preferred them to bagels and that raspberry jelly were her favorite.

"I see you got a cinnamon stick for yourself," Katie said, her eyes twinkling.

"Hands off," Syd replied, though it pleased her beyond words Katie had remembered her favorite donut, too. As much as she missed the physical intimacy of a relationship, little things like paying attention to donut preference mattered almost as much. Katie seemed to get this. It was another check in the plus column. Syd couldn't wait to add more. She found herself hyper-focused on everything Katie did, watching her facial expressions for clues. Syd wanted to be near her, please her.

"What else did you accomplish?" Katie asked.

"I put the Snowy Egret Chair in the garage," Syd told her.

"You did?" Katie asked, and looked out at the clear spring morning. "Is it supposed to rain?"

"Not that I know of," Syd admitted, feeling sheepish. Why exactly had she moved the chair into the garage? Auda-Bonnie had tarped the thing like it was the infield at Yankee Stadium, and there wasn't a cloud in the sky. "It felt safer that way."

"You really are the sweetest woman in the world, aren't you?" Katie said, tilting her head as if the fact had just landed on her. "With everything else going on last night, I actually kind of forgot about the chair," she said, and then looked worried. "That probably sounds unprofessional."

"Not at all," Syd assured her. "The chair was fine in the truck. I was trying to find a way to impress you."

Katie licked jelly from the corner of her mouth. "You drove me all the way to Alabama yesterday," she reminded Syd. "That was impressive. I also remember some pretty impressive stuff that happened in the pool the other night. But that was so long ago, you probably don't remember."

This time, when Syd rose from the table, she brought the cat with her. Katie offered her hand for Anna to sniff, and then rubbed her chin. "This girl is a lover. I see why you missed her so much," she said. Her wrist grazed Syd's bicep and they locked eyes.

"Annapurna is a great cat," Syd replied, stressing the last syllable. "My lover is much hotter, and much taller." Leaning in, she grazed Katie's lips.

"Oh?" Katie asked, smiling. "Tell me more about this tall, hot person."

"I'd love to," Syd said, and the cat jumped from her arms and waddled into the dining room. Syd tugged at the belt of Katie's bathrobe and found the same pair of sexy, black panties from the night before. She sucked in an appreciative breath. "First of all, she's gorgeous," she said, and leaned in to kiss Katie's jaw.

Katie put her arms around Syd's neck. "Really?"

"Hm," Syd said, and moved her lips to Katie's ear. Pushing aside the robe she palmed her breast. "Also, she may have perfect breasts."

"You're not sure?" Katie pretended to pull away.

Syd held her steady with one hand, while stroking her nipple with the other. "I'm fairly certain, but I'll need to conduct further, lengthy investigations to be sure."

"Can we please go back to bed?" Katie asked, her voice suddenly sounding strangled.

"What about breakfast?" Syd looked at the half-eaten donut in Katie's hand.

"I'll be your breakfast," Katie offered. To prove her point, she took Syd's hand and slid it down the front of her panties. "This is what you do to me. Can you feel that?"

Syd pushed her fingers farther into Katie's underwear. "Oh, yeah," she said, and tipped her index finger so the hard edge of her guitar callus rested lightly on Katie's clit. Applying the tiniest bit of pressure, she moved the finger in a tiny circle. "Can you feel that?"

"Oh, shit, what is that?" Katie gasped, and arched into Syd's hand.

"Just me," Syd whispered, and leaned in to lick Katie's neck. She changed the motion of her finger from a circle to a figure eight, and Katie began to tremble. "You want me to stop?"

Katie covered Syd's hand with her own. "I wanted you to take me back to your bedroom," she gasped, and pushed harder against Syd's fingers. "But now we need to wait a minute because I'm about to come in your kitchen."

"Just let go," Syd said, but Katie wasn't waiting for permission.

Letting out a long, low moan, she jerked against Syd's hand. "Put your fingers inside me," she directed, and bore down harder when Syd complied. "That's it, fuck me, just like that," she said, and cried out again. "Yes, shit. That's so good."

Syd carried Katie all the way to the bedroom, luxuriating in the feeling of Katie's lips on her skin, Katie's hands in her hair.

Once on the bed, Katie flipped their positions, pushing Syd flat on her back. Towering over her, with delicious intent, she announced her plans as if she were going sightseeing. "First, I'm going to take off your shirt," she said, and indicated that Syd should lift her arms. "I want to see your breasts while I fuck you with my tongue, okay?"

"Okay," Syd choked. Struggling into a seated position, she lifted her arms like an obedient toddler. Katie tugged off Syd's T-shirt and black sports bra and flung them across the room. She was in complete control and it felt wonderful.

"I love your ink," she said, and took a moment to stroke Syd's sleeved arm. "The art is just extraordinary."

"Thank you," Syd somehow managed to reply. Normally, she loved talking about her famous tattoos. Right now, other less-celebrated parts of her body were crying out for attention.

Katie seemed to know this and ran a hand up Syd's forearm to caress her shoulder. "You're so strong," she said. "No one has ever carried me to bed before."

"It was the quickest way to get us here," Syd admitted and tried to capture Katie's lips in a kiss.

"Not yet," Katie said, and pushed Syd back on the bed. "I want you to lean back, okay? I didn't get to properly taste you in the pool, and it's been driving me crazy. I need to know."

Syd didn't argue. Having someone else call the shots was electrifying. Katie seemed to know exactly the effect she was having on Syd. A small smile played at the corner of her mouth, as she unbuttoned Syd's jeans and slid them down her hips bringing her underwear along in the process. Syd watched her work through hooded eyes. Her body was fire. She wanted to flip Katie on the bed and cover her body with her own but Katie was in control.

Murmuring quietly as if talking to herself, Katie continued to lay out her plan of action. "I'm going to kiss your whole body, starting here," she said, and nibbled the inside arch of Syd's foot like it was a taco.

The sensations shot up Syd's leg, causing her to squirm. Katie made a tsking noise. "Not yet," she said and pulled Syd's pinkie toe into her mouth.

"Oh, my God," Syd cried. "That feels incredible. You're killing me," she gasped, as her need ratcheted higher. Reaching up, she grabbed on to the bedpost to steady herself. Never before had she known having her foot kissed could be so erotic. Katie acted as if there was a rule of equality demanding every inch of Syd's skin be treated with equal care. Methodical and thorough, she used her tongue, teeth and hands to apply tender ministrations, winding Syd even tighter. Syd didn't know how long she could possibly last but Katie didn't seem to be in a hurry. She strolled up Syd's body like it was an orchard walk on a spring day. Sampling things at random, she took her time, paying extra attention to the soft tissue behind her knee. By the time she reached Syd's thighs, Syd's whole body was trembling with anticipation.

"Are you okay?" Katie asked, her knowing smile inches from where Syd wanted it most.

"I'm wonderful," Syd choked, and almost came right then.

"I'm so glad," Katie said, and settled between Syd's legs. "You sure that you're okay?" she teased.

"I promise." Syd whimpered at the sensation of Katie's breath against her skin.

"Good, now spread wider for me," she commanded. Using her thumbs, Katie peeled back Syd's upper folds to expose her clit. "There she is," she said softly, as if she were playing peek-a-boo. Using the tip of her tongue she licked the exposed bud delicately until Syd started to thrash.

"You're killing me," Syd breathed, and gasped when Katie's tongue slipped lower.

"I told you. I want to taste you," Katie murmured, not sounding the least bit apologetic. Syd felt her bones go limp as all the energy in her body collected toward her core. Every time she got close to orgasm, Katie would change what she was doing just enough to throw her off. It was as torturous as it was intentional. Syd loved every second. The pressure built so high she feared she'd use all the energy on the ascent. Was it possible to float free forever in orgasm purgatory? There were worse places to spend her time, Syd mused, and then exploded into a million little pieces.

# CHAPTER –TWENTY-THREE

## *The Robin Chair*

"Hi, Flora," Katie said, trying her best not to sound as if she wasn't lying naked on top of Atlanta's premier lesbian musician. "How was New York? How's Dad?"

"Both are fine, but two weeks is more than enough time for a visit. I'm happy to be back in Beaumont."

"Welcome home," Katie said, and wondered if Flora expected her to account for her whereabouts. If she was already home, she'd know Katie hadn't slept in her bedroom. Was that why she was calling?

"I just heard the exciting news," Flora crowed into the phone. If she cared where Katie was spending her Sunday afternoon, it wasn't her first priority. "You must be over the moon."

"Are you talking about the Snowy Egret Chair?" Katie asked, searching her mind for what else her grandmother might be referencing. They'd texted several times since Katie had secured the Snowy Egret Chair, but what else could it be?

"I'm talking about the Robin Chair. Don't you know?" Flora paused dramatically. "Bootsy Jenkins found it in Macon!"

"How would I know that? And who is Bootsy Jenkins?" Katie whispered, and slid off Syd, naked onto the floor. Pulling a blanket from the end of the bed, she gathered it around her shoulders and ducked her head inside to muffle her voice.

"Bootsy Jenkins is a friend of Nancy Littlejohn's."

"Okay," Katie answered, knowing there was more to the story.

"She was in Macon, Georgia, yesterday, for her grandson's birthday party, and saw the Robin Chair at a medieval-themed restaurant," Flora said. "Can you believe it? It was just sitting there, next to the front desk."

"Not the Medieval Times?" Katie asked, flashing to an image of an outlandish bar mitzvah she'd attended in NYC before moving to Georgia. How many people had suggested that's where the ZAP chairs might be found?

"That's not the exact name, but it's something similar," Flora replied. "They have knights and jousting and damsels in distress. Bootsy's grandson loves it."

"How did Bootsy know about the Robin Chair?" Katie asked, hopeful the social media posts had paid off. Flora had never said it outright, but Katie felt like her grandmother thought that the enterprise had been a waste of time.

"It was your social media campaign," Flora said immediately. "I'm sorry I wasn't more supportive in the beginning. Bootsy was a ZAP at Auburn. She follows the national chapter on Instagram and saw your post about finding the Snowy Egret Chair. I'm simply amazed."

"Social media is a powerful tool," Katie agreed. She was glad her idea worked but it wouldn't be fair to take credit for the entire Internet.

"The Board is very pleased with your efforts," Flora replied, graciously. "Check your email—there are several complimentary letters. Nancy wants to start planning the opening. We'll need to set a date."

"Yes, ma'am," Katie said, as her mind raced ahead through the details. If the last chair had been located, it meant Katie could begin the real work of curating the exhibit. She'd need to write copy for the brochure, interview conservators, secure the loan of the Graham ledger from the Beaumont Library. Every action was another domino falling toward her ultimate goal of getting a real job in a real city. It couldn't happen fast enough.

Flora seemed to read Katie's mind. "If everything goes well, Nancy Littlejohn, who you remember from the Board meeting, has offered to introduce you to the director of the High Museum in Atlanta."

"Nancy knows Morton Van Cleve?" Katie asked, surprised. "He's really famous."

"Morton plays bridge with Nancy's husband," Flora told her. "He's expressed interest in your exhibit. She's going to invite him to the opening."

"That's wonderful," Katie said. She doubted the nationally renowned museum director would come to Beaumont to see her exhibit, but you never knew. She pressed Flora for more information. "Did Bootsy buy the Robin Chair? Where is it now and why did you think I already knew about it?"

"It's on Instagram," Flora said, sounding sixteen. "Bootsy commented on your last post. Nancy saw it and called me. The Robin Chair is still in Macon. I'm not sure what happened. The owner may be a little odd."

"Odd, how?" Katie asked, now on alert.

"You'll need to go down to Macon to sort it out. I'm sure it's just money." Flora dismissed the problem as a non-issue.

"Okay, I'll drive down there today," Katie said, hoping the problem was purely monetary. She'd gone under budget on the Snowy Egret Chair, so there was extra cash available if the restaurant owner tried to gouge her. "If everything goes well, I can bring both chairs to Beaumont tonight."

"I'll meet you at Maguire House!" Flora said, sounding positively giddy. "Think of it, all the chairs together at last. We'll need to issue a press release."

"It's really exciting," Katie agreed, "but maybe wait until we have all the chairs before going public. I'd hate to be premature."

"Of course, you're right," Flora crowed. "That's why we put you in charge. Tell me, where is the Snowy Egret Chair now? And, where are you?"

"I'm in Atlanta," Katie said. "The chair is in my friend Syd's garage." She said a silent thank you for Syd's thoughtfulness. Telling Flora the chair was in the back of the truck didn't sound nearly as professional.

"Not Syd Collins?" Flora said, mimicking Beth's high school voice.

Katie smiled into the phone. "Syd came to Dothan with me. I'm sure she'll want to come to Macon, too. She's become very invested in the project."

"The project or the project manager?" Flora asked, still sounding girlish. "You had such a crush on her in high school," she mused. "Isn't it wonderful the chairs brought you together?"

"I won't argue with that," Katie agreed, and tilted her head out of the blanket to look at Syd sleeping on the bed. Every moment she spent with her made her want a hundred more. "But Syd's grandmother is the one to thank. I still can't believe she had two of them."

"Virginia Clairmont was an interesting woman," Flora said, surprising Katie.

"You knew her?" Katie asked. She was sure she'd never heard this piece of information before.

"Not well," Flora replied. "I only knew Virginia to say hello. She was two years ahead of me at Beaumont. A ZAP until she went inactive. She was best known on campus for being a poet."

"She wrote poetry?" Katie asked in surprise. Syd had talked a fair amount about her grandmother but Katie had never heard this detail. But it made total sense. Syd was a gifted lyricist, and creativity often ran in families.

"They used to publish Virginia's poems in the Beaumont Beacon," Flora continued. "Everyone thought her wonderfully wild and free. She eventually married her psychology professor, you know. It was a huge scandal."

"I did know that," Katie said, "but I never heard about her poetry."

"I knew Virginia's younger sister, Arlene, better," Flora explained. "Though I don't care for her."

"I don't think Syd is close to her aunt, either," Katie said, keeping her voice low. As much as she wanted to know every scrap of information about Syd's family, crouched naked on her bedroom floor was not the best place to collect it.

"I haven't seen Arlene in years," Flora went on. "At one point she made inquiries about joining the ZAP board, but no one would nominate her. Some of the girls in college called her Snarlene because she's so unpleasant."

"Flora, that's awful," Katie said, and shook her head. It was odd to think of Flora as a younger woman. "Poor Snarlene."

"Snarlene should've been nicer to people," Flora said, giving Syd's aunt no quarter. "She liked to stay up late and report girls who came in after curfew. Terrible tattletale. It may have been why Virginia went inactive at ZAP."

"That's horrible," Katie said, a little louder than intended, causing Syd to stir. Loath to wake her, Katie hastened to end the call. "I want to talk more about this later." She kept her voice low. "Right now, I need to go on Instagram and see what Bootsy Jenkins has to say about the Robin Chair."

"Let me know when you have it," Flora replied, as if the acquisition was a foregone conclusion.

"You'll be the first to know," Katie said, and rang off.

"Where are we going?" a sleepy voice murmured behind her.

Katie turned and saw Syd was awake. "How much of that did you hear?" she asked, hoping she hadn't said anything compromising.

"I heard Bootsy Jenkins found the chair," Syd said, and opened the covers, inviting Katie back to bed. "When are we leaving for Macon?"

"I hoped you'd want to come with me," Katie said, and crawled beneath the blanket. Syd's body was deliciously warm as Katie snuggled against her.

"Of course, I do," Syd said, and pressed her lips to Katie's neck. "Coming with you is my new favorite thing."

"Mine too," Katie replied, shivering with pleasure. She wanted nothing more than to while away the rest of the day in bed making Syd come over and over again but retrieving the Robin Chair was too important. Katie couldn't let the trail get cold. "How long does it take to get to Macon?" she asked, as Syd nibbled her ear.

"Less than two hours. It's just southeast of Beaumont," she said, and palmed Katie's breast. "We can leave anytime you like."

"Options are nice," Katie said, and wriggled her bare bottom into Syd's center. The day that had begun so deliciously was continuing to improve. A thought occurred to her and she stopped moving. "What about Annapurna? We can't leave her alone. She just got here."

Syd's hand stilled. "You're right, I'd forgotten Anna," she said, and then began stroking Katie again.

"What are we going to do?" Katie gasped, as Syd licked the back of her neck.

Cats were notoriously hard to transition, and they didn't travel well either. It didn't seem fair to bring Annapurna to Macon so soon after getting her settled. Leaving her home alone also seemed cruel. Anna had been in Syd's house less than twenty-four hours. She'd barely found the litter box.

"I'll ask Joe to watch her," Syd said, and slid lower down Katie's body.

"All night?" Katie asked, trying to stay focused on the conversation and not Syd's hands, now firmly holding her hips against the bed. "What about the club? Won't Lori mind?"

"The Pig's closed tonight," Syd said. "I'll drive back to Atlanta after dropping you and the chairs in Beaumont. It'll only be a few hours."

"Are you sure?" Katie asked. She tried to process the idea but found her mind more concerned with Syd's fingers. "Isn't that too much driving?"

"Not really," Syd whispered. "Shh."

"What about Joe?" Katie tried one last time. "How do you know he'll do it?"

"Joe will do it for the beer. Now please, be quiet?"

"Okay," Katie said, and gave in because she had no other choice. Closing her mouth, she opened her legs.

# CHAPTER TWENTY-FOUR

## *Knight Times*

Two hours later they were pulling out of the driveway, while Joe, beer already in hand, waved goodbye from the front porch. Syd would miss Annapurna, but knew the cat would be fine without her for the evening. Maybe that was just wishful thinking. Maybe Syd was a bad cat mom. Right now the most pressing thing on her mind was also pressing on her thigh.

"If you don't stop that, I might drive off the road," Syd warned Katie, and clenched her legs together.

Katie let her fingers linger, before pulling them away. "I can't seem to stop touching you," she admitted. "It's a problem."

"It's only a problem when we're going seventy miles an hour on an interstate highway," Syd replied, missing the pressure of Katie's hand. "In most circumstances, touching me is encouraged."

"I wish we could play the cow game," Katie said, and looked out the window. "There's nothing out there to count but power lines."

"Backroads add at least an hour," Syd said. "If the nap hadn't gotten away from us, we could have gone a different way."

"I liked that nap a lot," Katie said, matter-of-factly. "I really liked it when you flipped me around and ate me out from behind."

"I liked that too," Syd choked, and tightened her grip on the steering wheel. "I also like it when you talk about sex."

"Yeah?" Katie replied. "Didn't you ever talk dirty with Carrie? I'm sorry if that question is too invasive."

"That's okay," Syd said, "and, no. We didn't talk dirty. Carrie wanted people to think of her as a sex queen. She only got it half right."

"So, she wouldn't have told you how beautiful your reflection looked against the window this morning," Katie asked, and rubbed Syd's thigh. "Watching you made me come even harder."

Syd sucked in a breath. "Maybe I should hang a mirror," she joked. "There are several of Honey's in my garage. You might have noticed."

Katie took her hand away, jarring Syd from the thought. "I'm really concerned we'll have a problem getting the last chair," she said, looking worried. "In her comment Bootsy Jenkins said the owner was prickly but I'm pretty sure she meant prick. I wish I could get her on the phone."

"Everyone has a price," Syd said, trying to be reassuring. She had no idea what the issue was with the man in Macon but was confident they would work it out.

"That's my hope." Katie tapped her hand nervously against the window. "I can't decide if I should call him myself before we get to the restaurant or just show up. I'm also worried other people who saw the post might show up and make things weird. I'm glad Bootsy found the chair, but I wish she hadn't posted about it publicly. What do you think? Should I call the guy?"

"I think you should bring a wad of cash," Syd replied, touched Katie had asked her advice. The answer only seemed to stress her further.

"I've only got the ZAP Visa card," Katie said, drumming her fingers more quickly against the window.

"I'm sure that's fine," Syd said, wishing she could take back the comment. She searched for a way to alleviate Katie's stress.

"Maybe you should call the restaurant first. At least you'll have a better idea of what you're up against."

"Really?"

"Yeah, I'll stop at the next exit, and you can check in with the owner. The truck needs gas, anyway, and I'm a little hungry."

"I'm starving," Katie said, looking more relaxed. She reached a hand over and squeezed Syd's knee. "Thanks, Syd."

"I hope it works out."

But it didn't. Syd came back with fast food and found Katie wide-eyed in the truck. Calling the owner had only made the situation worse.

"What's the matter? Is everything okay?" Syd asked, and put the bags on the console between them.

"The owner said that the Robin Chair belonged to his mother. He's never selling it," Katie said, and picked up a bag.

"Oh, no," Syd said. Earlier when she'd said everyone had their price, she hadn't considered nostalgia. Of course, there were things on which you couldn't place a value. "Did you ask if you could borrow it? You know, like the library is loaning you the ledger? Don't fancy art people loan stuff to museums for exhibitions all the time?"

"That's the best I can hope for, now." Katie nodded, and took a burger from the bag. She began munching and Syd was glad to see the circumstances hadn't affected her appetite. "The guy hung up on me before I could ask him."

"He hung up on you?" Syd asked. This did not bode well for negotiation. "What exactly did he say?"

Katie swallowed her food. "He told me to fuck off. But he was Irish so it sounded more like feck."

"What a dick," Syd said, and felt a rush of anger followed by concern. "Do you still want to go to Macon?"

Katie shrugged and took another bite of her burger. "We're halfway there. Might as well go talk to him in person. Aren't you a huge star in Ireland?"

Syd unwrapped her burger. "He doesn't sound like my demographic," she said, and started the engine.

An hour later, they arrived at the restaurant. The building was a mile out from the square of downtown Macon and looked more like an abandoned barn than a medieval-themed restaurant. A hundred yards off the road, it was surrounded by a dusty gravel parking lot and a huge shallow ditch. Syd parked the truck and squinted up at an old billboard in front of the property. Paint flaked off the calligraphy but the writing was legible.

*Knight Times*
*Serfs and Turf*

"This isn't the franchise I was thinking of," she said, and chanced a look at Katie.

"It's a punny knockoff," Katie said, and opened the door of the truck. "I can't wait to see the menu."

"We're eating again?" Syd asked, following her into the parking lot. How could Katie possibly be hungry after the cheeseburgers they'd inhaled not an hour ago? Syd couldn't possibly eat another bite.

"God, no," Katie said, her feet crunching purposefully into the gravel. She turned and gave Syd a half-smile. "I want to see the menu because I want to see more puns. There are four on the sign alone."

"That is impressive," Syd agreed, and returned the smile. She was relieved Katie wasn't planning to order food. Puns, as obnoxious as they may be, were far more palatable than mutton or whatever else might be on offer at the Knight Timz. The place barely looked open. Katie's worry that Bootsy's Instagram comment would cause people to throng to Macon was thankfully baseless. Besides Katie's truck, there were only a few other vehicles in the parking lot and a shabby-looking bus.

Hand in hand, Syd and Katie approached the large shallow trench surrounding the structure. "I think this is supposed to be a moat," Katie said, eyeing the bottom, which contained a mass of tangled vines and rusty barbed wire.

Syd peered into the trench and then took an involuntary step back. "That's poison ivy," she said, yanking Katie away from the edge.

"Are you allergic?" Katie asked.

Syd shook her head. "No, but that doesn't mean I won't be one day. The more exposure you have to poison ivy, the more likely you are to contract it. I can't believe someone planted it here on purpose."

Katie looked down at the rough-hewn wooden planking beneath their feet. "I'm glad the drawbridge is down."

"Yeah," Syd replied. "Getting to the building without this bridge would not be fun." She wondered who in their right mind purposefully planted a pit full of poison ivy and then remembered it was the man they were about to meet.

Katie pressed the doorbell, and a faint gong echoed inside the building. She squeezed Syd's hand. "Wish me luck?" she asked, and pressed the bell again.

"Good luck," Syd said, and kissed her cheek.

Minutes passed and no one answered so Katie tried the doorknob. It opened easily into a room decorated to look like the front hall of a medieval manor house. No one appeared to be inside so they stepped cautiously forward, still holding hands.

"Do you think this is okay?" Katie asked, and gave Syd a nervous look. "The website said the restaurant opens at noon."

"I'm sure it's fine," Syd said, but worried it might not be. It was difficult to know if the cobwebs clinging to the heavy iron chandelier were there on purpose. If it weren't for the cars in the parking lot, Syd might be convinced the place was closed. Katie seemed paralyzed with indecision so Syd made a suggestion. "Let's check in here," she said and pointed to a set of double doors labeled Great Hall. If anyone was in the building this was the most likely place to find them.

Syd pushed through the doors into a cavernous room smelling of stale beer and cigarette smoke. Dimly lit chandeliers, similar to the one in the entrance hall, gave off just enough light to see that Knight Times had seen better days. Syd looked around at the furniture and realized none of it matched. How had Bootsy known for sure the chair she saw was the Robin Chair? Maybe it was all a mistake.

"I see some people back there on the right," Katie said, quietly at Syd's side. "Look in the corner."

Syd peered across the dining room and saw two men sitting in big wooden chairs. She knew one was most likely the jerk who'd told Katie to feck off and wondered if that's why Katie seemed hesitant. Syd didn't want to put them in a dangerous situation but honestly didn't think there was anything to fear. It was possible the whole thing was a wild goose chase anyway. Perhaps Katie just needed a little prompting. "Do you want to go talk to them?"

The question seemed to surprise her. "Yes, of course. Let's go," Katie said, but held firmly to Syd's hand.

Silent, they walked across the wide cement floor toward the duo in the corner of the room. Syd could only see the man facing her, and the back of the other chair. If the man noticed her, he didn't react, not even when Katie and Syd came within earshot of their conversation. He seemed to be telling a story about his mother. They paused to listen.

"'Twas me Mam's favorite stick of furniture," the man facing them said in a thick Irish brogue. He stroked the arm of the chair he was sitting in which did indeed appear to have robins carved on it. "I'll never part with this chair. I already told the other lady," he said, and took a sip from a metal tankard.

"As long as you don't sell it to Syd Collins," another voice said and Syd felt as if she'd been punched. Sitting across from the restaurant owner, casually draped in another big wooden chair was her former bandmate Paul, a.k.a Florida Man.

"What the hell are you doing here?" Syd asked, and felt her free hand ball into a fist.

"I noticed you'd been hunting chairs on Instagram," Paul said, looking proud of himself. "Thought I'd come down here and see what it was all about."

"Why?" Syd asked. "What does this have to do with you? It doesn't make sense."

"Florida Man don't have to make no sense," Paul snarled and gave a nasty laugh. "Go feck yourself, Syd."

"Yes, feck yourself, Syd," the restaurant owner chortled. "No one's getting me mam's chair."

"I'm the person buying the chair," Katie spoke for the first time. "Syd has been helping with the search but it's me who wants to buy your mother's chair." Katie tried to give the man a business card. "Your mother's chair was one of eight in a collection. I'm staging an exhibition."

"A what?" The man was too drunk to process what Katie was saying. The only piece of information in his head was on repeat out of his mouth. "No one's getting me mam's chair." He took the business card and ripped it into pieces, earning a laugh from Paul.

"I understand if you don't want to sell it," Katie tried, but he was no longer listening. Eyes closed he took another sip of beer and then belched for effect.

"Good one, Declan," Paul said, and raised his own tankard in salute.

Syd knew better than to engage but couldn't stop herself. The idea that Paul had come to Macon to disrupt the sale of the Robin Chair made her furious. "Seriously, what are you doing here, Paul?"

He gave her a churlish look. "I already told you. Carrie showed me that online shit about the chairs. I thought it would be fun to come down here and fuck your shit up. You know? Like how you fucked up mine?"

Syd steadied herself. "If memory serves, you're the person who betrayed our friendship. I'm not sure how that qualifies as me fucking up your shit."

"It's not about the girl, dude. It's about the song." Paul rose from the chair and stumbled drunkenly toward Syd. His long lean body was almost a mirror of her own. "I can't go anywhere that someone doesn't play "Florida Man." I'm like a baseball player with a walk-on song."

"You're lucky I only wrote one song about your sorry ass," Syd said, hating herself for admitting the truth. "Because if anyone fucked over anyone, it was you." She pointed a finger in Paul's face. "Now, leave us alone before I write a whole album about you."

Paul narrowed his eyes. Syd wasn't worried he'd throw a punch but knew anything was likely to come from his mouth. She hated that Katie was there to witness the spectacle and worried Paul was making Declan even more determined not to sell. Stepping over to the Robin Chair, Paul placed a hand on the restaurant owner's shoulder. "You're never getting this man's chair," he sneered.

"I'm never selling it," Declan said, and let out another burp.

Syd feared the moment was lost. It was possible Katie might be able to come back later and talk Declan into loaning the Robin Chair to the ZAP exhibit but a purchase didn't seem likely and nothing was happening today.

"Let's have another round," Paul said, prompting Declan to pick up a small bell attached to a stick.

He waved it incessantly until two women dressed as serving wenches appeared through the door behind them. One held an old-fashioned walkie-talkie, the other a bucket full of potatoes. Both looked angry, but their expressions changed abruptly when they noticed Syd.

"Oh, my fecking God, it's herself!" Bucket Wench said in an Irish accent identical to Declan's. She turned to the wench with the walkie-talkie. "It's her! It's Syd Collins as I live and breathe!"

"Holy fecking feck!" Walkie-Talkie Wench shot back, flashing a mouthful of braces incongruent with the bonnet perched on her head. Her accent was even thicker. "We just listened to "Florida Man" in the car. I can't believe you're here."

"The Florida Man is here too." Syd smirked and pointed to Paul.

"Hey, ladies," Paul drawled slowly as if they were all old friends. "How are y'all doing?"

"Horrified to see the likes of you," Bucket Wench said, looking genuinely stricken. "What are you doing in my restaurant?"

Paul looked surprised. "I have business with Declan."

"As you may have noticed, our brother is indisposed," Walkie-Talkie Wench said, glaring at Paul as Declan slid obliviously to the floor. "I suggest you leave while you still have the teeth you came with. My sister's a fair shot with a spud."

Bucket Wench tipped the pail at Paul and then picked out a large potato. "I'm better with darts."

Paul took a step back. "This is bullshit."

"What's bullshit is bird-dogging yer mate's wife," Walkie-Talkie Wench said and grabbed a potato of her own. "Syd carried you on her shoulders fer years and that was the thanks you gave her? You're lucky we don't toss you in the moat." She turned back to Syd, hand over her heart. "If you haven't guessed, we're huge fans. Just give us the word and we'll run this blighter out on a rail."

"Let him go on his own speed," Syd said and watched pleased as, muttering to himself, Paul slunk out the door.

"As you wish, Syd," Walkie-Talkie Wench replied and returned the potato to the bucket. "I can't believe you're here. You never came to see our hideous show?"

"We're here to see the owner," Syd said, and nodded toward Declan who was now snoring gently with his head on the foot of the Robin Chair. "We may need to come back at a more convenient time."

Walkie-Talkie Wench brightened. "But the owners are right here. I'm Siobhan, and this is my sister, Sheila."

Bucket Wench made a low curtsey. "We're very pleased to meet you, Ms. Collins. What business could you possibly have with the likes of us?"

Syd wondered what to do next. She doubted the sisters would be any more agreeable to parting with a family heirloom. Maybe Katie could talk them into loaning it out. It was too important to the ZAP exhibit not to inquire. Katie gave her a nod and Syd pushed forward. "This is my friend Katie. I believe she spoke with your brother earlier today."

"This isn't about the chair?" Siobhan said, and shared a look with Sheila that Syd couldn't read.

"Actually, it is," Syd said, holding her breath.

Sheila squealed. "That was never you," she said, and let out a loud laugh. "What do you want with that wretched thing? Declan swears he won't be parted with it. Is it very valuable?"

"Only to us," Katie told her. "Your mother's chair is one of eight in a collection. We've already got the other seven. They're going to be part of a museum exhibit at the university in Beaumont. I understand…" she started, but Siobhan cut her off.

"How much?" she asked. "If you don't mind me asking?"

"The going rate is twenty-five hundred dollars a chair," Syd said, and Sheila dropped the bucket. It hit the floor with a thud and potatoes spilled out, rolling in all directions.

"For that hideous thing?" she asked.

"Your brother seemed very attached to it," Katie said. "Isn't it a family heirloom?"

"Family heirloom?" The sisters collapsed with laughter. "That's rich," Sheila said. "Our blessed mother bought this pigsty of a venue on Craigslist last year, complete with all the furniture, including that ridiculous chair. Said it was her retirement plan. As if. The fecking gnats sent her shrieking back to Dublin in one season, leaving us to deal with this mess. It was supposed to be a grand lark, wasn't it? But we're dressed as serving girls while Declan swans around like he's laird of the manor."

"I'd like to buy the chair," Katie said. "But it would have to be a legitimate sale. The foundation I work for won't be happy if it's contested."

Sheila took a ring of keys from her pocket. "I find twenty-five hundred dollars to be extremely legitimate," she said, and turned to her sister. "What'cha think, Siobhan?"

"I think Declan will get over it," she said. "And if he doesn't, we're all equal partners so there's nothing for it. His lordship has been voted down."

"Only if you're sure," Katie said, and stuck out her hand.

"We are." Siobhan clasped Katie's fingers. "Two thousand and five hundred percent."

# CHAPTER TWENTY-FIVE

## *I'll be Damselled*

When Katie and Syd arrived at Maguire House, pedestal lights illuminated the six ZAP chairs already in their possession. The two vacant pedestals had been left dramatically dark.

"There you are," Flora said, and placed the last napkin on a table set with takeout containers. "Our heroines of the hour. Congratulations on completing the quest. Well done, ladies."

Katie let go of Syd's hand to embrace her grandmother. Katie didn't know if it was the change of scenery or the news that Katie and Syd had recovered the last two chairs, but Flora looked visibly more relaxed than when she'd left for New York. Whatever it was, Katie was thankful. She squeezed Flora's shoulders. "Welcome back," she told her grandmother. "You look fantastic."

"I feel amazing," Flora said. "I had a very pleasant time in New York. Your father spoils me, you know."

"He's a sweet man," Katie agreed.

"And now I've come back to the most wonderful news," she said, and her gaze lingered warmly on Katie. "I'm very proud of you, dear."

"Thank you, it means a lot," Katie told her, and smiled quizzically when Grace and Arthur stepped forward to say hello.

"Grace and I, were…um…nearby, when Miss Flora called," Arthur said, and scratched innocently at the back of his neck.

"Hey, y'all," Grace said, and gave them each a little wave. In proximity to Syd, their resemblance was even more pronounced.

"Hey, Grace. Hey, Arthur," Syd said, smiling fondly as she greeted her niece and the ZAP houseboy.

Katie took the opportunity to introduce Syd to her grandmother. "Flora, this is my friend Syd Collins. I see you've already met her niece Grace," she said and shot Arthur a questioning look.

"Grace wanted to see the new chairs, too," he said, quickly. "I thought it would be okay to bring her by."

"It's more than okay," Syd said, and clapped Arthur on the back, "it's fortuitous. Y'all can unload the truck."

"Okay," Grace said. Taking the opportunity for a graceful exit, she all but ran from the room, with Arthur just steps behind her.

Syd smiled at Flora. "It's nice to meet you, Mrs. Simmons. I've heard a lot about you."

"Call me Flora." It was not a request.

Syd nodded. "It's a pleasure to meet you, Flora."

"I assure you, the pleasure is all mine," Flora replied, and took Syd's hand. "I understand you've recently moved back to Georgia. How do you like being home?"

"I like it a lot," Syd said, shyly, and moved to stand behind Katie.

"We've been big fans since the early days," Flora assured her, and Katie just managed to suppress an eye roll. She ached to turn and press herself into Syd's body but held back. Early adapter of Syd's music or not, Flora did not support public displays of affection. Certainly not the type Katie was imagining.

"I'm flattered," Syd said, and placed a discreet hand on the small of Katie's back.

"I hope you're hungry," Flora replied, and nodded to the takeout containers on the table.

Katie felt Syd stiffen and remembered the cat. "Syd only has a few minutes before she needs to leave for Atlanta," she explained to Flora. "That's why I asked you to bring my car here tonight. After we see the chairs, Syd's driving the Mini home."

"But you just got here," Flora said, and then seemed to catch herself. "Certainly, whatever it is can wait a night?"

"Syd has an emergency with her cat," Katie explained. She didn't like to disappoint Flora, but it wasn't fair to make Syd uncomfortable. Leaving Annapurna with Joe for a few hours was favor enough. Katie could only imagine the emotions Syd must be processing at the return of the beloved pet. She wouldn't ask Syd to be away from Anna overnight. Later in the week, or sooner if Katie could manage it, she'd return the pickup truck to the board member's farm in Atlanta. Syd could meet Katie there in the Mini Cooper. Hopefully, they'd spend a long weekend together.

Thankfully, Flora was too polite to press Syd any further. "You must take your dinner to go," she said, and nodded to the containers on the table.

"That's not necessary," Syd replied.

Flora wouldn't be put off. "If you don't like crab cakes, I'm sure your cat will be delighted to have them."

"I'm sure she would, but not as much as me," Syd said, giving in graciously. "I hope I'll be able to join you, one day soon."

"I hope so, too," Flora replied.

Voices in the small courtyard behind the building heralded Grace and Arthur returning with the first chair. Katie rushed to open the door. She couldn't wait to see the eight Bird Chairs of Zeta Alpha Pi reunited. What had started as a concession prize, a means to a finding a better job, now felt like a triumph. Later tonight, she would make a formal announcement on social media. Soon the Board would be able to set a date for the opening.

"Take your time. This isn't a race," Katie told Grace and Arthur, and then willed her heart to follow the advice. Her life was coming together at a pace she hadn't imagined. The moment felt charged with electricity, too good to be true.

"Put it on the last pedestal, just over here, on the right," Flora said, showing Grace and Arthur where to deposit the Snowy Egret Chair. It was barely discernable through the dense packing material. Erring on the side of volume, Auda-Bonnie had double bubble-wrapped the auction prize, and then shrouded it with a tarp secured with duct tape. Unveiling would take effort. Fortunately, Flora seemed up for the challenge and gleefully set upon it with a pair of shears, while Arthur and Grace trudged back outside for the Robin Chair.

Katie noticed Syd checking her phone and remembered they needed to keep an eye on time. "Everything okay?" she asked, and reached out to squeeze Syd's elbow. "Do you need to get on the road?"

"Pretty soon," Syd said, looking genuinely unhappy. "I don't want to get home any later than eleven. Joe just texted and Anna's still hiding under the couch."

"Poor girl," Katie replied. She knew Syd was worried about the cat, and wouldn't pressure her into staying. "Transitions are tough."

"I won't argue with that," Syd said, and surprised Katie with a flirty wink. "Though I'm finding, some transitions are easier than others."

"Are you calling me easy?" Katie asked.

Syd laughed. "You're funny," she said, and then grew serious. "I won't leave until we see the chairs reunited."

"Okay," Katie agreed. She loved how invested Syd had become in the museum project, almost as much as she loved Syd's use of the word "we."

"It won't be long," Katie told her. Feigning calm, she approached the seminal painting; Eight austere women in eight elaborately carved chairs.

"Was this the last time the collection was all together?" Syd asked.

"We can only speculate," Flora called, from the other side of the room.

Katie turned to see that her grandmother had freed the Snowy Egret Chair and flipped on the pedestal light beneath it.

Seven of the eight chairs were now together. Only one pedestal remained dark. In a matter of moments Grace and Arthur would bring the final chair inside and all eight chairs would be reunited. The task would be complete.

"I'm getting excited," Syd said, and touched Katie's elbow.

"Me too," Katie agreed, and leaned back into Syd's body for a moment before Flora called her away to help clear the debris.

Arms full of bubble wrap, Katie opened the door to the courtyard, and a fine spring night. The gnats and humidity had abated with the daylight, and Katie ferried her cargo across the small patio to the recycling bins, wondering what was keeping Arthur and Grace. She could see they'd paused under the street light, holding the Robin Chair. Was everything okay? Why weren't they moving?

"Everything all right?" Katie asked, suddenly questioning the wisdom of sending college kids to move valuable pieces of furniture.

"A drawer fell out," Arthur called, sounding excited. "It looks like some kind of secret compartment. There's a bunch of papers inside."

"Don't touch anything," Katie screamed, and ran the small distance across the courtyard. Grace and Arthur were holding the Robin Chair tipped toward the ground. *Secret drawer.* The only two words more thrilling to an exhibition director were fully and funded. "What happened?" Katie asked, eyeing the spot where a two-foot panel was missing from beneath the chair's leather seat cushion.

"I'm so sorry," Grace gushed, looking terrified. "I was adjusting my grip on the wood, and a board just popped off. I tried to catch it, but I didn't want to drop the chair. I'm so sorry," she said, again.

"You did nothing wrong," Katie assured her, and bent to examine the drawer. It was filled with papers, just as Arthur said.

"What are the papers?" he asked. "Are they old? Can you use them in the exhibit?"

"Let's see," Katie said. Hands shaking, she activated the flashlight on her phone. Arthur was right. If something in the drawer belonged to one of the founders, it would be additional material for the exhibit. It seemed too much for Katie to hope for, and it was.

"What is it?" Arthur asked, eagerly.

The small beam flashed across the print illuminating a poorly drawn cartoon princess. Despite her disappointment, Katie giggled. "It's a lesson to be careful what you wish for," she said, and lifted a stack of menus for *I'll Be Damselled in Distress Thursdays* at the Knight Times restaurant.

"That's disappointing," Grace said, and shifted her weight to the other foot.

Katie realized the couple was still holding the heavy chair. "Let's bring everything inside," she said, and picked up the drawer from where it lay on the pavement. "I'll explain why these menus aren't disappointing at all."

"It's just amazing!" Flora said, as Grace and Arthur placed the Robin Chair on the remaining pedestal and flicked on the light.

Katie slid the drawer halfway into the recess beneath the seat. "Now that I know it's here, I can't believe we missed it." She fingered the simple spring lock activated by a strategically placed carved berry.

"Was there anything about drawers in the ledger you found in the library?" Syd asked.

Katie shook her head. "Not that I saw. I guess I could have missed it."

"It's quite possible the drawers were intentionally left out of the ledger," Flora said. "Sororities are notoriously secretive."

"Drawers?" Grace asked. "You think there might be more than one?"

"That's what I was talking about," Katie said. She slid over in front of the Snowy Egret Chair on her knees, Flora close behind.

Even though they knew precisely where to look, the release was still difficult to find. Katie had to reference the Robin Chair twice before locating the dime-sized release beneath the egret's food. "Care to do the honors?" Katie said, and made way for Flora. She didn't have to ask twice.

"I'd love to," Flora answered, and jabbed a finger into the berry. There was a clicking noise and the drawer popped open like it had been shut the day before.

"What's inside?" Arthur asked, and Katie shone her flashlight into the drawer.

"It looks like a Bible," Flora exclaimed, and reached in to take it.

"Don't," Katie said, and caught her hand. "Not without dust gloves," she said, and rose to grab a pair from the work station. Excitement welled inside her. Bibles were the quintessential American artifact. Tying one to the founders' exhibit would be thrilling. Her mind raced ahead to the other chairs. The odds they'd find additional nineteenth-century artifacts were slim. Katie cautioned herself not to get carried away. Pulling on the gloves, she took a clean tray out of a cabinet. "Should we examine the Bible first or check to see what's inside the other drawers?" she asked.

"I kind of need to get going," Syd said, jarring Katie out of the moment.

"Oh, right. Your cat," she said, realizing immediately that she'd sounded callous. Syd had been very clear about her time constraint. "Let me get you my car keys," she said, and set down the tray.

"I'm sorry," Syd said, and looked nervously toward the door. "This is beyond cool. But I promised Joe."

"You got a new cat?" Grace asked, sounding surprised. "When did this happen? No one tells me anything."

"I got Annapurna back," Syd told her niece. "Carrie dropped by my house last night. Says she'd had a change of heart. Gave me full custody."

"No way," Grace said. Eyes narrowed, Katie thought she looked like her mother. "I bet her new apartment doesn't allow pets."

"You're probably right." Syd nodded, sadly. "I feel bad for Anna. She doesn't deserve to be treated this way. I left her with Joe."

"Wait five more minutes?" Grace begged. "I want you to see what's inside Honey's chairs. Please?" Grace walked across the room and stood in front of the Hummingbird Chair. "This one was Honey's, right?"

"It was," Katie said, trying to gauge Syd's mood. "The two chairs that came from your great-grandmother's estate were the Hummingbird, and the chair to the left of it, the Brown Thrasher. We don't have to open them tonight. Whatever is in there may have waited a hundred years, it can wait a few more days."

Grace's face fell. "But I want to see what's inside tonight! Please, Aunt Syd?" she said again. "There might be cool, old jewelry in one of them."

"If there's anything in the drawers that belonged to Honey," Syd said, and moved to stand next to Grace in front of the Hummingbird Chair, "it's probably just more old letters. Deb is still going through the correspondence we took out of her cottage."

"Historians love letters," Flora said, and came to join the group.

"Love letters?" Arthur said, impishly.

Grace shushed him. "Go ahead, Aunt Syd. You're wasting time. Let's open them."

Katie took this as a sign to move forward. Peeling off the gloves, she offered them to Syd. "It's okay to wait."

Syd took the gloves. "It's not every day you get to open secret drawers."

Katie activated the flashlight on her phone, and leaned down to find the hidden spring. Similar to the Robin Chair, the button was positioned on a dime-sized berry. "Here it is," she said, pointing it out to the group.

Syd pressed the button but nothing happened.

"What's wrong?" Grace asked, sounding disappointed. "Is it broken? Press it again."

"I heard a click," Flora declared, swiveling her hearing aid. "Maybe the drawer is stuck on something."

"I thought I heard a click too," Arthur agreed.

"Let me see," Katie said, and knelt next to Syd. Their shoulders touched and she gave Syd a playful bump with her hips. "I want you to press it again. This time, hold it down."

Syd put her finger on the button. Katie heard a definite click though the drawer remained closed.

"I heard it that time," Grace shrieked and grabbed at Syd's shoulders. "Can't you open it?"

"Maybe if we tilt it?" Katie suggested, and rose to her feet. "Give me a hand, Arthur?"

"Sure," Arthur said, and positioned himself on the other side of the chair.

Syd kept her finger in the button while Arthur and Katie leaned the chair forward. Gravity did the rest. The secret drawer slid open, and four fat bundles spilled to the ground.

"Letters," Grace said in disgust.

"Big surprise," Syd said.

Returning the chair carefully to its pedestal, Katie bent to read the name on the address line. "They're all addressed to Virginia Clairmont."

"I told you," Syd told Grace. Still wearing the dust gloves, she picked up a bundle. "When I was little, Honey wrote a letter every morning before breakfast."

"It's a lost art," Flora mused.

Katie was glad for Syd to have more of Honey's keepsakes but her mind was racing ahead to what they might find in the other chairs.

"Can you read the return address?" Flora asked.

Katie scanned the name and felt a small tingling in her chest. Just because the bundles of letters didn't pertain to the ZAP founders, didn't mean they couldn't still have other historic significance. "Oh, wow."

"Who is it?" Flora looked over her shoulder.

"It says F. Whitaker, Statesboro, Georgia," Katie said. Looking up, she caught Syd's eye. "Any chance Honey was friends with a famous reclusive writer?"

Syd shrugged. "I wouldn't be surprised. Honey knew lots of famous people. She also knew how to keep a secret."

"Frances Whitaker famously taught one semester at Beaumont," Flora informed them. "She set the town on its ear with her feminist notions. I was still in high school. Virginia would have been a freshman."

"Letters are so boring," Grace said, eyeing the Brown Thrasher Chair. "Can we see what's in the other one?"

"Don't get too excited," Syd warned her niece. "Anything inside the chairs belongs to ZAP. We sold them, remember?" She gave Grace the gloves.

The drawer popped open to yield four more packets of letters. All were addressed to Virginia Clairmont, all from F. Whitaker.

"Honey was really tight with this woman," Grace observed. "How many letters are here?"

"There was no texting back then," Syd reminded Grace.

Katie eyed the bundles. Tied together in velvet ribbon, they seemed overtly romantic. Katie estimated there were nearly eighty in the collection. If they were truly written by Frances Cecile Whitaker, biographers and literary historians would be keen to see them. She began to get excited. "Whitaker scholars are going to freak out."

"Will the family be allowed to read them before you bring in the experts?" Syd asked, suddenly looking more serious than Katie had ever seen her.

She hesitated. Not two minutes ago, Syd had correctly pointed out that items found in the chairs belonged to the ZAP Foundation. This included any compromising information that might be discovered in the Whitaker letters. Katie was sensitive to Syd's need to protect Honey but the decision wasn't hers to make. It belonged to the ZAP Board of Directors.

Fortunately, the president was standing in the room.

# CHAPTER TWENTY-SIX

## *Aunt Snarlene*

"I warned you that Katie might be a starfucker," Jennifer said, and plucked an olive from Colette's martini.

"Hey!" Colette said, and moved her glass out of reach.

"I'm starving," Deb said, and nabbed the other olive. "Syd wouldn't share dessert with me last night."

"Just because I didn't want a piece of blueberry pie, yesterday, doesn't mean you can't order food now," Syd pointed out. "And please, don't call Katie a starfucker. Y'all know what happened. It's not accurate."

"The jury is still out," Deb replied and popped the olive into her mouth.

Seated in a small, midtown Atlanta bistro near Syd's house, Deb, Jennifer, and Colette were helping Syd drown her sorrows over Sunday brunch. It had been nearly a month since the discovery of the Frances Whitaker letters and three weeks since Syd had last spoken to Katie. It was still unclear who'd leaked the excerpts to the *New York Times*, but the chaos surrounding the event had overwhelmed the fledging romance. Stymied by doubt, Syd had stopped answering Katie's texts weeks ago.

Colette made a face. "It might be construed that Katie is starfucking y'all's grandma."

"Their dead grandmother," Jennifer corrected her. "How can you trust someone who wants to anchor their career on Honey's sex life?"

Deb looked thoughtful. "Syd's right. Katie's only a starfucker if she's the person who leaked the letters. We still don't know who did it. There's no proof it was her."

"Did Katie deny it?" Colette asked, and took a sip of her martini.

Syd nodded. "Katie called me the morning the story appeared on the front page of the NYT. She was freaking out. I don't think she was lying. I really don't."

"Then why did you blow her off?" Jennifer asked. "If you don't hold her responsible for leaking the letters, why are you so angry?"

"I'm not actually sure," Syd admitted, and sipped her bourbon. "Katie stopped texting me a couple of days ago. And it's kind of driving me crazy."

"When was the last time you texted her?" Jennifer asked.

"A few weeks," Syd admitted, feeling sheepish. "But as long as Katie kept texting me it didn't seem as final."

"How long did you expect Katie to keep texting an empty screen?" Jennifer asked. "I know you're a hot-shit rock star and all that, but there are limits."

"That's what worries me," Syd admitted.

"Did the family know Honey had been involved with a woman?" Colette asked Syd, gently. "Maybe that's why you're so upset."

"I suggested the same thing," Deb said, "and no, I never knew a thing about Honey's romantic life until I saw the letters. Did you, Syd?"

"No, I didn't," she admitted.

"Can you please tell us what's in the letters," Jennifer interrupted. "Syd said y'all got to read them but never gave us any details. We only saw the snippet in the article."

"Read them for yourself," Syd said. Pulling a thick binder from her messenger bag she flung it across the table.

"Are these the Frances Whitaker letters?" Colette asked, in surprise.

"You brought them here?" Jennifer said, pouncing gleefully on the binder.

"These are copies," Deb corrected her. "Katie had the letters scanned for the family. Everyone got a copy."

Colette moved her chair closer to Jennifer's to better see the binder. "This is really nice." She fingered the binder. "Katie had no legal obligation to do any of this."

"I didn't say she was the devil," Syd said defensively.

"Then why are you angry with her? I don't get it," Jennifer asked again.

Syd dodged the question. "There's a lot going on in my head right now. I'm going to wait for the dust to settle before I decide what to do."

"The last time you said that no one saw you for six months," Deb said and held up her hand to flag down a waiter.

Jennifer agreed. "As far as I can tell, you're hiding out in your house with an old cat right now. You don't have to reconnect with Katie but, please, don't go backward."

"Yes." Colette nodded. "There are plenty of other women out there. Your website has exploded since the world found out your grandmother corrupted Frances Whitaker." She shook the binder at Syd. "Everyone is giving you credit for this."

"That makes no sense," Syd said, though she knew it shouldn't surprise her. There was no gauging what the public might hold true on any given day.

"The Honey I knew didn't seem like a sexual creature," Jennifer said. The waiter appeared and she ordered a Cobb salad, no egg. "It's hard for me to think of her that way. Maybe that's what's bothering you."

"Maybe," Syd agreed, and ordered a steak sandwich, though she wasn't the least bit hungry.

"I'm angry because the letters leaked before we had time to process their existence," Deb said, and ordered a cheeseburger.

"When did you first read them?" Colette asked and also ordered a burger.

"Katie set up a viewing a few days after we found the secret drawers," Syd told them and recounted the visit to Beaumont University Library. Under the supervision of a librarian, the family had been issued special gloves and allowed to examine the letters. At the time, Syd had still been hopeful they'd have some say in how the information was made public.

"There was no legal obligation to do that either," Colette said and flipped a page in the binder.

"That's why it was so shocking when the story broke," Deb mused. "We thought the family was being taken into consideration and then suddenly the whole world knew."

The *New York Times* article opened a floodgate to public curiosity. It was late June. Everyone wanted Pride-centric material. A famous literary woman who was also a secret lesbian was simply too good to pass up. Honey's privacy had been collateral damage.

"It really is a complicated situation," Jennifer conceded, and put a hand on Syd's arm. "I'm not advocating for Katie. I'm advocating for your happiness."

"Me too, that's how I feel," Colette echoed.

"I appreciate your concern," Syd said.

She was lucky to have people who forced her to parse the details of her first romance after the divorce. It was the only way to get closure, and cheaper than therapy. Though painful, Syd was glad for the exercise.

"So, how are you feeling, now?" Deb asked, gently.

"I'm okay," Syd lied. Even though Katie had stopped texting, Syd had continued to dream of her. Each morning, she woke to an ache between her legs and a matching one in her chest.

"You're allowed to call her," Jennifer said, annoying Syd with how well she could read her. "Maybe wait until the story dies down."

"Let me know when that happens," Syd said, wryly. The story was now being reported from seemingly every angle. Most pieces highlighted the hidden love letters between Frances Whitaker and Honey, while others made Syd the primary focus.

"For a recluse you look amazing," Jennifer said, and fluttered her fingers at Syd. "Have you been in a tanning bed?"

"I've been in the pool," Syd replied. As Honey's story had gained traction, the only way to tune out the news had been to swim. Syd had swum so many laps she'd gone down a rung on her belt.

"We should capitalize on this," Colette said. Switching over to manager brain, she pulled out her phone. "I'll book a photo shoot."

"Whatever you think," Syd said. Publicity was her least favorite part of being a performing artist. She'd hired Colette to make these decisions and trusted her to do so.

"Will you attend the VIP opening of the ZAP Museum, next week?" Jennifer asked.

Deb nodded. "Grace and I are going. Owen is still on the fence."

Syd flashed to Katie standing seductively next to the Hummingbird Chair in her garage. *When would she stop thinking about her?* "No, I'm not going to the opening."

"Do you know if the letters will be part of the exhibit?" Jennifer looked down at the binder, and Colette snorted.

"Are you kidding? The Frances Whitaker letters will get their own exhibition, probably a book too, maybe even a movie." She looked to Syd who nodded.

"Once we read them, we realized Frances and Honey were genuinely in love." Syd took a sip of bourbon. "They saw each other once a year at Frances's house on Hilton Head Island."

"That's so sad," Colette said, paging through the binder.

Syd didn't argue. Yearning for the object of your affection was a brutal way to pass the time. If the past few weeks were any indication, Honey's life must have been unbearable.

"Isn't Whitaker's most famous short story set in Hilton Head?" Jennifer asked.

"Yeah," Deb replied. "Martin's Place. Whitaker actually references the story in one of her letters to Honey. I marked the page. It's somewhere near the middle."

"That adds significant value," Colette said, and flipped to the page.

Deb nodded. "People are suggesting Honey was the inspiration for the effeminate man who has the affair with the protagonist in the story."

"The character Brad Pitt played in the movie?" Colette asked, looking impressed.

Jennifer raised her hand to flag down the waiter. "I'm going to need another drink." She shot Syd a look. "I can't believe we didn't know Brad Pitt played Honey. Why didn't she tell anyone?"

"We'll never know," Syd said. Perhaps that's why she was feeling so out of sorts. Honey had chosen not to share an important part of her life. Had she not thought Syd trustworthy?

"What else was in the letters?" Jennifer asked. "I can tell by the look on Syd's face. Something else is bugging y'all."

Syd bit her lip. "It's not a huge deal, but Deb figured out that Frances Whitaker was the first person to call our grandmother Honey."

Jennifer slapped the table and a spoon bounced to the floor. "No way, I thought you gave her the name."

"That's the story we were told." Deb shrugged, looking a little hurt. "More than half of the letters are addressed to Honey. We think grandmother orchestrated the nickname to keep Frances present in her daily life."

"How romantic," Colette exclaimed.

"There's a lot of sweet stuff in there," Syd conceded. "Who knows what's really true?"

Jennifer looked sympathetic. "Trusting your instincts after a divorce takes time. Give yourself a break."

"I'm trying."

Syd Ubered home full of frustration and bourbon. Annapurna's ankle cuddles at the door only made her feel marginally better. Syd yearned for Katie's touch. The feeling was primal. Every so often an image of Katie, spread naked and wide, would pop into Syd's head. It never failed to amaze her, though she was also left confused. Why did her body crave something that wasn't good for her?

Deb had said goodbye at the bistro and gone back to Beaumont. Syd was touched her sister had come to check on her but was glad to have the house to herself again, if only to lick her wounds in peace. When the doorbell rang, Syd was browsing streaming services searching for a movie to take her mind off the real world. She wasn't expecting anyone and hoped it was Joe, who now sometimes stopped in to bring treats to Annapurna. The person framed in the peephole caused Syd to take an involuntary step back. *What the hell?* The doorbell rang again.

"I can see your shadow through the transom, Sydney," a deep, clear voice said from the front porch. "I drove all the way from Beaumont to talk to you. Please, open the door."

Reluctantly, Syd turned the knob. Standing on the doorstep, purse clutched to her chest as if any moment robbers might spring up from the hydrangea, was Great Aunt Arlene.

"Hello," Syd said. Still tipsy from the bourbon, she squinted against the light. There was no point asking why Great Aunt Arlene was standing on her doorstep. It almost certainly had to do with Honey's letters. According to Deb, Arlene had been livid when the *New York Times* story appeared, and called her daily to rant.

"Hello, Sydney," Arlene replied. As always, her eyes went directly to Syd's tattoos. She studied them for a moment and then wrinkled her button nose. "I've hired a lawyer to stop the exhibition of my sister's letters. We'd like your cooperation. He'd like to depose you first."

"Yeah, that's not happening," Syd said, wishing she'd been in the pool when the doorbell rang. "Would you like to come in and talk about it? I have sweet tea."

Arlene looked at Syd as if she'd suggested they picnic in a truck-stop bathroom. "Thank you, but I don't have time."

"You just said that you came all the way from Beaumont to talk to me," Syd countered. "How did you get here?" Blinking against the light, she saw an unfamiliar car parked in the driveway.

"Cindy Peters was good enough to drive me," Arlene explained. "I don't want to keep her. We'd like to get home before dark."

"You made Cindy Peters drive you all the way here just to tell me you'd hired a lawyer?" Syd asked, incredulous. Why hadn't Deb said anything about this?

"I came with Cindy to watch her granddaughter's tennis match," Arlene said, looking defiant. "Susan plays for Georgia Tech."

Syd wondered at the tinge of pride in her voice. She didn't know much about Arlene's private life. Their great aunt had always kept herself at a far remove from the rest of the family. Deb swore she was an evil witch who had no friends. It looked as if this might not be completely true. "Did Susan win?" Syd asked, curious to see Arlene's reaction.

"In straight sets," Arlene replied, with evident relish. "Susan is very good. Georgia recruited her too. But Susan wants to be an engineer, so she chose Tech."

"Good for Susan," Syd said. "I appreciate you taking the time to stop by and talk with me, but I'm not interested in talking to your lawyer. When I sold the chairs to the ZAP Foundation, the letters were part of the sale."

Arlene's eyes flashed. "My lawyer thinks we can contest it."

"On what grounds?" Syd asked. "The ownership of the letters is not in question."

"Morality," Arlene stressed each syllable. "My sister embarrassed me enough during her lifetime. I won't have it continue after her death."

"I'm sorry you feel that way," Syd said, and felt a surge of rage. How dare Arlene trash-talk Honey? "I can't help you."

"I knew it was a long shot coming here." Arlene curled her lip. "I bet you're thrilled to have our dirty laundry aired in public," she spat. "You're just like Virginia," she said, and looked disdainfully at Syd's tattoos, again. "Both of you, perverted."

"What's perverted," Syd said, no longer trying to disguise her anger, "is to make moral judgments on other people. Is that why you cut Honey out of your life? Did you know about her relationship with Frances?"

"Virginia brought shame on this family, just like you have." Arlene pointed a stubby finger at Syd, like a cartoon schoolmarm. "My lawyer is going to file an injunction against the ZAP Foundation to stop further publication of the letters. All this nonsense about them being of historic value. The letters are pure smut and no one else's business!"

"They're certainly none of your business," Syd shouted. "If Honey's letters help one person overcome the bigotry you're spewing right now, then I hope they make a movie."

"How dare you!"

"How dare you?" Syd shot back. "The minute you started withholding your love from Honey, you lost the right to weigh in on her life. Now, please, get off my front porch."

"You'll be hearing from my lawyer." Arlene sniffed.

"I'll look forward to it," Syd said, and imagined the glee with which Colette would attack whatever billboard attorney Arlene had hired. "I bet you a hundred bucks I've got a better one."

Slamming the door, she returned to the couch and fell against the cushions as if she'd been shot. Had that really just happened? Syd's entire life, Deb had regaled her with stories of evil Great Aunt Arlene. This was the first time Syd had truly seen her in action. No wonder Honey had been so fiercely protective of her private life. Syd couldn't imagine a world where a sister didn't offer unconditional support.

Syd was suddenly very keen to share Honey's letters with the public. Not just as a fuck-you to Arlene, though this would be a nice side benefit, but as a reminder to everyone not to take equality for granted. At least now if you couldn't count on your family to support your choices, the law was on your side. Honey had had neither.

Maybe it was adrenaline from the confrontation, or finally coming to terms with the historic importance of her grandmother's letters, but Syd felt lighter than she had in weeks.

Deb would wet her pants when she learned that Syd had booted Great Aunt Arlene from her porch. Giggling, Syd picked up the phone and dialed her sister's number. When it went to voice mail, she frowned. The only other person Syd wanted to talk to had stopped texting a few days ago. How would Katie react if Syd suddenly called to apologize?

There was one only way to find out.

# CHAPTER TWENTY-SEVEN

## *Warm Reception*

"I wish you'd sit down, and eat something before our guests arrive," Flora advised Katie. "The exhibit looks perfect. Stop fussing with that old ledger and have a piece of fried chicken."

"Maybe in a second," Katie said, putting her off. There were too many butterflies in her stomach to allow for the addition of poultry. "I can't decide which page in the ledger to leave open for display," she said, and carefully flipped from the Owl Chair to the Eagle.

"Does it matter?" Flora asked. She waved her hand at the back wall of the exhibition room. Enlarged, digital renderings taken from the ledger hung behind the actual chairs along with photos of the founders. The ledger, on loan from the Beaumont University Library, sat on a pedestal beneath a glass box. It wasn't everything Katie had planned for the final exhibit, but it was close, and more than enough to dazzle the Board and a few VIP guests attending that evening. "Just pick your favorite page and come eat something. I had the cook next door at ZAP House make you a plate."

"Thanks so much," Katie murmured, and turned the page to the Hummingbird Chair because it reminded her of Syd. The butterflies in her stomach rumbled as she slipped off the dust gloves and replaced the casing over the ledger.

"Is everything okay, dear?" Flora asked and Katie considered the question.

Last week, out of the blue, Syd had texted to apologize for the disappearing act. Katie didn't know what had happened to thaw the frost that had settled on Syd after the fiasco with the letters going public, and she wasn't sure she cared. Hearing from Syd again, after three weeks of silence, felt like seeing sunshine for the first time after a monsoon. Katie wasn't ready to talk about her feelings with Flora yet, so she told her grandmother a version of the truth. "I'm a little nervous about public speaking."

"That's perfectly normal," Flora said. "But you've nothing to worry about. The exhibit looks wonderful." She smiled. "I'm sure you'll do a marvelous job."

"Thank you," Katie said, her mind still on Syd. When Katie had asked when they might see each other again, Syd had been vague but Katie was hopeful it would be soon. She'd invited Syd to attend the ZAP reception tonight but Syd had been noncommittal, which was probably for the best. A public event wasn't the ideal place to stage the kind of reunion Katie was imagining.

There was a tap on the back door, and she started.

"Eat something," Flora implored and went to see who it was. A minute later Beth walked into the room, holding a bouquet of flowers.

"Hey, y'all, I hope I'm not too early," she said, looking shyly around the exhibit.

"You're welcome anytime, dear," Flora said, and kissed Beth's cheeks. "How've you been? How are the boys? I haven't seen them since the lovely picture on your holiday card."

"Everyone is doing well," Beth replied, and smiled over Flora's shoulder at Katie. "The twins are a handful, but I love being a mother."

"That's fortunate, because there's no going back," Flora said, and they all laughed.

"Thanks for coming a little early," Katie told Beth. Her old friend had been the one bright spot during the long weeks of Syd's silence. Preaching time and tolerance, Beth had been certain things would work out. Her optimism had helped keep Katie's hope alive. When Syd finally contacted her, Beth had been the first person Katie had called. She hugged her now, and the flowers crinkled between them.

"Don't crush the gladioli," Flora said, and whisked the bouquet away into the kitchen to find a vase.

"How's the land of tiny men?" Katie asked.

Beth gave her a pained look. "Everything smells like pee," she said, and shook her head. "Potty training is not for sissies. When Jimmy got home tonight, I had to stop myself from actually running out the door."

"I love that you don't want to hurt their feelings," Katie said, touched at Beth's consideration for her family.

"Are you kidding? I didn't want to fall on my butt," Beth said, and turned her ankle so Katie could admire the three-inch heels that matched her teal-colored dress.

"Dang, girl," Katie said, and bent down to look properly at the shoes. "You clean up nice."

"You're not so bad yourself," Beth said, eyeing Katie's outfit. "That pantsuit is très sophisticated, very New York. And the exhibit looks fantastic. The board members are going to be impressed."

"Thanks for saying that," Katie replied. She was genuinely proud of what she'd accomplished but it was nice to hear it from Beth who didn't give undue compliments.

"Have you heard anything else from Syd?" Beth asked, and Katie nodded.

"She texted me a picture of a herd of cows yesterday," she said and laughed when Beth raised an eyebrow.

"I hope that's an inside joke," Beth said.

"It's an outside joke," Katie replied, grinning.

Beth smiled back at her. "I'm praying it'll work out for y'all," she said, looking sincere. "And not just because I want free tickets to Syd's concerts."

"Thanks, Sensei," Katie said and gave Beth a warm hug. "And thanks for coming early to help me play hostess."

Beth squeezed Katie's shoulders. "That what sisters are for, Grasshopper," she said.

Flora walked back into the exhibit room just in time to witness the exchange. Katie knew her grandmother was pleased she'd reconnected with Beth but was surprised when Flora joined their hug. "Isn't sisterhood marvelous?" she said, enveloping them in a cloud of Dior. "Zeta Alpha Pi, forever."

The reception began an hour later. The Board and several honored guests assembled in the exhibit room where Katie took them through the search for the chairs. Beginning with the chairs found by the ZAP Board members before she'd been hired, Katie chronicled the quest spotlighting each individual who'd played a role. The inclusive program made for a festive evening. Twice Katie gave up the podium to allow someone to relate an impromptu story. Auda-Bonnie nearly brought the house down reenacting how the Snowy Egret Chair had almost taken out her eye. It was nothing like any exhibit opening Katie had ever attended in New York, but the Bird Chairs of Zeta Alpha Pi were one of a kind. The fact that the quest had quite literally ended in a medieval setting was almost too good to be true.

Attendees were particularly interested in the secret drawers and the objects discovered within them. A hush went over the room when Katie put on a pair of white gloves and beckoned Grace forward.

"As you all know, ZAP alumni Virginia Clairmont had two of our founders' chairs in her estate," Katie said and gestured to the Hummingbird and Brown Thrasher Chairs. "The *New York Times* has the whole world excited about the correspondence from novelist Frances Whitaker Virginia kept inside secret drawers we found under the seats." She paused for effect. "What the *New York Times* didn't tell you was that it was Virginia Clairmont's great-granddaughter Grace who found the hidden lock."

There was a smattering of applause and Grace stepped forward looking confident. The way she stood reminded Katie of Syd who she wished, more and more, had been able to attend the reception. Several times while recounting the quest for the chairs Katie had been obliged to mention Syd's name and the words lingered in her mouth like the sweetest taste of honey.

"I only found the lock because I almost dropped the chair," Grace said and the crowd laughed appreciatively.

Katie spied Deb in the audience and hoped she was having a nice time. She'd spoken to Syd's sister only briefly and had been relieved to receive a warm reception.

Grace couldn't have been nicer, readily agreeing to participate in the night's program. Katie handed her a pair of white gloves and together they kneeled by the Hummingbird Chair.

"The lock is activated by a spring behind this berry." Katie indicated the dime-sized carving of the mulberry beneath the seat. "Grace? Would you care to do the honors?" she asked.

"I'd be happy to," Grace said. Reaching over she carefully pressed the button releasing the drawer.

The crowd made approving noises as Katie slid the drawer open for everyone to see.

"What's inside there now?" someone asked and Katie pulled out a small box she'd stashed inside the drawer earlier in that day.

"Another surprise," she said and winked at Flora who was standing off to the side with a pack of her friends. Katie opened the box and pulled out the commemorative buttons they'd had made to celebrate the opening of the exhibit. Beth had done the artwork. Beautiful, whimsical illustrations of all eight Bird Chairs of Zeta Alpha Pi.

"Beth, will you come forward?"

Beth joined them by the Hummingbird Chair and Katie pinned a button carefully to her dress. She gave Grace the box with the remaining buttons to pass them around the room. Nothing made event attendees happier than giveaway swag.

The program complete, Katie moved through the crowd, joining as many conversations as possible. She'd never been the center of this much attention and took a moment to marvel at her poise. When had she grown so comfortable in her own skin?

Katie smiled listening to Bootsy Jenkins tell a pocket of women about finding the Robin Chair at the Knight Times restaurant.

"I was picking up Randal from a birthday party and saw the chair sitting by the front desk," she said, eyes wild with excitement. "I remembered seeing the wanted poster on ZAP Instagram so I went back and compared the chair to the post."

"That was smart," Beth said.

Bootsy bobbed her head. "I thought so too." She beamed and went on to detail her fractious encounter with the owner. "I never met the sisters. They sound like they were much nicer than the man I met."

"It's a shame they weren't able to make it to the reception," Katie said, thinking fondly of Sheila and Siohban who'd had a conflict with a jousting match.

Bootsy nodded. "I was following the whole thing on Instagram. Is Syd Collins here tonight?" she asked and looked around the room as if it were possible to miss the presence of such a luminary.

"Syd couldn't make it," Katie said and glanced at Deb who was posing with Grace by the Hummingbird Chair.

"If you're talking about Syd Collins, I just saw her in the parking lot," Flora said, approaching the little group.

"You did?" Katie asked, and felt her pulse quicken.

"Yes," Flora said, and gave Katie a knowing look. "Someone may need to offer her assistance."

"Why? What's happened to Syd?" Katie asked. She stared at her grandmother in bewilderment. Was this some kind of joke? If Syd needed help, why was Flora acting blasé?

"I fear she's been swarmed by sorority girls," Flora said, dramatically. "I just saw her signing a woman's thigh."

"Those girls must be freaking out." Beth giggled. "Remember how we acted when we were younger?"

But Katie was already moving toward the door. It was fortunate the program had concluded because she floated outside with no notion of professional obligation. The fact that Syd had driven to Beaumont was suddenly the only thought in her head.

Just as Flora had said, Katie found Syd chatting with a group of sorority girls in the parking lot. Stopping to watch, she was reminded of Syd's effortless star quality. Dressed in a pair of basic tailored slacks and a pressed shirt, Syd still looked as if she'd stepped off a magazine cover. What the sorority girls couldn't see was the sweet woman who'd rushed home to be with her cat, the woman who counted cows on country roads and performed at benefits to support animals and old friends. Katie understood why the girls were in a swoon but also why the people closest to Syd felt protective. She was a very special person. Katie's fondest wish was that they'd be able to move beyond the Whitaker Letters, and take up where they'd left off.

She began walking again. The girls didn't seem in any hurry to leave and, contrary to Flora's observations, Syd didn't look as if she needed assistance. When Katie finally caught her eye, she was finishing a story about a local bar, and the girls were laughing hysterically.

"It was nice meeting y'all, but I need to go, now," Syd said, and smiled intently at Katie.

"Okay!"

"Thanks, Syd!"

"See you later."

The girls spoke all at once, and then tittered away like a flock of pigeons.

Left alone under the street light, Katie didn't know what to say, so she led with a hug. Her emotions were so much easier to express physically. Katie hoped they'd have time to talk later. Right now, she just wanted to luxuriate in the feeling of Syd's body against her own. The last few weeks had been misery. If it hadn't been for the distraction of the exhibit, Katie might have driven to Atlanta and become a stalker. Exhaling, she sniffed and was shocked to feel tears on her face.

"Is everything okay?" Syd asked, pulling away just enough to look Katie in the face. "Did something go wrong with the exhibit?"

To Katie's astonishment, Syd was crying too.

"No, I'm just so happy to see you," she said, and wiped at her cheeks. Standing on her tiptoes, she kissed Syd's eyelids, and tasted salt on her tongue.

"I didn't wait too long?" Syd asked, sounding nervous. "I'm worried that I've messed things up."

"What? You didn't mess up anything," Katie said, and melted back into Syd's body. They clung to each other for several moments and Katie felt her temperature climbing. "You just needed time," she whispered in her ear. "I knew you'd come back to me."

"You did?" Syd choked. "How could you know that, when I didn't have a clue?"

"Well, I hoped you'd come back," Katie confessed, and hugged her more tightly. "I've never felt this way about anyone before and can't imagine losing you."

"I don't want to lose you either," Syd whispered.

Katie pulled away and took Syd's hand. They were both still crying but the tension had broken.

"Finding the letters must have been really confusing for you," she said, and tried not to get lost in Syd's eyes. "You're still mourning your grandmother. I get it. When my mother died, I was sensitive to anything involving her memory. Flora couldn't mention Mom's name without me biting her head off."

"That's exactly it." Syd sniffed. "Learning about the Whitaker letters felt like losing Honey all over again."

"I understand completely," Katie replied. She looked away for a long moment and then back into Syd's face. If she and Syd were truly going to move forward, there was one last thing Katie had to clear up. "I need you to know it wasn't me who leaked the letters," she said. "I don't know who did, and I'm sorry it happened, but it wasn't me."

Syd made an odd face. "I'm sorry if I ever implied it was you," she said. "I found out this afternoon it was the librarian."

"Ernest?" Katie asked, and felt her mouth drop open. Her shock was followed by a rush of relief. "I've been with Deb and Grace all evening and they didn't say anything. How did you figure it out?"

"Grace and Deb don't know yet." Syd shook her head. "I got in the car the minute I heard."

"Who told you it was Ernest?" Katie asked, still in shock. The friendly librarian was the last person she'd have expected to have behaved unethically.

"My Great Aunt Arlene hired a lawyer with a special set of skills." Syd shuddered. "Ernest sent a copy of one of the letters to a scholar friend who leaked it to the *Times*. No one made any money but there's a digital trail that proves everything."

"I can't believe it," Katie said.

"That's not everything," Syd continued. "Great Aunt Arlene came to see me in Atlanta last week. She's livid the Whitaker letters have gone public and wants me to co-file an injunction against future exhibition."

"Oh, shit," Katie said then felt the relief rush away. Though lawyers for the ZAP Foundation were satisfied Syd's family had no legal claim to the letters, lawsuits took time and resources. They were also divisive. If Syd and Katie found themselves on opposing sides of a courtroom, the relationship would almost certainly be affected. "What did you say?" Katie asked, holding her breath.

"I told her to shove it," Syd said, grinning. "Turns out Honey's relationship with Frances was the only reason Arlene was so intent on getting Honey's stuff in the first place."

"Honey's sister knew about the letters?" Katie was shocked.

"She knew about Frances," Syd said. "She came at me pretty hard spewing crap about family and shame. She said Honey and I were cut from the same cloth."

"That's horrible," Katie said.

Syd raised her eyebrows. "I took it as a compliment."

"Not the part about Honey, the part where she attacked you," Katie clarified, and Syd smiled sweetly.

"I knew what you meant," she said, took Katie's hand. "Part of me wants to thank her. It wasn't until Arlene's rant that I was able to truly understand why Honey had to keep that part of herself private. It also made me realize why we have a responsibility to make it public now."

"Hooray for Aunt Arlene," Katie said, and gave Syd a lingering kiss.

Syd giggled. "Yay, Arlene," she said, and then pulled gently away. "You probably need to get back inside."

"I think we have a few minutes," Katie said, and must have looked desperate because Syd laughed.

"I hope we've more than just a few minutes," she said, and squeezed Katie's fingers.

"Yeah?"

"Well, not right now, unfortunately," Syd replied, and made a pouty face. "Unless there's somewhere nearby we could sneak off to be alone."

After a month apart, these were the words Katie most wanted to hear. "I might know a place," she said and squinted up at Maguire House.

"Oh, yeah?" Syd asked.

Hand in hand, they walked inside the building.

# CHAPTER TWENTY-EIGHT

## *On a Wing and a Chair*

"I'd like to thank everyone for attending our housewarming party," Syd spoke to the small group of friends and family gathered in her living room. "I'd originally hoped to have y'all over when I first moved back from LA but Honey got sick and I had to postpone the party."

"Here's to Honey," Grace said and raised a big glass of sweet tea.

"Indeed," Syd replied. "Here's to Honey," she said and tapped glasses with Katie who was standing directly to her left. "Postponing the party turned out not to be such a bad thing because there are now two more individuals warming this house that we can celebrate."

"Yay for Katie," Grace said and raised her sweet tea again.

"And yay for Annapurna," Emma said, lifting the big, white cat in the air.

Party guests clinked their glasses, while Syd gave Katie a quick kiss on the lips. "Here's to you, baby. Congratulations on the new job."

"Thanks, but I can't focus on that right now," Katie said and smiled into Syd's eyes. "Did you hear the news? I'm moving in with Syd Fucking Collins."

Though Katie hadn't formally moved in with Syd until three days ago, they hadn't spent a night apart since the ZAP reception. Once she'd found Katie again, Syd had seen no reason to let her go. When Katie had been offered an opportunity to curate an exhibit of the Whitaker Letters at the High Museum in downtown Atlanta, Syd had invited her to make the living arrangement official. To her delight, Katie had accepted and now they were toasting each other before family and friends.

"I thought you were going to sing something from the new album," Joe said. He picked up Syd's guitar, from where it was perched against the wall, and handed it to her.

"Yeah, play us a song, Squid," Owen said, his arm wrapped firmly around Deb.

"I *have* been working on something," Syd said and winked at Colette who turned on her cell phone and began recording.

"What are you doing?" Katie asked, staring at Syd's guitar. "I don't know anything about a new song."

"Because it's a surprise," Syd said, sweetly. Picking the strings of the Rockbridge, she addressed the crowd once more. "I was in a bad place before Katie came into my life. All of you know what happened because most of it was in the newspaper." She grinned and strummed the instrument.

"Play the song, Syd," Joe called and Syd waved him quiet.

"Because of Katie I now know my grandmother in a whole new way," Syd said. "The song is dedicated to her and to Honey who was never able to live openly. In World War II lovers were said to have sent letters on a wing and a prayer. In honor of my grandmother's love for Frances Whitaker and the Bird Chairs of Zeta Alpha Pi, I'm calling this song *On a Wing and a Chair*."

Smiling into Katie's eyes, Syd began to sing.

*It's early days and I'm early dazed*
*I still can't believe it's true*
*I'd just come through a heartbreak haze*

*And suddenly there's you*

*Green eyes, green light, flashing go, all night*
*I felt like my finger was in a socket*
*Laughing singing it's all so right*
*Tucked in your tiny pocket*

*It's not your looks but how you looked*
*I knew you saw. I felt you see.*
*You're the answer to my prayers*
*Love has finally come for me…*
*On a wing and a chair*